AND
ONE
OTHER

A NOVEL BY

Beth MacDonald

North
Ink
Books

*"A family is a web
so delicately woven
that it takes almost nothing
to set the whole thing shuddering
or even to tear it to pieces.
Yet the thread it's woven of
is as strong as anything on earth."*

—*Frederick Buechner*

PROLOGUE

I'D FOUND MY third-grade essay with Pops's papers while I was looking for his birth certificate. Ironically, the government required proof of life to declare him dead. I don't know how he'd managed to hold onto that ragged piece of spiral notebook paper. Why hadn't it, like so many of the people and things in my father's life, fallen through the cosmic cracks over the years?

MY FAMILY

My Pops says that we are manely Irish. That means that his parents parents, people I never new, came from the country of Irland.

My moms parents came from some were in South Dkota. My Pops told me that my mommy is part Soo indian and part some thing else. Maybe English he dont no. Her last name was Dickenson before she married my Pops just like aunt Marlyss. His name is Patrick O'Connor. He says you cant get much more Irish then that.

There are three kids in my family. Two boys named Joel and Gary who are both litteler then me and one other kid whose a girl. Thats me. My name is Jicky.

My Pops is strong and fun. He works for the lumber company and sometimes brings me little pieces of wood to make houses and boats from. Sometimes he brings me paper to draw things.

Mommy is pretty and smart and fun but when Gary got born she got sad all the time. She was sad sometimes before but she always got happy again. She sleeps allot. I wished she wakeup. Sometimes Joey pulls on her when shes in bed. I try to play with Joey but Gary crys cuz he needs things. Gary is like my baby. Joey just stays mad. I wish I could play with him more and he and mommy would be happy again.

BOOK
ONE

CHAPTER ONE

AS WE'D CLIMBED into the car, our last ride as a family, Joel claimed shotgun, my usual seat of honor beside our father. The change had set off another of Gary and Joel's perpetual squabbles. I'd just managed to quiet them when Gary slid across the backseat of the station wagon, wrapped his skinny arms around my neck, and sobbed, "J-Jicky, don't leave me."

"Don't be silly, sweetie—I'm not leaving you, you're leaving me. And, don't worry, you won't be alone—you'll have Joey and Pops. They'll take care of you."

"Not like you. Joey's not even nice to me anymore."

I shook my head. "I'll talk to him. I'm sure it'll get better once you're on the road." My voice had been loud enough for Joel to hear in the front seat, and I thought I'd heard him mutter, "Fat chance." I hoped I was wrong.

Pops stopped the station wagon in front of Aunt Marlys's house, got out, and cranked down the back windshield. He grabbed my stuff from the top of the piles of clothing and assorted household stuff in the way-back. Gary had hopped out too, but Joel refused to leave the passenger seat.

I hugged and kissed Gary atop his sweaty red hair. At nine he still had that sweet-sour little boy smell. By early autumn of 1977, he had been *my* little boy for over four years. It was hard seeing him leave, but it would've been harder to stay with my brothers as they turned into moody teenagers. Joel, at twelve, was already a handful for me. He was turning mean and I was worried that it was my fault—something I'd done. I kept hearing a voice in my head saying, *Gary will be better off without you.* I now suspect that it was my subconscious attempting to lessen my guilt.

Pops gave me a big hug and told me there was still time for me to change my mind and join them, but he was just trying to make me feel wanted. There wasn't room for me in his life anymore. He was on his way to meet his newest love, Louisa, in Connecticut. She and Pops had met at a resort (dude-ranch, really) where he'd worked over the summer. Louisa had agreed that the boys needed their father, but she had said nothing about housing me. While she seemed like an okay person, I sensed she didn't want a teenage girl underfoot. I was hoping, really hoping, that she would be kind to my brothers.

I went to the front window and once again asked Joel to be good to Gary, then whispered, "Watch for the money—I'll send something as soon as I can." Joel was now as old as I had been when our mother left us. He was old enough to help Gary, and I was hoping that the responsibility would be good for him. Boy, was I trying to convince myself of it.

∗ ∗ ∗

POPS DROVE AWAY while Gary hung out the back window frantically waving his freckled arm. I stayed on the street outside my aunt's house until the beat-up Country Squire was out of sight, then I let myself in the unlocked back door. Aunt Marlys had lived in the little house for years, having bought it with her divorce settlement when she'd first moved to Gareth to be closer to her younger sister, my mom. A few years ago *Uncle* Jim had moved in with her. I really didn't want to call

Jim "uncle," but Aunt Marlys had insisted. The man creeped me out.

I carried my things through the kitchen to the laundry room which would double as my bedroom for the next two years. While I hadn't been thrilled about living in the laundry room, the luxury of having a washer and dryer that I could use whenever I chose made it seem like a small price to pay. Growing up, the local laundromat, or more often, washing things out by hand, were my only laundry options. I'd tried to keep the family clean after mom had left, but the boys and I were pretty ripe most of the time. The kids at school made sure we knew it.

Uncle Jim had scored an old army cot and set it up just inside the door along the outside wall of the small orangish (emphasis on *ish*) room. The only window was above the bed —a nice arrangement in hot weather, but I was sure I'd need some extra blankets come winter. Parallel to the cot, on the other side of the room, was an old washtub on a rusted metal stand and a newer model washer/dryer set. A hose with a hooked end draped from the bottom of the washtub to an open standpipe sticking out of the wall; a similar hose went from the washing machine to the washtub. Aunt Marlys had explained that the washtub was a necessity—the plumbing was too old to handle the speed and pressure of the water expelled by the new laundry equipment. With this ugly workaround, the used washer water could build up in the washtub then drain slowly (via gravity) into the antiquated plumbing inside the wall.

A couple of sour dishrags hung on the edge of the tub giving the small room an unusual funk. I hated the washtub. Without it I would've had room for a chair or a place for my art equipment. I thought of my mom saying, *"If wishes were horses, beggars would ride."* At sixteen—who am I kidding, by twelve—I'd already learned that wishing was completely pointless.

A small three-drawer chest for my clothes sat beside the head of the cot where it could also serve as a nightstand. I thought if I could find a lamp (and an outlet) I'd be okay. I unloaded my things into the chest of drawers, shoved my art supplies under the cot, and spread the sheets and blanket Aunt Marlys had left for me over the stained mattress. My chores completed, I went for a walk in my new neighborhood and later killed time watching soaps until my aunt arrived home. She'd asked me to wait around for her so that she could fill me in on the extra household duties expected of me since she and *Uncle* Jim were giving me such a good deal on room and board.

* * *

I'D FLOPPED ON my cot and was thinking about my brothers as I watched dying leaves fall from the ragged cottonwoods just outside my window. Joel and Gary would have already been attending their new school for over a month. I hoped they were happy and that Louisa was being a good substitute mom. Pops (or one of the boys) owed me a letter, but I was coming to the conclusion that I needed to give up waiting for a response and write to them again. Maybe then one of them might get the hint and write back.

It was Sunday morning, the only time I had to myself between school and work. I'd taken a shower earlier and was wearing the thin cotton robe Aunt Marlys had loaned me so that I could wash both my pairs of jeans at the same time. As I began towel drying my hair, the washing machine started banging and hopping. I'd carelessly put all my dirty clothes and towels together in one load—evidently it had been too much for the machine. Ignoring my wet hair, I threw the damp towel over the edge of the washtub and opened the washer. I had just finished rearranging the off-balanced load and restarting the machine when the telephone rang. I usually paid little attention to the phone—seldom did anyone call me—but both Marlys and Jim were gone that morning. I hurried to the living room.

"Hello."

"Well, Jicky, I didn't 'spect you to answer. How ya doin', hon?"

"POPS! It's so good to hear your voice. I was just thinking about you."

We talked for the next twenty minutes—first me and Pops, then Gary, and finally Joel, who didn't seem as excited to chat with me as had Pops and Gary. I already knew from Pops that they'd gotten the letters I'd sent. I quietly asked Joel if he'd gotten the money. He said he had. I reminded him that half of it was for Gary, but if there was nothing Gary needed or wanted, he should save it for him in a safe place. Joel grunted and gave the receiver back to Pops for goodbyes.

I SCURRIED THROUGH the kitchen puzzled by the sound of falling water. I reached the laundry room to find the washtub overflowing—sudsy water was spreading toward the outer edges of the room. I panicked. By the time I'd figured out how to stop the washing machine, water had completely covered the laundry room floor, wicked up the blanket on my cot, and inundated everything stored beneath it. All my completed paintings and drawings, the pieces I was most proud of, were now a soggy stack of garbage. My treasured stash of watercolor papers and drawing pads was ruined as well. I grabbed the cardboard box with my art supplies and tossed it on top of the dryer to look through after I'd figured out what had gone wrong with the washer.

I reached into the washtub, still full of lukewarm water, and pulled my towel from the drain. The thin terry towel was just long enough to have been caught by the water as it gushed from the washer hose, but not small enough to have gone down the drain. I wrung it over the washtub while tears filled my eyes. I was upset that I'd ruined my artwork and supplies, but even more upset thinking that my aunt might see the flood in her house as a reason to evict me—I had nowhere else to go.

I thought about getting towels from the bathroom to soak up the mess on the floor, but figured that would make Aunt Marlys even more angry. I grabbed the top sheet and blanket from my cot and threw them on the floor to start absorbing the water. I was wringing the blanket over the washtub when *Uncle* Jim walked in the back door and found me soaked from the cleanup, my aunt's old robe clinging to me from calves to neck.

"What the hell happened here?" Jim said, while looking me over, his eyes lingering too long on the wet robe sticking to my breasts. I crossed my arms in front of me while I explained that I'd accidentally blocked the drain hose while doing my laundry.

"God, you'd better get this cleaned up by the time Marlys gets back—she's gonna be pissed for sure. You're just damn lucky you didn't get her new kitchen carpet wet."

"Yeah, Jim, I know. I caught it before it got very deep. I hate to ask you this, but could you finish wringing out the blanket and put it in the washer with the sheet? I've gotta get ready for work."

"I s'pose I could Jik, but you're gonna owe me."

"Yeah. Oh, shit. My jeans are still wet—I don't have anything to wear to work."

"Go take a shower. I can find something of Marlys's for you to wear. Do you need anything besides *bottoms*? Marlys has some pretty sexy bras and panties that would look even better on you."

I tried to keep my voice even, "No, I've got everything else. Thank God my shoes were by the back door."

I grabbed my clothes from the chest of drawers and ran to the bathroom. By the time I'd taken a quick shower to warm up, Jim had left a pair of Marlys's sweatpants outside the locked bathroom. I dressed and went back to the laundry room to find it looking, other than the cot being bare, as though nothing had happened. Jim was still in the room pulling apart my wet artwork over the washtub.

"What are you going to do with these?" Jim asked.

"There's no save. Would you mind throwing them in the garbage for me? I've really gotta run—thanks for your help."

"No problem, Jik. I'll change out the wash when it's done. Your aunt doesn't even have to know anything happened. It can be our secret."

As I sprinted to the back door I called to Jim, "Thanks, but I'm gonna fess up." There was no way on earth I wanted to share a secret with that man—that I now felt indebted to him made my skin crawl.

AUNT MARLYS TOOK the news of the flood better than I'd thought she would, but she told me, in no uncertain terms, that I'd better not let it happen again. She shook her umpteenth cigarette of the day from her pack of Merits, then offered one to me. I hadn't smoked before moving in with my aunt, but she seemed to consider coffee and cigarettes a part of our room and board arrangement. I was an adult now, certain behaviors were expected and encouraged. I'd begun to rely on caffeine and nicotine to get through my long days.

"Jicky, you look so much like your mom when you've got a cigarette in your hand. Not your coloring so much, but the shape of your face and the way you do things. God I miss her."

"Yeah, I do too. I've always meant to ask you—do you have any idea where she went? Pops'd never talk about it. When I'd bug him about it he'd just tell me to remember her from when I was little and forget the rest."

"Maybe back home? South Dakota? But your dad's right—she doesn't wanna be found. She called me once—long time ago—to tell me she was doin' better, but that was 'bout all she said—nothin' 'bout where she was or if she was ever comin' back." Marlys paused to take a drag and a long exhale. "Doesn't make it much easier, does it? I mean, you were just a little girl."

"Did she ask about us? Do you remember?"

"Sorry, I don't think so. We didn't talk long." Marlys stared off toward the kitchen wall like she was trying to remember their conversation, or maybe it was her little sister she was trying to remember—my beautiful, sad mother who didn't want to be found.

CHAPTER TWO

"GET THE FUCK away from me Jim or I swear I'll scream." Jim was hovering behind me while I tried to wash the evening dishes. Aunt Marlys, oblivious to what was happening in the kitchen, sat in the living room watching *Three's Company*.

"Awww come on, babe, you know you love it. I got my own *Three's Company* here…what with you and your auntie."

He pushed me closer to the cabinet. His massive belt buckle jabbed me in the lower back, while his hands, one on either side of my body, trapped me against the edge of the stainless steel sink. When I couldn't stand it any longer, I took a paring knife from the dirty dishwater and sliced his right hand between his middle and ring finger.

"God damn it!" he yelled as he grabbed the dish towel to bandage his wound.

Marlys called from the living room, "What'ya done now, Jimmy?"

Before he could answer, I yelled, "Come here quick! He's cut himself helping me."

Jim glared and hissed, "Just you wait, you frigid little bitch. Don't think you're gonna get away with this, cuz you ain't."

* * *

I'D THOUGHT I'D been so clever a year earlier when I'd confessed to Marlys that I'd flooded the laundry room and that *Uncle* Jim had helped me clean it up. I thought I'd left him with no power to blackmail me. Unfortunately, Jim had seen through my strategy and had come up with a new one. A few months after the first flood, he'd staged a second by taking a pair of my knee socks and plugging the drain of the washtub while I was in the shower. Aunt Marlys was home that Sunday morning, and when she discovered the washtub overflowing, she went ballistic. After stopping the washer, she came and pulled me from the shower.

"What kind of fucking idiot did your father raise?" she bellowed as she pushed me onto the flooded floor of the laundry room while I tried to keep a towel wrapped around my wet body. I suppose I could have tried to deny that I'd hung my socks over the tub. I could've told the truth; the last time I'd seen those socks they were on top of my chest of drawers. But it would've been a waste of breath—she wouldn't have believed the truth. I don't know that she loved Jim, but she wasn't about to admit that she'd made a mistake by choosing such a scuzzbucket for a boyfriend.

Jim walked into the kitchen from the back yard as I was mopping up the washer water with my blanket. "Oh God, Jik —what happened?" he said with a smirk. "Betcha hope that doesn't happen again."

I could've killed him.

It was shortly after that Sunday that the *accidental* touching started. It was as though the hall leading to the bathroom was too narrow for Jim to pass me and not brush against my hip. It became impossible for him to put a dish in the sink while I was doing dishes without patting my butt or breathing in my ear. I avoided him as much as possible during daylight hours, and, one night after waking from a sound sleep to find him standing in my doorway, I started bringing a kitchen chair to the laundry room and wedging it under the doorknob of my closed door before I went to bed.

* * *

THANKFULLY, AS SAD as my housing situation was, not everything was horrible the two years I spent in Gareth after Pops and the boys left. I missed them, but not taking care of my brothers gave me more time to earn money and study. I'd always been a fairly good student. I excelled in art classes, enjoyed most English classes, and science and math had been easy for me, although I hadn't taken anything too advanced. One of my teachers, Miss Harris, sort of adopted me as her pet. She saw something in me that my other teachers had missed. Maybe it was because she was new and didn't know my family history, or maybe she just had a more generous spirit than most folks. She taught American Lit, and it became my favorite class.

One day, as I was checking out a book from the library, Miss Harris asked me what college I planned on attending. It was something I'd never been asked, and I loved the way she'd asked it—not *if* I was going, but *where* I was going. I don't think that most of the teachers in my small high school had thought I'd make it to my junior year given my home life, and, in truth, I hadn't been considering college. But, once Miss Harris planted the idea in my head, I started thinking of the little bit of money I'd been squirreling away as my *college fund*. My Pops had been at the University in Laramie when he'd met my mom. He had dropped out, but I figured he'd be proud if I could get into UW.

A few weeks after Miss Harris had asked me about my college plans, I told her that I'd decided I'd like to go to Laramie. She was so happy for me. To me it seemed as good a plan as any, and it gave me something to look forward to, even though I had no idea what to envision, never having seen a college campus. I just knew I'd be learning new things, and, of more immediate concern, I'd be hundreds of miles away from *Uncle* Jim.

* * *

AUNT MARLYS WAS livid. The rubber soles of my tennis shoes made sucking sounds as I lifted them from the sopping kitchen carpet. Marlys slapped my face and hissed, "How could you do it again! What sort of idiot leaves a washing machine running when they leave the house?"

I didn't say, *You do—You do it all the time.* Instead I said, "I'm sorry."

I'd left the washer going when I took off for work, but it was something that I'd never been told not to do. I didn't know what had happened to cause the flood, and I didn't know why Marlys thought it was my fault until she walked to the laundry room and brought back one of my bras and pairs of underpants. She held the soaking lingerie in the air— "These are yours, aren't they?"

"Yes, but I didn't—" Marlys cut me off.

"The hell you didn't! Who else would have left them on the washtub?"

I wanted to scream, *"JIM, JIM, JIM—WHY CAN'T YOU SEE HIM FOR THE SLEAZEBALL HE IS!"* But I didn't. It was less than a month until I graduated and could leave her house for good. It would all be over soon. I'd made my last room and board payment to Aunt Marlys a day earlier—I had to put up with Jim's torture for just a few more weeks. I was not about to let him win and make me homeless.

Marlys loudly explained what I had to do to make amends. First, clean up the mess. *Not a problem.* Second, pay for new kitchen carpet and any necessary cabinet, wall, and floor repairs. She said that I should be grateful—Jim had offered to fix everything at a discounted hourly rate so that I wouldn't have to pay some expensive carpenter. We could keep the labor costs "in the family," as Aunt Marlys put it. I nearly puked. The bastard had set me up, and I was going to have to pay him for it.

I sloshed to my dresser and from the bottom drawer, where I now kept my few art supplies and other important papers, I pulled out the envelope with my savings and handed it to Marlys. I'd managed to save $132.56 over the past two years—my college fund. "If it's not enough, you'll have to give me a little time. It's all I've got right now."

Marlys took the envelope, opened it, and fanned the bills. "We'll see," was all she said.

At least she'd calmed down and I wouldn't have to physically put the money in Jim's hands. At the thought of his ugly paws, I picked up the bra and underpants that Marlys had dropped on the wet kitchen carpet and threw them in the grubby plastic garbage can under the sink. It was my only good set, but I knew I would never again wear them knowing that Jim had handled them.

* * *

THE DAY I graduated, I gritted my teeth and said "thank you" and "goodbye" to my aunt and *uncle*, then headed to Laramie looking to start the rest of my life. Without my savings, college was no longer in the cards, but I hadn't told anyone at school about my change of plans. I'd set my sights on the university town months ago. Laramie seemed as good a place to start over as any, and thanks to Miss Harris's generous graduation gift to me, I had an open-ended bus ticket.

The Greyhound rolled into Laramie at four-forty-seven a.m. I grabbed the pillowcase full of my belongings and walked toward the closest twenty-four-hour diner. A sign in the window read, HELP WANTED: WAITRESSES and

DISHWASHERS. I could do either. *Good*, I thought, *once I have a place to stay, I'll be set.*

I wasn't aiming to be swept away by anything or anybody, but I now realize, I must have looked as vulnerable as a pinfeather in front of a storm drain.

CHAPTER THREE

RICHARD WECKWERTH started talking to me at the diner when he noticed "JICKY" on the plastic rectangle pinned above my left breast. At the Never Empty, the customers usually weren't thinking about reading (except, maybe, in braille) when staring in that general direction. He was the first customer to question me about my name, which was a gift from my father.

Pops's mother had been a dancer of sorts—fans, feather boas, real boas? I never knew what to believe when Pops opened his mouth, but according to him, the French cologne, *Jicky*, had been her signature scent. Pops loved the scent and my dead Grandma Frannie. He named me for both: Jicky Frances O'Connor. My mother didn't care for the name, but she'd once told me that voicing an opinion to Patrick O'Connor was like talking to a post. So, I grew up suffering from all the issues that arise from having a weird name. One that, besides being unusual, rhymed with *icky*, thereby making elementary school an even bigger challenge for me (as though our family living in our car part of the time and me being a head taller than any other girl in my class weren't challenges enough). By my twelfth birthday, Mom still wasn't talking to Pops or anyone else. That was the day she chose to carry her things out the front door and disappeared from our lives.

***

"CARE FOR MORE coffee?"

"Yes, p-p-please...by the way, how's your name pronounced? I've never seen it before."

I poured Rich's coffee and told him in French it was pronounced "JEE-kee," but people usually called me Jik.

Without stuttering, he responded, *"Jicky, un jour, tu m'épouseras."* While I didn't know what he had said, I could pick out my name in the phrase. I thanked him for his pretty words and told him that I would stop back to top off his coffee. By the time I'd made the rounds of the diner with my thermal pot of the singed dishwater we served as coffee, he had gathered his books and disappeared. He'd left me a tip as big as his bill. I hoped I'd see him again, and it had little to do with the tip. I would've felt the same way if he'd left only a dime... or if he hadn't left a tip... or if he hadn't paid for his coffee...

THE DINER WAS never lacking in male customers. I didn't realize until after I'd accepted the job that the Never Empty was known for hiring young, good-looking women. Had I known, I might not have applied after my two years around *Uncle* Jim, but at least at the diner there was an unwritten look-but-don't-touch policy. So as it turned out, I poured coffee for a lot of ogling ranch hands who thought of themselves as cowboys, college students with enough cash to eat out, a few cocky crop-dusters, and the occasional trucker who'd make his way downtown from the interstate.

In general, the ranch hands never said much—they just stared and nodded. I never knew what the students would do. They tended to be loudest when they had the numbers to fill a booth. Usually, when loud, they weren't terribly nice. The truckers and the crop-dusters were the most talkative. Given the chance, they'd chat my ears off. Maybe it came from being alone most of the time. It was a crop-duster who uttered one of my more memorable compliments. As he was leaving he motioned me to his side and told me that I had the best ass he'd ever seen. Now, that's not the kind of charming line a girl hears every day.

Richard wasn't like any of them. He visited during the Never Empty's slow hours, always taking the small corner table by the side window. He ordered food, but never much, and coffee. He drank cup after cup of coffee, which guaranteed that I would stop by his table often. After a couple of weeks he asked me to sit with him during my fifteen-minute afternoon break. I'd sip a fountain Coke and smoke a cigarette while Rich talked about his classes or plans for the weekend. Those few minutes soon became my favorite part of the day.

I learned that he was a student at the University's School of Law and that he shared a house with his best friend, Tom, and his friend's new wife, Pam. He said it was both a good and bad arrangement. He hadn't counted on the awkwardness of sharing a home with newlyweds when he and his friends had made their original plans (why his friends hadn't thought of it, I couldn't fathom). Rich said he would like to move out, but it wasn't in the cards for a while. For now, he was just trying to stay out of the house as much as possible. He told me he spent most evenings in the law library—then, with a smile he added, "the d-d-diner provides a nice d-daytime escape." And, he said he liked seeing me, which pleased me a lot more than hearing that I had a nice ass.

A month after we first met, Rich asked me on a date. Two weeks after that, he introduced me to Thomas and Pamala Streator. On July Fourth, 1980 we married with Tom and Pam by our sides. It was exactly ten months from the day we'd first set eyes on one another, when Rich had said, "*Jicky, un jour, tu m'épouseras."* By the Fourth I knew it meant, "Jicky, someday you will marry me."

* * *

THERE WERE LOTS of fireworks on our wedding night, but only because it was Independence Day. As we drove the barren highways up through Wyoming toward Chadron, it sounded as though the few rural towns and clusters of double-wides we passed were being shelled. By dusk I was sure they were. The beauty of the noisy bombs bursting in air as we neared Lusk almost made up for the incessant heat and dust on our drive north.

We stayed at a roadside motel called The Kennedy. Had we driven a bit longer we would have made it to Rich's hometown, but I assumed he was being romantic and didn't want to stay in his childhood bedroom on our wedding night. Considering the amount of activity in the motel room, we could've just as well slept in the twin beds at his parents' house. Rich apologized for his lack of enthusiasm, saying that he was tired after the long drive. Which may have been true, but it still hurt.

Our wedding had been nice—we were married by a court magistrate at Tom and Pam's place. Rich had made sure that we had flowers. Pam, my matron of honor, had loaned me a dress for the occasion. Tom, Rich's best man, ran the stereo and snapped a few photos. It was very nice. Not every girl's dream, but nice. I had just figured that our first real night together was going to be more than just *nice.* We had kissed a few times during our short courtship, but we'd always been rushed. We had no privacy, and we were both private people. I was not, however, as Jim had called me, a "frigid little bitch." I was looking forward to my wedding night—I loved Rich, and I thought once we had a room, and a whole night together with no one else around, I might finally understand what made sex such a powerful force in the world. As it turned out, I was wrong.

WE DROVE INTO Chadron before lunch on the fifth. Rich's parents lived in a beautiful old house close to the Methodist Church that they attended every Sunday and, in the case of Rich's mom, many other days of the week as well. After carrying our suitcase inside, Rich took the car and headed to the insurance agency to greet his father and bring him home for lunch. He whispered in my ear as he was leaving that this was a request from his mother, who wanted some time alone with me. He said, "She t-t-t-told me she wants to get to know her new daughter without her old son around answering all the q-q-questions." Obviously, she knew her "old son" well. I didn't mind talking, but Rich rarely let me answer questions when we were together—it was as though he didn't trust what would come from my mouth.

Gloria, who had asked me to call her "Mother," was warm, but *sooo* formal. When I asked if there was anything I could do to help her prepare lunch, she gave me a firm, "no, thank you," but she patted one of the kitchen chairs and said I should sit so that we could chat while she finished making a fruit salad.

She told me she was disappointed Richard and I hadn't had a larger wedding—she would have loved to have met my family and celebrated our big day. She said she'd been so happy when Thomas had married Pamala, and had thoroughly enjoyed their wedding the previous summer. She stated that she had always hoped she would see her only son take a bride. As she spoke I thought, *not a good beginning*. Her tone hadn't been judgmental, just a little sad—at least she seemed genuinely pleased that Rich and I were married.

I wanted to tell her Rich had planned it all, but I was afraid it would sound as though I was somehow blaming him for the arrangements and his parent's exclusion. I had asked him if he wanted his parents to come and he'd said "no." At the time I hadn't asked him why, though I should have. I thought maybe he didn't get along with his folks. I now realized it had most likely been for my benefit. He knew my family would not be part of our big day, so his wouldn't be either. He would have seen it as the only fair way to handle our parental inequality.

I told Gloria that in order to spare my feelings, her generous son had deprived himself of his parents' participation. I explained that my mom was out of the picture and that my father and brothers couldn't have afforded the trip from Connecticut. Gloria said she was very sorry to hear about my family's situation. "Under those circumstances you should have had the wedding in Chadron at *our* church."

I thanked her for her generosity, but said both Rich and I were happy with our small ceremony. "Well, we're legally hitched, and I'm pretty sure our vows are gonna stick even though we didn't get to say them in a church." Gloria winced at my remark, but asked me to tell her all about the ceremony as she carefully scooped little balls of watermelon from large slices left over from the church's Fourth of July picnic. She said she wanted to know every detail; she wanted to feel as though she had been with us.

So, I explained that at nine o'clock, after packing my things, I'd met Rich, Tom, and Pam at the Never Empty, the diner where I worked (and where Rich and I had met), for a big pre-ceremony breakfast. I told her how my colleagues at the diner had surprised me by picking up the tab for our meal and giving us a big laundry basket full of kitchen gadgets and household items. I explained that much of our courtship had been on view at the diner and how a few of the girls felt they knew Rich almost as well as they knew me.

I told her when we arrived at Pam and Tom's house after breakfast it was so clean and polished that it sparkled. Pam had decorated the living room with red, white, and blue crepe paper streamers and puffy bows to make it extra festive. Shortly before the ceremony, the neighbors brought over flowers that Rich had stored in their air-conditioned bedroom overnight because the florist wouldn't deliver on the Fourth. He'd surprised me by ordering a big bouquet of red roses in a blue vase and white rose corsages and boutonnieres trimmed with red, white, and blue ribbons.

I told her about the vintage off-white dress with the royal blue sash that Pam had loaned me. And, I showed her my wedding band that matched Rich's—with those items we thought we had covered the "something old, something new, something borrowed, something blue" tradition.

She asked who had performed the ceremony and I explained that a court magistrate who was an adjunct professor at the law school had stopped by to do the honors, and even though he was on his way to a picnic he had been dressed appropriately. He'd waited until after the ceremony to change into shorts and a T-shirt in Tom and Pam's bathroom.

She said, "I suppose you didn't have music?" When I told her we had played the stereo, she wanted to know our selections. I said we had both chosen a piece for Tom to queue up. For my processional I'd chosen "Annie's Song" by John Denver. Her response was, "Oh, I see. What did Richard select?" I told her Rich had chosen a pretty "innermetzo" from some opera to be played after the magistrate declared us married. When I said I couldn't remember the name of the opera—that I had a hard time remembering words in foreign languages—Gloria asked, "Might it have been the

'Intermezzo' from *Cavalleria Rusticana*? It's one of his favorites."

"That's it! Rich told me it means 'rustic chivalry.' He told me (I lowered my voice to imitate Rich), *'while the music's beautiful the story doesn't end well'*." Raising my voice to its normal pitch I continued, "He's so sweet—he asked if I would mind if we played it at the wedding. Like he needed my permission. I mean, he was the one making all the plans—I said if he liked it, it would be fine with me. I don't know much about opera, but the one thing I do know is that most of the good ones don't end well."

* * *

RICH AND HIS dad roared into the kitchen talking with more animation than I had ever seen in my new husband. It was as though his dad gave him an extra boisterousness that I had only seen a few times when Rich and Tom had popped into the Never Empty to see me at work. When Pam was around, Tom might still fire on all cylinders, but Rich would always tone it back.

It didn't take me long to see Rich's mom had the same effect on him as did Pam. Even his dad became more subdued once he'd stepped off the throw-rug by the back door onto the kitchen linoleum. In this house it was clear that my new mother-in-law was the person in charge. Perhaps that was the way it was in other homes too, but it wasn't anything that I'd seen while growing up. Even as demanding as Aunt Marlys could be, she alway let scuzzy *Uncle* Jim think he was the boss.

Rich's dad gave me a big hug and said, "Rich is right, you are a pretty one." Then to Gloria he added, "Have you two girls had fun getting to know one another?"

"Of course, Westerly. Go wash up. We are eating in the dining room today."

Rich had warned me it was his parent's custom to say grace before meals. I was thankful for the heads-up—I'd never lived in a praying household and would have been mortified seeing his folks bow their heads while I reached for the dinner rolls. Rich hadn't warned me, however, that his mother would ask me to offer the table grace. I could have tried to fake it, but I didn't even know where to start. I suppose I could have recited the Pledge of Allegiance, but I don't think Gloria would've laughed. In the end, I was truthful and told my new family that I didn't know how to pray. I asked if I might say a table grace in a day or two after I'd heard a few. Rich saved me by offering the lunchtime blessing, and that afternoon, while he drove me around his hometown, he taught me the subtleties of Methodist prayer. Another honeymoon surprise.

* * *

AFTER TWO DAYS in Chadron I learned that everyone we met near the Methodist Church knew Gloria, and everyone we met anywhere in town knew Westerly Weckwerth. Wes greeted everyone, young and old, with the same enthusiasm and familiarity. He remembered their stories and, at least for the moments he spent in their presence, empathized or celebrated with them. He was a man easy to like. I saw some of those qualities in Rich, but in most ways my husband was more his mother's son.

Gloria had an internal compass that seemed to keep her pointed toward the direction of "good," or at least her interpretation of the concept. She was a planner and a true behind-the-scenes person—the kind of person who got things done and often failed to get recognized or appreciated for her contribution. If that bothered her, I never noticed. She was self-confident, self-contained, and very hard to get to know.

Tuesday evening, our last evening in Chadron, Gloria made a pork roast, riced potatoes, and green beans for supper even though it was still ninety-three degrees at five o'clock. The spring before, Rich's folks had installed central air-conditioning in their sixty-year-old house, making oven dinners a more comfortable possibility in the summer. Evidently, this dinner was Rich's favorite, and it was the one I was asked to bless. I had heard several different table graces over the visit, so chose the one that I liked best: "Be present at our table, Lord; Be here and everywhere adored; Thy creatures bless and grant that we, May feast in paradise with thee." I figured I had pulled it off by the family's collective, "Amen."

CHAPTER FOUR

THE DRIVE HOME from Chadron was going to be longer than the drive there. It was definitely hotter. My sweaty legs stuck to the vinyl car seat and wrinkled my cotton wraparound skirt, while the wind from the open windows twisted my auburn hair into tight coils guaranteeing me an hour of effort with with a comb and brush.

We'd taken off from Rich's parents' house early Wednesday, giving us a full two days before I had to be back at the Never Empty on Saturday morning. We were going to drive through the Black Hills of South Dakota before turning west. Mountains weren't anything special to me, having lived in or near them most of my life, but Rich wanted to show me Mount Rushmore—the mountain carved with the faces of the presidents. At least that was the plan.

As we neared the town of Hot Springs, the car started whining worse than bagpipes in the hands of a novice. Then the sputtering started. At the edge of town the Chevy gasped, coughed, and stopped. We spent the next six hours in Hot Springs having our fuel pump rebuilt and our checking account depleted. When we finally left town heading north, it was evening. We hadn't arranged for a place to stay thinking that we would be stopping early enough to find something. But now it was late, and there were no rooms. Even though it wasn't part of his plan, after paying for the fuel pump, Rich thought it a blessing for our budget—no motel meant no motel bill.

We stopped at the Ruby House in Keystone for a late dinner, then drove the short distance to Mount Rushmore. We got to the parking lot just as the rangers were escorting people to their cars. Rich didn't seem perturbed by our timing and told me he had a new plan. He said that the Black Hills were full of back roads—we could just find a quiet spot, park, and spend the night in the car. We'd see the presidents in the morning while it was still cool, then quickly tour the Hills before heading back to Laramie. We'd be home by late-afternoon. I was relieved. Thanks to our stop at the Ruby House, my stomach was now full of fried chicken, and we had an adventurous plan for the night. After a childhood full of uncertainty, it felt good to be with a man who could make a plan and wanted to take care of me.

Rich turned onto a logging road in the National Forest and drove until he spotted an area wide enough to turn the sedan around so that it would be headed back toward the highway come morning. It had been dusk before we'd left the main road, but now, deep within the trees, the velvety dark felt thick enough to cut. As we stepped from the car, the only light we could see shined down from the large stars straight above our heads. In the new-moon sky the shiny orbs looked so close I thought it might be possible to reach up and unscrew them like lightbulbs.

"Leave your door open, Jik and open the back door on your side. I'll t-t-take the front seat and you c-c-can have the back—it's easier to sleep when you don't have the steering wheel to c-c-contend with. My friend K-K-Kevin and I used to do this all the time … It'll be fine. The seats in Chevys are like sleepin' on a c-c...sofa."

I said thanks, but thought it was another pretty unromantic way to spend what now appeared to be the last night of our honeymoon. My only consolation was the night air. It felt cool after the afternoon's heat, and it smelled sweet like the sap on the ponderosa pines. I took off my skirt, laid it on the flat area below the back window, then slid head first into the backseat, angling my neck so that the door's armrest served as a pillow. My feet hung off the end of the bench seat, but Rich was right, it wasn't uncomfortable.

I woke hours later with Rich reaching into the back seat from the open door trying to spread a blanket over my prone body. He may have succeeded had I not reached up and pulled him on top of me. We started kissing and in the darkness of that mountain night, thrashing in the backseat of his yellow Chevrolet, I finally started to figure out why sex makes people act like such idiots.

Rich and I woke a little after four o'clock, the birds just starting to sing. We were a tangled mess of legs, clothes, and blanket. I would've liked to have snuggled or, even better, started the whole process over, but Rich had already turned back into the Rich of the past week—his reserve was now far more abundant than his passion from a few hours earlier.

He climbed from the car and suggested that I do the same. His head turned away from me, he said in a ragged voice, "We c-c-can leave now and d-drive to Mt. Rushmore to watch the morning sun illuminate the faces." Then he walked into the woods until I couldn't see him.

I squatted beside the car's back tire to relieve myself and attempted to clean up from the night. I'd never been a *girly* girl, but I was thinking that a gas station restroom, or even a cup of water, would have been handy. It was still too dark to find my Baggie of toiletries in the suitcase, and, besides, without water there wasn't much point. I dressed, straightened the backseat, and savored memories as I folded the blanket.

Rich eventually returned to the car, his face puffy and his eyes red. I asked if anything was wrong. He didn't reply at first, just shook his head. A bit later, after wiping his nose, he told me he thought he was having an allergic reaction to something in the air—he'd be better once we got back to Wyoming.

We left our spot in the woods, and, after a short and quiet drive, Rich parked the Chevy in the empty lot at Mount Rushmore. As we walked toward the Visitors' Center, Rich held my hand and led me up the winding and still dark path to a bench facing the carved mountain. He'd grabbed the blanket as we'd left the car and now wrapped it around both of us while we watched the mountain being bathed by the orange sunrise. Rich was right—it was spectacular. As I rested my messy head on his shoulder I thought about the decision I'd made to marry this sweet, peculiar man. It had been a good one.

* * *

WE'D STOPPED AT a truck-stop near the Wyoming border to clean up and have a late breakfast. I felt so much better after having washed, braided my hair, and eaten my fill of pancakes and bacon. As we turned back onto the highway, Rich asked, "Jik, do you want to k-k-keep working at the Never Empty?"

I was surprised by his question, because I'd never thought not working was an option, and I thought once you'd landed a job you kept it. In my experience, good jobs weren't easy to find.

Rich continued, "I d-don't mean not working, but now that we're married are you g-g-gonna feel c-c-comfortable with all those guys leering at you? You know what I mean, it's why guys go there. G-G-God knows it's not for the c-c-coffee."

"I guess you should know, you drank enough of it... I figured I'd stay there—the tips are good and no one's ever really hassled me. Do you want me to quit?"

"I'd just rather you worked somewhere else. It's up to you, but if you're okay with it, I'll ask around at the University to see if there are any c-c...job openings. You c-c-can t-type, right?"

"Yeah, I can type—I took it in school, but I'm prob'ly a little rusty."

"N-no problem, I've got an electric. You c-c-can practice at home."

* * *

WE DROVE ON, passing rusty oil wells, sagging barbed wire fences, and wind-beaten mobile homes.

I'd been quiet, thinking about what I could do for a job if I wasn't waiting tables. Rich had been quiet too, obviously lost in thoughts of his own. When he finally spoke he said he had a request of me. Maybe, because it was our honeymoon, I thought it was going to be something personal. In a way it was, but certainly not what I'd expected. Rich asked me to quit being so openly inquisitive. He suggested that I keep my questions for him. He said when I heard something that I didn't understand, I should look around the room and take my facial cues from others, but remain silent. Or, if I had to say something, it should be a noncommittal, "Oh," or "I see," or "Is that so?" Rich said he would answer my questions when we were alone.

I was at a loss; I had no idea what he meant, and I told him so.

"Jicky, you're an adult. There are things that you should already know that you d-d-don't seem to have learned— things I'd thought you'd have p-picked up on from reading the p-paper or listening to the news, like when you asked my d-d-dad about Saddam Hussein, or when you d-didn't get his joke about N-N-Nebraska having a unicameral legislature and asked him if unicameral meant a camel with one hump."

I told Rich that I had never been embarrassed by my lack of education, and while I hadn't known what unicameral meant, I'd thought my quip about one-humped camels was pretty funny. "I know what I know, and if I ask questions, I learn more. Isn't learning new stuff good?"

"Yes, of c-course it is, but now that we're married, we're a t-t-team, and I want our t-team to both look and *sound* intelligent."

I tried not to be hurt by his comment. I understood what he meant, and if he'd thought I was dumb he wouldn't have married me. But, I had never in my life not been myself. I'd been asked to do some odd things, some of them pretty embarrassing, yet this was the most hurtful request ever made of me—even though I knew that Rich hadn't meant it to be. In every other instance I'd been able to say no to jerks like *Uncle Jim* and get on with my life, but it now appeared, to get on with my life as Rich's wife, I was going to have to be agreeable and keep my mouth shut most of the time.

CHAPTER FIVE

I SAT IN THE old swiveling office chair behind the reception desk in the Math Department dressed in Pam's clothes and tried to figure out how I'd gotten there. Rich and I had only been married a little over two months, but he'd managed to change me so much in that time that I wasn't sure of who I'd been or who I was becoming.

"Hello, you've reached the mathematics department. No, Professor Scott isn't in today. He'll be back tomorrow, if you'd like to try back then." I paused before saying, "Certainly, Dr. Marshall, I'll give him the message."

I wrote, *You suck. It is on Friday.* on a pink message slip and put it on Dr. Scott's desk. It seemed rather rude, but my job was to write the messages as they were given to me, so I wrote what Dr. Marshall had said. From the few dealings I'd had with him, *you suck* was on the mild side. Scott and Marshall were good friends, and their banter could get raunchy, especially Marshall's.

Most of my message taking and call transferring was pretty routine. And, while the job was "respectable," (a term Rich deemed important) I found it terribly boring. I would have preferred waiting tables at the Never Empty, where my work days were predictable, but never exactly the same. Plus, I made tips. In the Mathematics Department I rattled around the front office listening to the clock tick and pondered how to dust the disgustingly overgrown cactus plants that filled the deep window sill.

I'd tried talking with Rich about the situation, but he'd just told me I should make the best of it. He reminded me that I could audit classes as long as they didn't interfere with my normal work day—it was one of the benefits of working for the University. So, I started reviewing the course catalog to see if there was a class that both interested me and would fit with a schedule that kept me tied to the mathematics office from eight to five. That's how I ended up in the Art Department one blustery afternoon a few days before Halloween.

* * *

I'D EATEN a bologna sandwich at my desk before leaving to cross the campus. One of the art professors, Janet Marley, had offered to meet me over my lunch hour to review my possible participation in a class or two. Evening classes were limited, but Dr. Marley had told me that Life Drawing-101 was usually held in the evening to make it easier to find models and that the ceramics and photography classes were also often held both day and evening because of limited potter's wheels and darkroom space.

I had twenty minutes for the rushed meeting, and when I arrived on the other edge of the sprawling campus, Dr. Marley was nowhere to be seen. The only person in the building willing to talk to me was a long-haired art student with a bum leg who introduced himself as Danny Ogden and then offered to show me around since it appeared I'd been stood up by the professor. Danny said that he was a graduate student and worked in the Art Department, so I figured he would do. By the time we had walked through the various studios and I'd seen the student projects, I was sold. I was wishing (yeah, there's that word) that I could do more than just audit a few night classes next semester when Danny said, "Come back Thursday at seven for the Life Drawing class to see if it might be something you'd like to be part of this semester."

"Sure, but isn't it too late to start?...and, won't I need the professor's approval?"

"Nope, you can start right away if you want, and you're already approved. I teach the Thursday night session. By the way, what's your name? I don't think you told me earlier, or if you did, I forgot already. Sorry."

"No...I'm sorry...I don't think I told you. It's Jicky. Jicky O'Connor." I reached out my hand to shake Danny's. His was strong, stained with paint pigments, and smelled of turpentine. It wasn't until I was rushing back to the math building that I realized I'd given Danny Ogden my maiden name. I'd been "Jicky Weckwerth" for three months, but on that October day, excited about a new beginning, I'd blissfully forgotten how much my life had changed.

That afternoon I started my quest to find out who in the Mathematics Department owned the dusty cactuses that blocked the light and air from my only window. When I found that no one seemed to own the cactuses, or had even noticed that they existed (to quote Dr. Scott who passed by them multiple times a day, "What cacti?"), I borrowed an AV-cart from the closet and transferred them, pots and all, into the dumpster at the back of the building. I'd buy a replacement plant over the weekend, something more pleasant—less prickly—maybe a philodendron.

It was time for me to start taking back part of my life.

* * *

THURSDAY QUICKLY BECAME my favorite day of the week. I would smile through my hours at the Mathematics Department, rush home to make supper, clean up, and be out the door heading back to campus by six-thirty. Danny started his class, or, session as he called it, promptly at seven. He said that while we may not be professionals yet, our models were, and he had promised to respect their time.

I'd taken art classes in junior and senior high school, but this was different. I'd always been naturally artistic and my work was often admired—here I was among talented and trained artists drawing the human body, something that I had never done. I was unsure of myself and unusually self-conscious, but I was learning so much from Danny Ogden, and he was always so generous with his praise for the few things I did well that I never thought of quitting.

Rich was supportive at home—I suppose that wasn't surprising since he'd been the one to suggest I take advantage of my auditing privileges at the University. While I didn't have to pay for classes, I found out at my first drawing session that I would need to buy supplies. Good art supplies are expensive and we didn't have much extra cash. Rich laughed when I asked about the purchases. "Of course you c-c-can buy what ever you need, Jik. You d-d-don't need my permission to buy your supplies."

We hadn't talked much about money—I'd just figured if I was going to spend our savings on something that was only for me, I should clear it with my spouse. Rich went on, "Now, if it's something big t-t-ticket, l-l-like an appliance or a c-c-car, yes, we would need to t-talk, but on the little stuff, just use your judgement. From what I've seen, you're more of a p-p-penny-pincher than me."

Rich was right. He had grown up in a home where money wasn't an issue. The Weckwerths were solidly middle class. They had enough money so as not to worry if their furnace quit or little Richie ripped a hole in the knee of his dress pants. That hadn't been the situation in my family. Not that my parents seemed concerned about money—we just didn't have any. If our furnace broke (or the gas got turned off for non-payment, which was more likely), we stayed cold or split up the family and found friends with heat. When my little brother, Joey, ripped his clothes during recess, he wore them with holes. Gary, being the youngest, always wore holes. I don't know that he'd ever had anything new to wear. That was the life I'd known, one of hand-me-downs and left-overs. Which was sort of the case for me again, and maybe that was another reason I thought I should ask before buying pastels and drawing pencils.

Part of the reason I didn't feel like myself during the work week was that I was dressing in Pam's hand-me-downs. Pam loved buying new clothes. The expense had never been an issue for her—she had wealthy parents who still supported her, and, following her graduation, she had a well-paying job as a dental hygienist. When she'd loaned me the vintage dress for my wedding she'd mentioned that her closet was full of things she no longer wore. For work, she now wore a uniform, and when not at work she preferred to wear her newest outfits.

I'd left home with enough clothing to fill a pillowcase: one extra pair of jeans, a wraparound skirt, three T-shirts, two flannel shirts, a sweatshirt, a jean jacket and a winter coat. I had two pair of shoes—one was a pair of sneakers (now food stained from wearing them while waitressing), the other, an old pair of cowboy boots that Aunt Marlys had given me when her bunions got so big she couldn't pull them on anymore. I wore a uniform at the Never Empty. Not that it had been free, I'd had to pay for it from my first four paychecks, but I always knew what I'd be wearing to work. It had made life simple, and it was another reason I'd been hesitant when Rich talked to me about working at the University during our ride home after our honeymoon. When I told him I didn't have the wardrobe for an office job, he told me that he had already talked to Pam about the situation. They had it covered—as it turned out, they literally had *me* covered.

Rich had gone through Pam's cast-offs and chosen a work wardrobe for me. My feet were a half size larger than Pam's, so he'd taken me to Baker's Shoes in downtown Laramie and bought me a pair of heels and a pair of flats. I had never owned so many beautiful things, but I also never felt like they were mine. Every morning when I dressed for work I felt like an imposter. I wasn't Pam, a girl who wore scratchy wool slacks and expensive sweaters. I was Jicky. I felt far more at home in my orange and brown polyester waitress uniform or my faded Ts and jeans.

* * *

IT WAS ANOTHER Thursday evening. I'd stripped off Pam's pink-plaid skirt and vest as soon as I'd come through the duplex door, and then quickly dressed for class in jeans, boots, and my old jean jacket. After fixing a rushed supper of Campbell's Chunky Soup over boiled rice, I kissed Rich, grabbed my art supplies and headed out the door.

I paused on our duplex's steps and looked up at the stars. After a big gulp of air, I exhaled for what felt like the first time since the previous Thursday and took off back to campus.

CHAPTER SIX

IN DECEMBER, RICH and I would be going to Chadron for Christmas Eve services at First Methodist and having Christmas dinner with his extended Nebraska family whom I hadn't met yet because, as Rich's mother often reminded me in her letters, we hadn't had a big wedding. Tom and Pam had made plans to join her family at their suburban home outside of Denver for the holiday, then visit the family cabin in Vail for some post-Christmas skiing. On their drive home, they would stop by Tom's family's ranch in northern Colorado for a New Year's Eve celebration. Our little foursome, having Christmas arranged, explained to our families that we wouldn't be traveling over Thanksgiving—not that Pops and my brothers had ever expected I would see them during the holidays.

Pam's dentist had given all his employees large turkeys for Thanksgiving, so she and Tom were tackling the bird and making desserts. Rich and I were put in charge of the side dishes. Pam seemed to have doubts about our ability when this division of labor was arranged, but we assured her that we could follow recipes—we had both been reading since the age of six.

* * *

"HELP, JICKY, THE potatoes are b-b-burning."

We'd let the water boil over and the peeled potatoes had adhered themselves to the sides of the aluminum pan.

Pops overheard Rich's voice through the receiver. "Oops, sounds like you're in trouble with the bossman."

"Don't worry, he's fine—he can turn off the stove as easily as I can. It's not everyday that I hear from you guys, even if all the boys wanted to do was give me their Christmas lists. I'm really glad you called, but I suppose I should go deal with the rest of the food so we won't be late for dinner."

"Wish we could see you someday, hon—it seems like it's been forever."

"Well, Pops, like mom always said, *if wishes were horses, beggars would ride.* It's been over three years. I couldn't believe how much older the boys looked in their school photos."

"God, Jicky, you should see how tall they're gettin'—those pictures don't show that."

"Who knows, maybe next year after Rich graduates I'll have the time and a few extra bucks to come see you guys, but right now Pops, I better go rescue the potatoes. Happy Thanksgiving."

I hung up the phone thinking about how seldom I'd spoken to my father over the past few years. We were all pretty good about writing during our first year apart, but after Pops and Louisa had parted ways it was months before I'd had an address so that I could send a note, let alone a phone number to make a long-distance call. I'd felt kind of bad about that. I'd been sending Joel money whenever I could, but when I'd thought he and Gary needed it the most (when I was pretty sure they were homeless), I hadn't known how to reach them. Rich didn't know, but I was still sending cash to my brothers. While Rich had always been generous with me, I wasn't sure how he'd feel about sharing our money with my family. I'd kept my mouth shut because I didn't want to risk having him tell me how to behave regarding my brothers—there were some things about my life that I didn't want to change.

* * *

WE CARRIED OUR "burnt offerings," as Rich was calling them, over to Tom and Pam's side of our shared duplex. The food wasn't burned; Rich had just panicked when the potatoes boiled over. I'd left any bits of brown-tinged potato in the big sauce pan now soaking in our kitchen sink. The potatoes that I'd mashed looked and tasted fine, the green bean casserole appeared perfect, and the packaged dinner rolls were guaranteed fresh for two weeks, so I was sure that they were soft. We were running a little late, not because of Pops's phone call, or the potatoes, but because Rich had asked me to change clothes before we'd walked to Tom and Pam's side of the house.

I'd been wearing jeans and a T-shirt while cooking. It felt good to wear my own clothes on a weekday and I hadn't planned on changing for dinner. Rich and I had lived with Tom and Pam for over a month (July Fourth until mid-August) before Tom and Pam had closed on the duplex. It wasn't like we were strangers—they had seen me dressed informally before, and I'd always felt a little funny dressed in Pam's clothes when I was with Pam. It seemed like a no-win situation. Either the clothes had looked better on her, making me feel bad, or worse, they looked better on me, which I'm sure felt like a punch in the gut to Pam. Nevertheless, I changed as requested by Rich, and we were fashionably late.

* * *

PAM'S TABLE LOOKED like something out of *Better Homes and Gardens*. She had placed orange placemats over a gold tablecloth and set them with brown and tan ceramic dishes. Cloth napkins that matched the gold tablecloth were gathered in wooden napkin rings and placed on the plates, and an arrangement of cut flowers in a wicker cornucopia anchored the center of the table. Ivory tapers glowed on either side of centerpiece. I had never seen such a lovely table—I thought displays like the one in front of me only existed in magazine photoshoots or possibly in the homes of very rich folks with servants.

The previous Thanksgiving I'd worked my usual shift at the Never Empty, where the special decorations had included colorful Thanksgiving themed paper placemats with scalloped edges. They'd been provided by one of the restaurant supply companies. The kids' version had had a line drawing of a turkey wearing a Pilgrim hat—it was meant to be colored at the table to give kids something to do while they waited for their food to be served. Unfortunately, the restaurant manager had been too cheap to buy crayons. Maybe he knew from past experience that there wouldn't be many kids. Since the Never Empty appealed to loners, most of the kids dragged in to eat dry turkey and salty stuffing came with their despondent divorced dads who "got them" for Thanksgiving, because their harried moms "had them" for Christmas. I'd wished we could've at least given the few kids who'd shown up packs of crayons so that they could've colored their sad black and white turkeys.

WE TOOK OUR plates from the table to dish up in the kitchen so that we could leave the centerpiece intact. Pam and Tom had done a great job roasting their first bird, and though Pam's gravy was lumpy, Tom's sausage stuffing was tasty. We pushed away from the table after main course seconds followed by hefty desserts and vowed to not eat again for days.

"I'd be happy to help you with the dishes, Pam," I said, as we carried our empty dessert plates into the kitchen. "I can wash—or dry—doesn't matter. You'll just have to give me directions on where to put stuff." I'd known Pam and Tom's old kitchen, but I'd barely seen Pam since we'd moved, even though Rich spent at least part of most evenings with Tom.

Pam brushed me off. "That's okay, Jik. Just help me cover the leftovers and put them in the fridge. Tom can help me later. There's a game starting in fifteen minutes that I want to catch."

Pam, a former cheerleader, was a huge football fan, probably as big a fan of pro-football as the guys. I found nothing quite as boring as sitting with them while they watched football. Well, maybe that's not true—I found the threesome's fascination with politics just as boring. Besides being obsessed with current governmental events, Rich had his gaze on a future in politics—specifically, getting Tom elected to office. They spoke about it all the time. Rich had the smarts, and Tom, while just as smart, had the charisma needed to win votes. Privately they considered themselves a team and they had since shortly after they'd met as freshmen at UW.

Pam had joined their political team after falling under Tom's spell. The two had met in a poly sci class that Pam was taking for her minor. She'd earned a B.S. in dental hygiene— her minor was in public policy. She was just biding time working for the turkey-gifting dentist while Tom finished his Master's in political science, but her sights were set higher. Like Tom and Rich, she wanted a life in government. She saw herself as a policy wonk in training. I was Rich's wife, part of his team (as he often reminded me), but I don't think any of them ever saw me as part of their political futures. I had quickly learned to tune them out.

I STUCK AROUND for the first quarter of the game, then went home to change clothes and take a nap. I promised to rejoin them at halftime, after asking what time it would be starting. How fifteen minutes could take so long was a mystery to me.

When I came back forty minutes later in my jeans and sweatshirt, Tom was on the porch having a cigarette. I knew there was no way that Rich or Pam would be joining him, so I asked if I could bum one. Rich hated to see me smoke, and I'd been trying to quit since before we'd gotten married, but that late autumn afternoon the temptation was too great.

"I thought you'd given up the coffin nails, Jickster—or is that only when Rich is around?"

"Well, yeah, I've been trying to quit, but somedays—like those when I see somebody I know smoking—it's just hard to tell myself no. Do you ever feel that way about anything?"

Tom handed me a Winston and pulled his monogramed lighter from his pocket. With a single squeeze of his thumb against his fingers, he flipped it open and the flame flared. He lit my cigarette while taking a drag on his own. As he tucked the lighter back into a pocket of his tight jeans, he finally answered my question.

"No, Jiks, I don't. I tend to do whatever the hell I like and like whatever the hell I do. Pam's been after me to quit since day one, but I figure I've been smoking since I was sixteen." Tom scoffed, "Shit, my mom gave me my lighter when I still lived at home—Pam knew I smoked—" he paused and took a long drag, "she married me anyway—why should I change now?"

"Well, maybe it's just different for me and Rich—he's made a lot of changes in my life. I'm okay with most of 'em, but completely giving up smoking... well, that's tough. Sometimes I feel like I need to smoke."

"Seems like Rich likes to play Svengali with you."

I answered with one of the noncommittal responses Rich had taught me, "You think?"

"Well, I'd say he's at least trying to be Henry Higgins to your Eliza Doolittle."

"You don't say," I mumbled, as I stubbed out my remaining cigarette, wiped my hands on my jeans, and pushed my way through Tom and Pam's front door.

I had no idea what Tom had meant by what he'd just said to me, and I think he knew it, but I was also certain that I couldn't ask Rich. I was going to have to remember the names until I could find someone to ask—*Spengolly*, or something like it, and *Henry Higgins. What, or who, were they?*

CHAPTER SEVEN

IT WAS ANOTHER Thursday, the first week in December. Danny Ogden and I sat on the half-wall outside the Art Building smoking. We'd been talking as we left the building, and when Danny stopped for his after class cigarette, I asked if I could join him. The day after Thanksgiving, I'd bought myself a pack of Winstons—the one I'd bummed from Tom had tasted so good. As I paid my sixty cents, I thought about what Tom had said on Thanksgiving afternoon—I'd decided to try to be like him and "do whatever the hell I liked" for a change. I knew that Rich's advice to quit smoking was good, but I just wasn't ready, and I was tired of feeling bad about myself.

Danny and I had been talking about the notion of negative space in drawing. It was a concept that I'd not been taught in my past art classes, and I was amazed at how helpful I'd found it when figuring out spacial relationships in my drawings.

"The more ways you learn to look at an object, or a person, the easier it is for you to capture your subject on paper," Danny said, as he exhaled, slowly blowing smoke rings into the cool night air. "Guess that only makes sense—it's like knowin' a person. The more you know about 'em the better you understand 'em—well, most of the time."

I thought he was probably right. "So what should I know about you, Danny Ogden?"

"Boy, did I step into that one—I hate to talk about myself, but since you asked…" Danny mused for awhile while he finished his cigarette, then stood up and ground the butt out on the sidewalk with his good leg. "What I know is, it's gettin' late, and I should get home to my wife and kids."

For some reason his response took me by surprise, maybe because I'd always pictured him as a loner. I tried to keep the disappointment I was feeling from my voice and said in an overly bright tone, "Kids? How many do you have?"

"Two little ones—a boy—he's four, and our little girl is just a bit over a year."

"So, you've got the perfect family."

"Guess so—they're the only *perfect* I got goin' for me." Danny turned and limped toward the parking lot calling out, "See ya next week. Only two sessions left this semester."

Fine dry snow fell as I walked home feeling disappointed. I knew it was stupid of me, but I was sad that Danny Ogden was married. It was like his being married meant nothing could happen between us; of course, I was married, too, but for some reason that knowledge hadn't dulled my imagination. Only two weeks left …

* * *

WE WAITED OUTSIDE the locked studio door. None of us remembered having ever gotten to the classroom before the instructor. Danny was never late. At ten past seven one of the senior students suggested we move to the always-open student workroom down the hall. With only two sessions left, we all wanted to continue working on the drawings we had started the week before.

Danny walked into the workroom about half past seven. He was visibly *off*. I couldn't tell if he was drunk or high, but he was something. He didn't say anything to the class—he just motioned to the senior student who had taken charge to keep doing what he was doing, then slumped in a torn vinyl chair at the back of the room.

I didn't hear him leave, but Danny was gone by the time class was over.

The following week our session was led by Dr. Janet Marley. She made no mention of Danny Ogden. It was as though he had never been our instructor.

CHAPTER EIGHT

RICH AND I walked the downtown streets enjoying the decorated store windows. Laramie, like other towns in the weeks before Christmas, had spruced up and was showing off her wares. In a way, Rich and I were doing the same—we were dressed for a luncheon hosted by one of his law professors, but had stopped downtown to run some errands before attending the gathering. As I noticed our reflection in the unusually clean plate-glass windows, I thought about what an attractive couple we made. It struck me as funny that I'd never thought about it before—maybe because I'd unconsciously compared us to Tom and Pam. I'd always known that they were striking —beautiful Pam with her pale skin and hair, next to her powerfully built ex-wrestler husband. Tom's hair was as dark as Pam's was blonde, and, for a man who studied all the time, he somehow never lost his rancher's tan. Tom and Pam were the kind of couple people noticed. I knew this because I'd noticed them around town months before Rich had introduced us (though I'd never mentioned it to any to them). They were the kind of young couple that people admired on sight. Kids wanted to be like them, and older folks wished their children would grow up to be so handsome and happy.

WE HAD JUST, that morning, sent a package off to Pops and the boys with their gifts, and I was hoping they would get it before Christmas. While I was fairly certain the box would arrive at the Waterbury post office before the twenty-fifth, I didn't know how often my father checked for mail. Maybe Joel and Gary, knowing I always sent presents, made him check more frequently in December. Rich'd been great about me sending gifts to my family and had encouraged me to spend even more on the boys than I had planned. Because of his generosity I'd managed to buy several things from the wish lists they'd rattled off during our Thanksgiving Day phone call. (Spending the extra money had made me feel even more guilty when I'd slid in the envelope of cash that I'd been hiding in my sock drawer.)

"What should I get your mom and dad for Christmas?" I asked Rich as we passed a trendy women's clothing store.

"Oh, Jik, you d-don't have to get my p-parents anything. I get them the same thing every year—we c-c-can just add your name to the t-t-tag."

"What *same thing* do you get them? Your answer didn't tell me much."

"I always g-get a new board game and a big c-c-can of popcorn—the kind with three flavors. We break open the g-game after dinner on Christmas Day, p-p-pass around the instructions so that we all have a chance t-to learn them, and then we start playing late afternoon. If the g-game's fun, we play into the evening. The popcorn usually ends up being C-C-Christmas Day supper."

"It sounds like fun, but your parents must have a huge backlog of board games by now if you've been doing it for years."

"You'd think so, but Mom always ends up d-donating the g-games to the church youth room, so no, there aren't any g-games in the house. T-T-Truthfully, I don't think Mom l-likes games much."

I didn't say anything to Rich, but I tried to figure out why, if he knew his mother didn't like games, he wouldn't at least get her a small personal gift. I decided that I would find something special for Gloria—it'd been years since I'd had a mom to give a present to.

*　*　*

JICKY ARE YOU okay? You've been awful quiet since you and Rich got here." It was Christmas Eve day and Wes and I were alone in the kitchen, Gloria having taken Rich over to the church to help the pastor move the crèche inside for the evening service.

"I'm fine, Wes," I shook my head slightly and smiled, "I mean, *Dad*… I guess I just don't have much to say."

"Well, *I guess* I'm just missin' all your questions. That's what I remember best from your visit this summer—you were a question-askin' machine. You made this old guy feel pretty darn smart."

"Oh, that…Rich asked me to tone it down. He said I asked you—well, not just you, *everybody*—too many questions about things I should already know. He told me it made me sound stupid. He didn't use that word, but that's what he'd meant."

"Well, keeping your mouth shut—that's what's stupid! How you suppose'ta learn new things if you aren't allowed to ask?"

"Oh, he wants me to learn—he just wants me to keep my questions to myself until I can ask him. Like earlier when you guys were talkin' about about using a 'mall' in the back yard— I had no idea what you were talkin' about, but I didn't say anything. I'm gonna ask Rich later."

"It's a *m-a-u-l*, not a *m-a-l-l*. It's just another name for a big hammer—like a sledge hammer."

"Okay, now it makes sense," I said, nodding. "My Pops would've called it a 'BFH'—I wonder if Rich knows what that means?" Wes howled with laughter. Obviously, he knew it meant *big fuckin' hammer*. When he quieted he said, "Jicky, I think Rich is wrong, but I'm smart enough to not wanna get between a couple of newlyweds. Just remember, he married you the way you were—you've got a kind'a spark that the world needs more of. Don't let that super-smart son of mine change you too much."

"Thanks, that's a really nice thing to say—though he's prob'ly right about my smoking—I know it'd be good for me to quit."

"Sure, but stoppin' smoking's hard. I managed to quit my daily five-cent Ben Franklins a few years ago, but I still like a Tiparillo now and then. Speakin' of, are you still lightin' up? Do ya want to join me in the garage for a smoke before our keepers get back from the church?"

* * *

WALKING BACK TO the house, beating the lingering smoke from our jackets, Wes muttered, "You don't have to mention this to Gloria."

"You got it. As far as I'm concerned, everything we've said today stays between the two of us." As I was saying the words I remembered the names that Tom had mentioned when we were alone on the porch on Thanksgiving. Since I knew that Wes would keep my secrets, I asked if he could tell me anything about Henry Higgins and Spengolly.

Wes laughed. "Well, Professor Henry Higgins was an old smarty who thought he could make a poor street gal into a fine lady—he's a character in the musical "My Fair Lady." Gloria's got the LP if you wanna listen to it sometime. And, I think the other name you're askin' 'bout is *Svengali*—A *v* instead of a *p*, and an *a* instead of an *o*. Truthfully, I don't know much about him, but I think he's kinda like ol' Henry Higgins. You'll prob'ly need to talk to a librarian."

"Thanks, Dad. I'll check it out at UW. I get to use the library since I work at the school. At least now I'll know what to ask since you told me how to say that crazy name."

"Well, you're welcome, Jicky— happy to help, and I'm understandin' why you didn't want to ask Rich about those two."

"Yeah, I didn't know for sure, but they're kinda who I thought they might be... Can I see that record album of Gloria's when we get inside?"

* * *

RICH TWISTED THE colorful cube back and forth, turning it upside down, then right side up again. "This thing is impossible, Jik. D-d-did you get it for me to d-drive me nuts?"

"No, I got it for you because I thought you'd think it was fun, and I've noticed that you haven't put it down since you opened the box."

"Well, from what I've read, l-lots of addictive things are fun at first. It's l-later when they become debilitating by t-t-taking over your l-life that you start to regret them."

Gloria interceded, "Richard, is that any way to thank your bride for such a nice gift?"

Rich didn't say anything, lost once again in the twists and turns of the Rubik's Cube.

"He's only kidding, Mother. Rich loves playing the put-upon husband—after half a year I'm getting use to it."

Gloria and I had just come back into the living room after cleaning up the Christmas dinner dishes. Wes was taking the cellophane off the Clue game that Rich and I had chosen as this year's Christmas Day entertainment (if we could get Rich to put down the Rubik's Cube long enough to play). I picked up and admired the beautiful tunic blouse that Rich's parents had given me along with a flowery Hallmark card and a fifty dollar bill to spend on more clothing.

While doing the dishes, Gloria had explained that she had the receipt if I wanted to return the blouse and then offered to take me shopping in Chadron. She said that she had determined from what Rich had told her, that most of my good clothes were cast offs from Pam. "It was kind of Pamela to share, but being the youngest girl in my family I know what it's like to wear hand-me-downs. I can still remember how wonderful it felt when I finally got to choose my own clothing. I hope that Richard's father and I were not being presumptuous thinking that you might feel that same way."

"Oh no, I'd never feel that way about you and Wes—and besides, it's kinda true—I would like to choose some nice work clothes. Pam's things are pretty, but not really what I'd pick if I got to do the picking. I don't know how you knew, but the shirt you bought is much more my style."

"Well, if the scarf you gave me is any indication of your taste, and I believe it is, because Richard has never given me anything so pretty, I think we will have a delightful shopping trip together."

"Me too, Gloria—Mother. I'm sorry—that's gonna take some getting use to."

"Oh, that's alright, Jicky. You'll have time to get *used* to it after you and Richard move here. Richard's father and I are so excited—it will be so nice having you two nearby. I suppose you will be living with us until you find a place of your own." It was a statement, not a question.

I swallowed hard, knowing that Gloria was not kidding. Kidding was not in her nature. That conversation with Rich's mom over Christmas dinner dishes was how I learned that I would be moving to Nebraska in June. *Richard* had not told me about that part of the team's grand plan as yet. After only six months of marriage I felt completely left out and out of place —sort of like a lone yellow square on the red side of an ever changing Rubik's Cube.

64

CHAPTER NINE

I WAS THE first one in the Mathematics office on January second. Wearing the new tunic top that Rich's parents had given me, I was feeling far more stylish than I ever had in Pam's clothes. I'd belted the top over a pair of fake-suede pants that I'd bought at a shop in downtown Chadron; for a change my ankle bones weren't showing. (Pam and I wore the same size clothing, but I was at least three inches taller.) I adjusted the shade in the large office window and inspected the philodendron. It appeared to have weathered my absence in fine shape—in all honesty, it didn't require any more attention than the cactuses, but it looked friendlier and was a lot easier to dust.

The conversation that Rich and I'd had on our ride back to Laramie was still playing in my head. Back in his childhood bedroom, on Christmas night, I'd asked him about his mother's comment about us moving to Chadron. He said that he had planned to move back all along—he actually seemed surprised that I didn't know. His father's best friend, Milton Edgerton, had offered Rich a junior partnership in his law office even before Rich had started law school. Milton would be retiring in a few years and wanted to make sure that he left his many clients in good hands.

I had to admit that the move made sense and the job was a wonderful opportunity for a new attorney. I had just never thought I'd be a Nebraskan, and finding out about the move from Gloria had been a shock. I screwed up my courage and told Rich that I wanted to be in the loop from then on. I was tired of being the last to know what was going on in my life. Rich promised to do better. That's probably when he decided it was time for me to know everything. He filled me in as we drove back to Wyoming on New Year's Day 1981.

"The Plan," as he and Tom called it, was a methodical process to get Tom elected to Congress, and it would begin as soon as Rich and Tom graduated in the spring. The abbreviated version went like this: First, we would all move to Nebraska and establish residency. Rich had never considered himself anything but a Nebraskan, but Tom and Pam, having been born in Colorado, would have to prove their allegiance— they would go to Lincoln where Tom would complete his Ph.D. in Political Science and Pam would get her Master's in Public Policy and Health Care Administration. Rich, during this time would be establishing his law practice in Chadron and learning everything he currently didn't know about party politics on the state level. Tom would eventually take a job in education, preferably as a professor at a Nebraska college or university; if nothing was available in education, he would go to work for a nonprofit organization. After winning several terms as a State Senator, Tom would make his first run for Congress in the late '80s or early '90s. Rich would be at his side, running his campaigns and later holding down the fort in Nebraska, while Tom and Pam moved to Washington to become the Capitol's fresh, new power couple.

As I listened to Rich's plan for our lives, I was struck by just how little I had to do with our foursome's future. I was the extra wheel on a tricycle—it would probably work fine with me attached, but it might roll more smoothly if I weren't around.

***

PROFESSOR SCOTT WALKED through the office doorway at nine o'clock balancing a pile of intra-campus mail on his briefcase which he was carrying like a serving tray. As he handed over the teetering bundle, he asked, "Who is Jicky O'Connor? Don't tell me you got married over the break?"

"It's me, and no I didn't get married. I've been married since I started working for you—O'Connor was my maiden name."

"Well whoever you are, you've got a package. I left it in the mailroom—I couldn't figure out how to carry it without dropping something. Why don't you go get it before things get busy."

I didn't say it, but I thought it was a good thing the man could do math—he could've never been a waitress. His concept of busy was a phone call every half hour and his physical coordination was…was…well, nonexistent. I happily threw on my coat and grabbed the cigarettes from my purse for the walk to the Commons.

The package was from Danny Ogden. I couldn't imagine why Danny would be sending me a Christmas gift, but I was so excited that I nearly ran back to the office. I slid the tip of my desk shears under the packing tape with more anticipation than I had felt since I was a kid. I ripped open the corrugated cardboard to find a letter and handfuls of scrunched-up newspaper cradling a beautiful Pentax SLR camera.

The camera wasn't a Christmas gift, but it was a gift. Danny explained that he'd bought himself a new camera several years ago—he wanted me to have his old one. He said he didn't mean to embarrass me, but he'd gotten the impression that I didn't have any extra cash lying around, and he knew from some of our conversations that I didn't own a camera. He wrote that the art department had scheduled a beginning photography course in the evenings during the upcoming semester and he hoped that I would take advantage of it. He told me I had an excellent eye for framing my subjects and that viewing the world through a lens would help me hone my natural gifts. The camera was already loaded and he had included an extra roll of black and white film.

I was ecstatic! I could barely wait until my lunch hour when I could run over to the Art Building to sign-up for the photography class and thank Danny in person.

By twelve-fifty-five my exuberance from the morning had faded. Even though I'd secured a seat to audit the evening photography class, I'd also learned that Danny Ogden had left the University. He and his family had moved over Christmas break leaving no forwarding address. I couldn't thank him for his gift, and the thought of never seeing Danny again pained me far more than I wanted to admit.

As I walked back to the Math office I smoked the lone Winston from the pack I'd bought after Thanksgiving. I thought about the last time Danny and I had spent time together, when we'd sat on the half-wall outside the Art Building smoking and discussing negative space. At the time I knew I was playing with fire—flirting without letting myself admit it. I'm not sure what would have happened had Danny not had the good sense to rush home.

I crumpled the empty red cigarette box and threw it in the trash can outside the Math and Science Building.

CHAPTER TEN

MONDAY MORNING I stood at the kitchen sink trying to wash off the purple ink of the cowboy-hat shaped tattoo the bouncer had stamped on my left hand as I'd walked into the bar on Friday night. Three mornings of showers hadn't faded it. The ink was as indelible as the memories.

RICH HAD CALLED from the kitchen as soon as I'd come through the front door Friday evening, "Tom wants us to go out with him t-tonight. There's a band playing at C-C-Cluster Ducks he wants to hear—they're from Denver and rumored to be p-pretty good. With Pam out of t-t-town, he doesn't think he should go alone."

The bar, Cluster Ducks, had the biggest dance floor in the area and had been busier than ever since *Urban Cowboy* had hit the theaters in the summer. Or, so I'd heard; Rich and I had rarely gone out together in the evening since moving into the duplex.

"T-T-Tom asked me to drive—that usually means he p-p-plans on drinking. Actually, with P-Pam gone, I think he p-plans on getting shit-faced. It's good she doesn't leave him alone t-too often."

Shortly after Rich and I married I found out that he didn't dance. Not that he couldn't—he wasn't half bad, it was that he wouldn't. Half bad was not something that you showed in public. Rich believed if you couldn't do a thing well, especially something that might draw attention, you shouldn't do it at all. Never mind that it might be pleasant. Never mind that your spouse might enjoy it.

MY EYES FOLLOWED couples as they two-stepped across the floor. I sipped a beer while under the Formica topped table my boots moved to the music. Tom, who had been doing far more than sipping, saw the longing in my eyes and asked me if I would like to join him on the dance floor. I looked toward Rich —he shrugged his shoulders and said, "Help yourself." I wasn't sure if his words had been directed at Tom or me, but by the time they'd passed his lips we were already out of our chairs.

Tom led me to the crowded dance floor as I yelled, "I've never done this with a partner before." He shouted back, "Yeah, like lotsa things, it's a helluva lot more fun with two people. It's a shame your husband is such a stick-in-the-mud. He's missin' out."

"Tell him. He might listen to you."

"Not about dancing, Jik—seem's like you'd have more sway there."

I shook my head as Tom took me in his arms. We started to move with the music, but not in the way I had hoped. It was as though there was an invisible tension to our movements. We were like two refrigerator magnets turned against one another. I zigged. He zagged. Then Tom stopped.

In the middle of the dance floor, with the music playing, Tom stopped.

He held me at arms length, my shoulders beneath his large hands. As soon I was still and quiet he let go, then reached into his jeans pocket and pulled out a quarter. "Flip you for the lead!" he shouted over a steel guitar riff.

Had it been anyone but Tom Streator I would have been totally mortified. Since it was Tom, my mortification was only partial. I punched him in the shoulder and told him he was a jerk, but then spoke into his ear, "If you can lead me, I'll try to follow. No coin toss necessary."

Three songs later we were partners. By the time the band played Johnny Lee's "Lookin' For Love," I felt like I knew how to Texas two-step. It felt amazing.

Rich greeted us back at the table with fresh beers and told Tom he couldn't remember the last time I'd looked so happy. Tom flashed his winning grin at both of us, but when he turned my way I thought I saw something more in his eyes. My body was humming. As predicted, Tom got shit-faced. Rich drove us home.

I PEELED OFF my jeans in the bathroom and hung them on the back of the door. I was about to put on my nightgown, but I knew I didn't want to sleep. I brushed my teeth and fluffed my hair, then gingerly walked back to the cold bedroom.

Rich was already in bed, turned on his side facing the door. I was both nervous and excited walking into the room naked, back-lit by the hall nightlight. I'd hoped he would see me and say something, but his eyes were closed even though his breathing led me to think he was still awake. I slid under the pile of blankets and slipped my hand under the oversized T-shirt he slept in. At first Rich didn't move; when he finally turned toward me he said, "Jicky, I'm tired."

"But I'm not, and we haven't made love in over a month," I said as I stroked his body.

"Jik, I said, 'I'm t-t-tired'—and you smell like b-b-beer and cigarettes—it's not exactly a t-turn-on. Sorry." He rolled away from me tugging on the blankets.

I walked to the bathroom and put on my nightgown. Back in bed I hugged the edge of the mattress. A silent tear ran from the corner of my eye and over the bridge of my nose, dripping onto the pillow. I felt caught, and I didn't know how to get out of my comfortable trap. I was not even twenty, and had to face that, while I was not in a loveless marriage, ours was going to be an almost sexless union.

I told myself that I would never again make the first move toward Rich. I'd live without sex as long as it meant living without the humiliation of his rejection.

* * *

IT WAS THAT night that the dreams started. The first one concluded with an orgasm. I didn't just dream I'd climaxed, I actually did.

In the dream, Rich, Tom, Pam and I were all sitting around a living room—not one I'd ever seen before. There weren't enough seats for all of us, so Rich and Pam were sitting on a couch. I was in an easy chair, and Tom was sitting on the floor leaning back on my chair cushion, the back of his head between my knees. Looking down on his thick dark hair, I could see the lumpy cauliflower cartilage on his ears, a remnant from his high school and college wrestling days. In the dream, I placed my hand on his head and ran my fingers through his hair. That was all it took. My body seized in the greatest pleasure I had ever felt. I woke up shaking, as Rich lay sound asleep beside me.

After that, the dreams changed. They were different from night to night, but all had a reoccurring theme. In my dreams, I couldn't understand why I was so alone. I would look at my reflection in mirrors or windows or puddles of water and think: *Why doesn't anyone ask me out? Why don't I have a boyfriend? Why does no one want me?* That was when I would suddenly recall I was married: *Ahh-ha, that's why I don't date. Got it!* But then, and this happened in every dream, I couldn't remember who I'd married. Men would float through my slumbering brain: Danny Ogden, Tom Streator, even the crop-duster from the Never Empty who'd told me I had a nice ass. But never Rich. Not once Rich. The dreams never resolved my problem—I would wake not knowing who my husband was.

CHAPTER ELEVEN

I'D WORRIED IN January when I'd brought Danny's old camera home. I was concerned Rich might think it an extravagant gift from a man I barely knew. Or, maybe worse, he would think I "knew" Danny in a way that might justify expensive gifts. But, when I showed Rich the camera, the letter that went with it, and told him I'd signed up for the photography class, he seemed genuinely pleased and proud that my former art professor believed in my potential as a photographer.

"I've been looking through the class materials. Owning the camera, I have the most expensive thing, but I'll still need some other pieces of equipment that are prob'ly gonna cost a lot. I don't know, but the info says I have to have something called a light meter and suggests I get a flash unit and a camera bag…I'll also have to buy film and pay a darkroom fee when we start learning to process film. It's gonna be expensive."

"Go ahead and b-b-buy what you think you'll need, Jicky."

"I could try to cut down on what I spend."

"Don't be silly—from what I've seen you b-b-barely spend anything on yourself and I d-don't want you skipping meals."

"There is some place I could get some extra cash." I paused then said, "I'm sorry Rich, I've been lying to you."

"What d-d-do you mean?"

"I've never quit sending money to Joel and Gary…I've been keeping a little from each of my paychecks. I'm sorry. I should've told you."

Rich hugged me, "Oh, Jik, I've known that all along. I d-don't c-c-care—no, that's not t-true—I d-do c-care. I c-c-care that you're a loving sister to your little brothers." He lifted my chin and looked me in the eyes. "It's okay honey, you d-don't have to t-tell me everything. Don't c-cut back on what you send them. I have money in savings—we c-can afford your equipment."

THOSE LAST FIVE months in Laramie would have been unbearable had I not been auditing the photography class. It turned out that Danny Ogden knew me better than I had known myself. I'd planned on registering for the pottery class, not photography—primarily because Danny had been right—I didn't own a camera, but also because I'd never thought of photography as an art form. I still wasn't sure that I did, but I enjoyed the heck out of it. Obviously, I liked composing my shots, viewing the world through the limited range of the aperture, but I also liked the feel of the steel and leather camera body, and the weight and girth of the lens as it rested in my hand. I liked the the sensation of smooth metal sliding on smooth metal as I adjusted f-stops, and the subtle duo-click when I squeezed, then released, the shutter. I even came to appreciate the sour acidic smell of the chemical fixatives and the red glow of the safety light reflecting off the enlarger in the darkroom. I loved it, and I was good at it. I only wished that I could've told Danny what he had done for me.

The camera gave me an excuse to drive around the area looking for subjects to photograph. One of my favorite spots was Vedauwoo—an outcropping of granite about half an hour from Laramie that looks like round-edged building blocks piled in unruly towers by some gigantic god-like toddler. I loved Vedauwoo for its expansive scenery, but also for the option it gave me to shoot a landscape while focusing on negative space. Instead of looking at the stones, I looked at the space between the stones—the areas of nothingness. *The areas of nothingness.* Those are the spaces where people don't normally focus. It's not that they don't exist, but that they are ignored. Those were the spaces I searched out—both to photograph and to live in. They were the only places that felt like home to me.

If people were interested in hearing about me, they wanted to know things like where I worked or if I was married—the big picture. I couldn't quit the big picture, but I quit focusing on it. I kept working at the Mathematics Department and I stayed married to Rich, but I set my sights on the spaces—the in-betweens. I lived happily for months in the negative space where I could just be Jicky again. I worked on my photography and began perusing the 550s aisle of the UW library. I looked for books about geomorphology and would spend contented hours trying to understand what I read. I learned everything I could about the landforms around Laramie and the natural sciences in general. The more the light shined on Jicky the secretary and Jicky the wife, the more I slipped into the dark crevasses around what people saw. But, I knew I'd have problems staying in my private world once we moved to Nebraska, so, by early May, I'd started trying to be like everyone else and focus on what could most easily be seen.

* * *

"MR. STREATOR, IF you could move to the right a little—no your right. That's it. Tom, step back just a tiny bit and shift to your right, too." I stepped away from the camera that I'd carefully situated on the railing of the duplex's little front porch and walked over to join the group while counting down. I slid into place beside Rich, "four…three…two… smile." Click.

I broke ranks and walked toward the camera saying, "That's it for today—I'm out of film and I'm sure everybody's tired of smiling. I think at least a couple of the pictures should turn out."

This was the second time in a week that I'd shot graduations. Rich's law school graduation had been the weekend before. His parents had driven to Laramie for the event. We'd had a nice time, even though they'd had to stay with Tom and Pam because we didn't have an extra bed, and no one wanted to sleep on our sofa-sleeper, the one inherited from Tom's parents when Rich and Tom started rooming together their junior year. It was in such bad condition we weren't bothering to move it to Chadron—considering we had almost no furniture, that said a lot.

Tom's parents had driven a truck and trailer to Wyoming for the graduation ceremony, and after the festivities they would drive Tom's three-year-old car back to Colorado. Tom and Rich would pack all of our belongings into the truck and trailer and drop Rich's and my stuff in Chadron, before Tom and Pam continued on to Lincoln. There they would meet up with Tom's little brother, who was driving up from Denver in Tom's graduation gift—a new Audi Quattro, which his brother would trade for the truck and trailer, and then take a little less flashy, and, I'm sure slower, drive back to Colorado.

* * *

I SETTLED INTO the driver's seat and made sure that the philodendron that I'd liberated from the Math Department window was securely belted into the passenger's seat. I was the tail end of our convoy to Nebraska. Rich and Tom were in the loaded truck and trailer at the head of the procession; Pam was in the center with her car; I, appropriately, was the tag-a-long in the old yellow Chevy.

I tried to convince myself that it was the beginning of a great adventure—a new state! a new home! I was going to be a Nebraska housewife!... how very exciting... I consoled myself with the thought that I could take pictures and do my art anywhere, and, also, that I had joined my life to the lives of good folks. My husband and his friends were the sort of people who envisioned a future so bright that it was blinding. I tried to feel fortunate that I would be a part of that future and assured myself that I would find a purpose.

It was the last day of May, 1981. The four of us were "a team" heading off to "work the plan." Failure was not an option for Rich, Tom, and Pam.

AUGUST
1982

CHAPTER TWELVE

IN MY DAYDREAMS I'm back in his arms. I've undone his tie and the upper buttons of his dress shirt so that I can feel his skin next to mine.

He was only about an inch taller than me, five-nine to my five-eight, so it was easy to nestle my face in the bend where his neck met his muscular shoulder. I'd drink in his scent. At that inner juncture his skin was smooth, soft, and warm.

Like a cat, I'd push against his jawline with my cheek. His dark afternoon-stubble never failed to excite me. I would reach under the starched cotton of his dress shirt and slide my hands up and over his chest—a move that never failed to excite him. He once jokingly told me that he'd messed up so many pairs of dress pants with his inevitable erections whenever I entered a room that his dry cleaning bills were going through the roof. I told him of the price we would have to pay for our relationship, his dry-cleaning bills were the least of my worries.

When I'd voice my concerns, he would give me one of his vote-winning grins, lift me off the ground, and swing me in circles saying, "My Jickster, my Jickums, my Jicky, I don't care, I don't care, I don't care. I will never let you go."

Memories …

But I'm getting the story out of order. He would have hated that. For being a free spirit, he was surprisingly disciplined with his schedule. He lived his life in a strictly planned order, although he'd once told me he would throw it all away for me—that I was someone special. But, now, knowing what I do, I'm pretty sure he wasn't being completely honest.

Strangely, it doesn't matter …

CHAPTER THIRTEEN

"C-C-COME ON JICKY, l-let me carry you over the threshold."

"What, and wreck your back? We've been married for over two years, Rich—it seems kinda pointless."

"It's n-not. It's symbolic. This is the first real home that we've owned t-together. It's our first big accomplishment as a c-c-couple—I want to celebrate it!"

I was proud that we'd been able to save the downpayment so quickly, but I also realized that we'd had a distinct advantage over many young couples—we hadn't paid rent or bought groceries in over a year. I'd been able to take nearly everything I'd earned as the receptionist at the *Chadron Record* and put it in savings. Even though I was still sending money to Joel and Gary once a month, the bottom line in Rich's and my savings account had grown rapidly.

"Okay, you crazy Husker, you win." I reached up and put my arms around Rich's neck and gave a helpful hop. I heard a slight grunt as he caught me, but I think it was meant as a comic gesture on his part; at twenty-one, I was still as thin as one of Wes's Tiparillos.

We had just closed on a small three-bedroom, one-and-a-half bath ranch-style house down the block from his parents' place. It was a nice starter home for us and was certainly going to be the nicest place I'd ever lived, if you didn't count the one-year-two-months-and-three-and-a-half-days that we'd lived with Rich's parents. We would be staying with the elder Weckwerths one or two more nights while we got our new house move-in ready, and though I appreciated all that they'd done for us over the past year, I was more than ready to graduate from twin beds.

My feet back on the floor, we walked through the empty rooms discussing where our few possessions should go. We chose the largest bedroom as our master and the next largest as a guest room (or, as we referred to it, "Tom's room"). Rich claimed the small bedroom as his home office and said until we got a dining room set, for which neither of us saw much need, the formal dining room could be my studio. I was thrilled at the prospect. The dining room had two large windows to the north—not great in the winter, but perfect light for painting, which was *one* of the things I dreamed of doing again now that we had space and privacy.

* * *

"WHERE ARE YOU going to put the beds?" Gloria asked as Rich and his dad carried the first set of head and foot boards from the garage of their house toward our place. My mother-in-law had been scouting for used furniture from the time Rich and I had started looking at houses, and she had found us some nice pieces. She'd asked me before she'd started making inquiries if I had any objections—if furniture hunting was something that I would like to do myself. I'd let her know that I appreciated her help; I really didn't want to furniture shop. I also let her know that I was ready to pay for whatever she found—I already felt like we owed far too much to Wes and Gloria.

"Rich and I decided we want the large bedroom set in the big bedroom and the other bed and small chest in the room next to it. Rich is putting his desk in the little bedroom."

"Oh, that surprises me. I thought that you would want the room closest to you for a nursery, but I suppose you can make those changes later. Babies don't really need rooms of their own right away. We kept Rich's crib next to our bed for his first six months."

I didn't know how to respond, so I just smiled and mumbled, "Is that so?" one of the handy noncommittal phases that Rich had taught me. How could I explain to his mother that her much anticipated grandchild was not going to happen as long as I stayed faithful to her son? Rich had not made love to me since we'd moved to Nebraska, and while I had once hoped that when we moved into our own place things might change, I was beginning to doubt it. The most recent demonstration of his reticence had occurred only the day earlier. After Rich had carried me across the threshold, when I thought he might seal the deal with a kiss—a pretty natural move under the circumstances—he'd just set me on my feet with a, "Well, there. We did it!" At least he hadn't shaken my hand as though we'd just closed a real estate transaction.

When I told Gloria that we didn't intend to get a dining table, she was surprised. When I told her my plans for the dining room, she grimaced slightly. I hadn't meant to upset her, but I had no intention of giving up the space Rich had allotted me. We did not need a big fancy table that we would never use. The kitchen had a breakfast nook that seated four. I couldn't imagine that we would ever have more than two guests at a time. To me our house was a place to live and work. Neither Rich nor I had ever been big entertainers, and we saw no need to change.

SEVERAL DAYS AFTER we'd settled in, Gloria gave me a call after supper. She'd found a sturdy old drafting table in a second-hand furniture shop in Valentine and would arrange for a friend from church to deliver it to me if I thought it might work for my *studio*. I told her I'd love it and asked how much it cost. At that my mother-in-law said, "Oh, don't worry about it, consider it a housewarming gift from me." I'm not sure that it was as much a housewarming gift, as it was an apology for her expression of dismay days earlier. I would have never assumed that I was Gloria's type of person, but she was determined to please me, even when I perplexed her, which always perplexed me.

CHAPTER FOURTEEN

"JIK, WOULD YA come in here."

The editor of the *Chadron Record*, George Jenkins, rarely called me into his office, so I was curious and a little worried by what he might want.

"Sit down young lady—I have somethin' I need to discuss with ya. You've prob'ly heard by now that Bob's leaving. He's been offered a full-time teachin' job in Valentine, so I'm losin' my photographer. I know ya know your way 'round a camera and I was wonderin' if ya might like to try your hand at some news photography. I'd pay ya thirty cents more an hour and expenses. You'd get bylines, but ya'd have to keep answerin' the phones when ya aren't out shootin'. What da' ya say?"

I didn't have to think it over and probably answered a bit too quickly. "I say yes! When can I start?"

"Well, Bob doesn't leave for another week, so start talkin' to him right away to learn the ropes. I'll make the jump in pay after he leaves—can't afford to be payin' two people for the same job. And, on that note, when I said I'd pay your expenses, I mean within reason. If ya wanna start doin' arty crap, do it on your own dime. If it's any good and I wanna print it, I'll pay ya extra by the photo."

THAT WAS THE beginning of my life as a professional photographer. Rich was so happy for me. He had always wanted me to have a job he could be proud of. He'd been less than excited when I'd taken the receptionist position at the *Record*. He had wanted me to find a job at Chadron State, so that he could've told people I worked at the college. But, when I'd looked around that little campus and remembered how bored I'd been in the Math Department at the much larger University of Wyoming, I knew I'd have to find something else to do or die of boredom before I turned twenty-three. A few days later, when George Jenkins was showing me around the office of the *Record*, I'd known instantly that I wanted the receptionist position.

The newspaper's offices were on the north edge of downtown in a two story building rumored to be one of the oldest buildings in Chadron. George had told me it once housed a funeral parlor in the basement, a furniture store on the main floor, and a bordello on the second—or as he'd called it "one stop shoppin' for randy ranchers." What had really sold me on the job was George's extensive tour of the darkroom. I loved the idea of working in a building that had a darkroom, even though, as the receptionist, I wouldn't be the person getting paid to use it.

So, when I told Rich that, now, as a newspaper photographer I'd be getting byline credit, he'd decided working at the newspaper was okay with him. While my name had never made the masthead as a receptionist, I was now listed as staff photographer in every issue of the *Chadron Record*. The one thing about the position that made Rich unhappy was my change of attire. After breaking a heel and ruining a pair of slacks on assignment, I asked George if I could start wearing jeans to the office. George responded, "I don't give a fat, flyin' fig what you wear—never did. If you wanna wear jeans, it's fine with me. Whatever'll make the job easier is what ya should be wearin'." From then on, if I knew I was to be shooting something solemn or formal I dressed up, otherwise I was in jeans and boots, whether I was answering the phone or toting my camera through a dusty field.

I happily donated the last of Pam's fancy hand-me-downs to the fall rummage sale at the church. Good riddance to nice clothes and bad memories.

GEORGE JENKINS DID me a big favor when he told me to do the "arty crap" on my own dime. He may have known what he was doing, but I've never been sure. The way it worked was, on my off hours, if I shot film that I'd purchased, I owned the copyrights to my photos. Even if I sold a shot to the *Record*, I could still do other things with the image—even sell it elsewhere. About three months after I started shooting, George started buying my scenery photos. By six months in, I had a regular feature on page three, called *Picture of the Week*. I shot most of my own work with my Pentax. Everytime George handed me my freelancer's paycheck I said another silent thank you to Danny Ogden for giving me his old camera.

* * *

IN 1984, MID-JUNE, I took a Thursday and Friday off from the paper. I'd convinced Rich to function without the car for a few days so that I could go on a photo shoot in the Black Hills. This was a first for me; I hadn't traveled alone overnight since Rich and I had married. I'd hoped to go east to see Pops and my brothers after Rich graduated, but that was before I knew we were moving to Chadron, and then, once we'd bought the house, it seemed impossible to get away. But, I was to a point where I thought I was going to explode if I didn't do something on my own. Nothing was particularly wrong, but the sameness of life was starting to get to me. I kept thinking: *Is this all there is?… Is this it for me?*

I TOOK OFF in the dark on Thursday hoping to get to Mount Rushmore before sunrise. Rich and I were soon to celebrate our fourth anniversary and I thought that I would take some pictures of Rushmore at sunrise as my gift to him. Surely he hadn't forgotten that amazing morning from our honeymoon trip. My other plans for my three day adventure were to get a few shots to sell to the paper and a passel of new landscape photos to serve as inspiration for the watercolors I'd begun painting for fun.

I had Highway 385 to myself at three-thirty in the morning. I should have worried about wildlife as I flew up the narrow road, but I was more concerned with beating the sun to my destination. Rich and I were still driving the old yellow Chevy, and thanks to Wes's tinkering, it was running better than ever. Even so, it was old enough that Rich probably should've been thinking about a new car, but I'd gotten the feeling that it would've broken his heart to traded away the *old banana boat.*

I pulled into the Rushmore parking lot with plenty of time to gather my equipment and head for the mountain. I found the bench where Rich and I had huddled that chilly morning four years earlier, positioned my camera on the tripod, and waited. It was just like I remembered it from the last morning of our honeymoon. Soon tourists would be crowding the paths, but now the rustling of pine branches and the songs of waking birds were the only sounds breaking the silence.

As I waited for the soft morning glow to hit the rock faces, I studied the wooden bench scarred with the pen-knifed initials of so many romances. Undoubtedly some of them were still thriving, while others were long over. I pondered my own *happily ever after.* I thought about Rich sleeping in our home in Chadron. I'd kissed his forehead as I'd left our bedroom that morning, a room that we no longer shared. He'd mumbled, "Bye Jik, have a good time…," his voice disappearing into his pillow as he rolled away from me. Rolling away from me seemed to be the perfect metaphor for our relationship. Rich had spent the last four years rolling away from me. I didn't doubt that we loved one another, but there was nothing physical about our marriage. I thought of the night we'd spent in the car four years ago. It had been the only night of real passion in my life.

I sat on the bench, my head in my hands, and cried.

Was this it? Was this going to be what my life was like? I was only twenty-four; I could conceivably live for fifty more years, maybe longer. The thought of that much empty life made me cry harder. I needed someone to love me and to *want me.* I wanted a man's arms around my body, his lips on mine, our bodies entwined. I wanted passion and I wanted to respond with passion. I didn't want to hurt Rich, but I was tired of hurting myself. I was tired of feeling alone, undesirable, and so damn old.

As I'd sat crying, the sun had risen. I'd not taken a single picture of the carved mountain. Soon the rangers would find me, or the tourists would, as they rounded the bend on their trek to the Visitor Center. It was time to leave—I had two more mornings to shoot the photo for Rich. I promised myself that I'd come back after I'd started to make things better.

I drove to Keystone for breakfast, found a payphone, and called the Hill's Family Planning Clinic in Rapid City. There was an appointment available at one o'clock that afternoon. I was determined that my life would change. It didn't have to change soon, but I vowed that it would change, and when it did, I would be prepared.

THE CLINIC WAS in a squat brick building close to Baken Park Shopping Center, not far from Dinosaur Hill, although I couldn't have told you how to get to the park with the green concrete dinosaurs from the clinic. I'd been driving around Rapid City most of the morning and was thoroughly confused by the strangely-shaped neighborhoods bordered by creeks, valleys, and hills.

"ARE YOU SURE you want a diaphragm? The pill is more effective and a lot less hassle. Most women your age prefer it." The nurse showing me the insertion technique for the little beige contraption seemed convinced that I didn't know what I wanted. Perhaps she was reading the uncertainty in my eyes or in my left leg that wouldn't quit bouncing. But, my appearance of doubt had nothing to do with my selection of a contraceptive method. How could I tell her that I was a married woman preparing for an affair someday in the future? How could I explain that I wanted children, but had a husband who didn't have sex with me, but, on the off-chance that he did, I wanted to conceive? *How could I tell her?* When I stayed mute and just kept studying a plastic model of the vagina and cervix, she offered to leave the room while I practiced inserting the diaphragm. She told me to leave it in place and to knock on the door when I was ready—the doctor would come in for a final check. He was thorough and wouldn't allow a patient to leave until she knew what she was doing.

I took the little concave disk and filled it with slimy spermicidal lubricant. Lying back on the paper-covered exam table in the gown provided by the clinic, I pinched the spring-loaded edges together in the way the nurse had instructed. But, instead of inserting it, I shot the diaphragm across the room like a miniature frisbee. It splatted onto the wall at the end of the exam table right below the bright-orange poster listing the signs and symptoms of STDs. As it bounced to the floor, I sat up and started to laugh so hard that tears came. I now realize that they were a release—it had been an incredibly tense day between getting lost in a strange city and planning an illicit affair with no-one in particular. Go figure. After washing my new little ufo, I attempted the procedure again, this time standing up. It worked much better.

The exam ended with the doctor telling me that while diaphragms were fairly effective when used correctly, he still recommended that my partner use a condom—both for protection from pregnancy and from the new and deadly sexually transmitted disease: acquired immune deficiency syndrome (AIDS). He said it was unlikely that I would come in contact with the virus living in a small town in Nebraska, but it was never wrong to error on the side of caution. I tried to think of any guys in Chadron who might be gay—it seemed as likely to me as finding someone shooting up drugs in the vestibule of First Methodist.

I DROVE EAST after my appointment and spent the rest of the afternoon photographing the Badlands. There'd been an afternoon rain, and the hillside bands of color were defined and glowing in the cloud-muted light. Before it cleared I even got some shots of a rainbow arching over those rugged pastel formations that had always struck me as though they belonged on another planet.

I stopped at Wall Drug for a late lunch—a buffalo burger that would serve as my dinner, too—then headed toward Keystone to check in to my motel. It had been a long day and I was planning another early morning. I was dead to the world by eight o'clock.

IN A REPLAY of the day before, I sat on the damp wooden bench looking out at Mount Rushmore waiting for the morning light. This morning, instead of feeling sad about my lot in life, I was looking forward to my future. Sure, I was feeling guilty knowing I was planning to cheat on my husband, but I knew it was cheat, or leave, and I didn't want to leave him. I loved Rich, but I needed more. I was thinking it would be nice to have a sign from the universe that what I was planning was the right direction for me to take—something like a flashing green light or a burning bush (although, I doubted from what I'd learned at the Methodist Church that God would give me a sign to break one of his Ten Commandments).

As the sun finally rose behind me, the pale granite of the carved mountain began to glow. Washington's face was shining, and though Teddy Roosevelt's likeness was in the shadows, Jefferson and Lincoln were magnificent. I had just taken two photos at different f-stops when a large bird flashed in the periphery of my left eye. As it flew in front of the tripod, I started shooting. It was a bald eagle! I had never seen one in person. In truth, I thought they were extinct. I had twenty-two exposures left—I shot them all, cost be damned. I was seeing a miracle and I knew that the Universe had given me her blessing, even if the God of the Old Testament had not.

* * *

I SPENT ONE more night in Keystone, then headed out on Saturday morning for the drive back to Chadron. I had originally planned on driving to the Badlands that morning and driving back home by way of Valentine, but since I'd gone to the Badlands on Friday, it felt like my adventure was complete. I'd shoot the gorgeous draw outside Valentine on another day.

I'd made a decision. I'd prepared. I'd been given a sign. And, I was now looking forward to the future again. It was time to go home.

CHAPTER FIFTEEN

I HURRIED TO have my film developed, but I kept the shots of Rushmore with the eagle a secret from Rich. I hid them away nearly as well as I hid the mound-shaped plastic case that held my new diaphragm. My husband would eventually see all my Rushmore photos. I don't believe he ever set eyes on the diaphragm.

I shared the best picture of the rainbow over the Badlands with Rich as soon as it was processed. He loved it, as did George at the *Record*; he ran it on the front page, above the fold, and in color. He also gave me full credit. A few fellow Chadronites razzed me for taking the photo in the neighboring state, but most of the townsfolk just congratulated me on capturing the rainbow in such a perfect spot. A week from the day the photo was published, George heard from the administrative staff at the National Park Service. They wanted to speak to me about using my photo when they reprinted the Badlands brochures and maps. When I told Rich my good news, he started practicing his profession on my behalf. My career as art licensor *J. F. Weckwerth* was born.

By July Fourth, when I gave Rich an enlargement of the best of the Rushmore eagle pictures, he went nuts. He loved the shot and the sentiment, but he immediately saw the potential of the photograph—it was so much more universal than my Badlands picture. With Rich behind them, it didn't take long before my landscape photos were everywhere. The Rushmore eagle or *"R-eagle,"* as we'd begun to call it, was eventually printed on everything from posters to playing cards.

In another bit of fortunate timing, Lee Greenwood's *God Bless the U.S.A.* was released in 1984. My photo became forever linked to that popular patriotic ballad. Every photo montage that featured a rippled American flag also featured the *R-eagle.* By the early '90s it was as familiar an image as a Thomas Kinkade cottage frosted with new-fallen snow, or a Terry Redlin pickup truck surrounded by well-groomed wildlife. While I didn't have the name recognition or make the kind of money those two did, I could have easily given up my day job at the paper had I wanted to forfeit my daily spats with George or all the juicy gossip shared every morning over the *Record's* front counter. I would've missed both far too much.

* * *

1984 WAS A monumental year for "The Plan" as much as it was for me. It was the year that Tom first ran for public office.

He and Rich had started at the State level, winning a seat in Nebraska's unicameral legislature (which I was now fully aware meant there was only one legislative body on the state level). Rich orchestrated Tom's campaign from Chadron, even though Tom ran in a district on the other side of Nebraska, having taken a professorship at a small private college outside of Lincoln upon completing his Ph.D. Everything was progressing just as the two of them had envisioned.

We'd all become involved in the Democratic party as soon as we'd moved to the State. My husband and the Streators blew in and took over the stagnant organization like a "gale-force-wind" or a "breath-of-fresh-air," depending upon who you talked to. There was a void and they filled it: Rich got to know the workings of the party from the ground up, Tom got to know the people, Pam got to know the policies. Those in power understood that the State House was just the starting point for Tom and Pam. Rich would see them off to Washington, D.C. before the '80s had passed into history.

My contributions were limited at first, but I went to meetings, set up folding chairs, and made sure that the people who wanted coffee or water had their choice of beverage.

Because I faithfully attended the monthly meetings with Rich, within a year I was elected to a seat as a precinct committee woman. While I wasn't always sure of what I was doing, I'd smile and say, "Is that so," or "Well, I'll be…" and then I'd wait until we were out of ear shot to ask Rich my questions (just like he had taught me to do shortly after we 'd married). But, my real service to the party came from wielding a camera. It was something I could do better than anyone else. I became the official, unpaid photographer for the local Party and later for one specific candidate. The Democrats in Nebraska had never been documented so thoroughly.

* * *

YOU COULD SAY our affair started when Tom needed publicity shots taken during the summer of 1984, when he first ran for the Nebraska Unicameral. Although, to say everything began for us that year would be incorrect. There had been a spark between Tom and me since our evening on the dance floor back in Laramie, but after my Black Hills trip, I'd finally allowed myself to act on my attraction. It wasn't as though I had targeted Tom to be my lover, and it wasn't as though we rushed into it—it took nearly four years and the thought of Tom leaving Nebraska for us to—I don't know what to call it —consummate? make love? finally fuck?

Over the next few years we did all three, but never often enough to suit either of us. We had four years together—really together. Around fifteen-hundred days, but fewer than fifteen encounters…assignations…fucks… What did that compute to? Fifteen every one-thousand-five-hundred days? One every one-hundred-fifty days? It was never enough, and now it could never be enough.

CHAPTER SIXTEEN

1988, WAS TOM'S first run for the U. S. Congress, and Rich had decided I should take a leave from the *Chadron Record* to document the race with my camera. He was looking toward a future where he thought such photos would be valuable—*The Early Career of a Political Superstar.*

We were at the big Marriott in Lincoln and running late. Rich had already left, and I needed to be on the road by ten o'clock to get to the next stop. Tom had a town hall talk at eleven, but when he walked into the living room of the empty hospitality suite that morning, punctuality lost all importance.

He had just taken a shower. His body was still damp and smelled of soap and English Leather. He had raked his thick hair back with his hands; wet, it looked even darker than usual. A few early gray strands shone in the ravines cut by his finger tips. My eyes tracked downward over his chest to the white hotel towel wrapped around his slim hips. I could see the outline of his erection.

He reached out and gently pulled me forward. I was partially dressed, having been changing into my jeans after our meetings that morning. I'd told myself that I'd be clothed and out of the hospitality room by the time Tom had finished his shower, but that was a lie. The campaign was going so well that I assumed it wouldn't be long until he left for

Washington, and while we hadn't seen much of each other living on opposite ends of a long state, I knew that once he was halfway across the country I would see him even less. We had been sharing rushed kisses and long phone calls for several years by then, but it seemed even those would become more difficult. I wanted this good-bye.

Tom slipped his smooth hands under my partially buttoned blouse and slid them around my ribcage. With one twist he deftly unhooked my bra then cupped my breasts. My involuntary moan made him smile. As I shrugged off my top, the towel fell from his waist. He pushed me onto the couch, unzipped my jeans, peeled them from my thighs, and dropped them to the floor. I felt the weight of his body and the thrust of his pelvis as he entered me. He murmured, "Oh, Jicky…I think you're going to be late."

"For what?" was all I whispered as I wrapped my legs around his torso. He was the man I wanted, and he wanted me. What was one lost hour when I'd been anticipating this moment for years and wasn't sure when it would happen again.

* * *

IT WAS A late afternoon in November 1990. Pam was at work, and Rich was at Tom's office on the Hill. Tom and Pam's Georgetown townhouse glowed golden in the low sunlight shining through the tall multi-paned windows. I looked up from the bed at the crystal chandelier dominating the center of the ceiling above me and then over to the windows swathed in heavy gold damask draperies tied back with thick silk cords capped by foot-long tassels. The raw-silk quilted bedspread lay heaped on the floor where Tom had kicked it half an hour earlier. It matched the drapes.

"Your life with me isn't going to look like this, unless you're the one who's been decorating your houses. You know what Rich's and my place looks like—decorating just isn't important to me. I mean, I like it when I see it, but it's not something I ever see myself doing."

"Damn, Jickster, do you you really think I care about this shit." Tom said as his hand swung toward the ornate headboard. "Pam's gotta have things just so. She's the one who keeps puttin' off having kids—says we've gotta keep entertainin' to impress folks. She loves this place so much I doubt she'll ever leave it, and that's okay, 'cause I'll be happier keeping *our home* to ourselves—'special'y if it means I don't hafta pick up my underwear."

"NO, don't quit picking up your underwear!" I playfully punched Tom's bicep and continued, "I'm not a slob—just not a decorator. Tell me, when have you ever seen my underwear on the floor?"

Tom rolled over me and pointed to my bra and underpants on the floor by the bed where they'd landed when he'd undressed me earlier.

"Okay, you got me this time, but as Rich would say in his legalese 'there were some extenuating circumstances.' But, really Tom, I'm not kidding, if we get married our home life is gonna be very different than the way you've been living."

"Got it, Jiks, and I don't give a rat's ass. I will live any way you like as long as I get to live with you and that pack of kids we're gonna have just as soon as we tie the knot. And, by the way, you can quit saying '*if*'—you *are* gonna be my wife."

* * *

IT WAS 1991, and we were preparing for Tom's next campaign. "Are you done yet, Jickster? I'd like you to take a few shots—some good ones—with my hat on."

"What, and cover-up that gorgeous hair."

"That *grayin'* hair don't you mean."

"No, I don't—women voters love your hair."

"Well, that may be so, but I like my hat, and I've felt like a damn fraud in all my campaign shots not wearin' it. No lecture, Jikums—I know why I couldn't wear it when I was runnin' on the east side of the state, but now it's time. I need votes from the west, too."

"Maybe you should switch to a white hat for photos," I said, with a smirk.

"Hell, no—you want me to look like a fuckin' Marlboro Man? Besides that, God'd prob'ly strike me dead."

We were shooting Tom's new portraits for his run for the U. S. Senate. Manchester-Mann, his D.C. ad agency, had given me a shot list. It had always been an unspoken rule that Tom had to ditch his black cowboy hat for campaign literature, even though he'd worn a hat all of his adult life (he'd probably worn one as a kid, too, having grown up on a ranch). The problem with wearing a cowboy hat in photos was the East vs. West battle that runs through all the Midwestern states; it's the same as the urban/rural divide in other places. Tom couldn't have looked too western and won his seat in eastern Nebraska's First District. But, now, if Tom could manage to straddle the divide, he could win the statewide Senate seat. He knew it. He adjusted his Stetson and grinned at his reflection in the mirrored closet doors of the hotel room.

"Okay, Tom, I'll shoot a roll with your hat. You can take it up with Rich and the bigwigs at Man & Mann…but you still hafta ditch that," I said, pointing to his cigarette.

"Shit, Jiks, I wish Nebraska were a tobacco growin' state so I didn't have to hide my smokes, too." Tom, still preening in the mirror, added, "God, with the hat and a cigarette I really do look like the fuckin' Marlboro Man!"

"Yeah, and that look would prob'ly get you elected in some parts of the State. I know the hat's gonna play well in Chadron."

"Darn, tootin', little shootin' lady," Tom teased as he stubbed out his cigarette in the glass ashtray on the nightstand. He plunked his hat on my head and twirled me around until I landed on the bed. "How'd you like to do a little playin' with me," he said, delaying the rest of our photo session.

* * *

TOM WALKED THROUGH the pulsing ballroom of the Omaha Hilton planting the heels of his cowboy boots into the polka-dotted, mauve and burgundy institutional carpeting. It looked like the Congressman meant business, but he was looking at me, not Rich. When he got to our table he took my hand and shoved a quarter in my palm just as the band started playing the opening strains of Brooks and Dunn's "Boot Scootin' Boogie."

"Flip you for the lead, Jickster."

"Ha, ha," I said, as I pushed the coin back into his palm and held it there. "Better keep your money—I understand this event is a fundraiser. I'll cede the lead to you—this time."

I looked over at Rich hip deep in conversation with some Dem fat-cat from the east side of the State. I'm not sure he even noticed as Tom and I rushed toward the dance floor.

Tom held me close for a second, then spun me out into the sweaty crowd. We'd managed to sneak away together for an hour earlier in the day, and I could still feel the weight of his body between my legs and picture the look in his eyes as he'd held my wrists to the over-starched sheets, pinning me to the hotel bed.

We danced to the lively crowd favorite, but it ended too soon. As we stood in the middle of the packed floor waiting for the next number, I hoped that it would be something just as energetic. I knew it was acceptable for us to dance the fast ones, but slow songs, meaning close contact, could raise eyebrows. When the female lead started singing a heart-rending version of "Someday Soon," I suggested I go back to the table.

"No way," he whispered in my ear, "I requested this one for us." Tom took me in his arms and looked at me as though we were the only two people in the room.

"Are you sure?"

"Never more sure of anything in my life, Jiks."

We danced slow… and close… and every time the refrain rolled round, Tom would whisper in my ear, *someday soon goin' with me, someday soon…*

The 1992 election was just days away. If Tom didn't win the Senate seat, our going public with our relationship would be of little consequence to the voters of Nebraska. However, if he won, I was worried. Not only would our affair blindside Rich, it could tank Tom's political career. I wasn't sure we could weather that kind of gossip. But, in the middle of the dance floor, during the largest fundraiser he had ever held, Tom was telling me that he was mine. I was the only thing that mattered to him… *"Never more sure of anything in my life, Jiks… someday soon."*

Tears of joy welled in my eyes as I buried my face in the yoke of Tom's western-cut sport coat. I lifted my head as the song came to an end and made my own vow in his ear, "Someday, Tom. Someday."

CHAPTER SEVENTEEN

BILL CLINTON HAD just been elected the 42nd President of the United States, and Tom had just won his first term in the U. S. Senate. Tom and Rich were planning a victory lap around Nebraska. Rich had wanted me to ride with them and take more photos, but I'd begged off. So far, Tom and I had managed to keep our affair private, and while we were talking of going public soon, I was getting more and more afraid that we would be found out before we could make the announcement. I didn't want to get caught at this late date and certainly not by Rich.

"HOW DID WE get here, Tom? We're smart people, why have we made such a mess of our lives and the lives of almost everyone who gets near us?" I was having one of those days when guilt was my constant companion. There'd been a few days like that toward the beginning of our affair, but lately they were becoming all too familiar.

"Jikster, don't make me feel guilty for lovin' you. I swear, it's the only big decision I've made without Rich in my entire adult life."

"Maybe so, I don't know… but, really, Rich hasn't done anything to hurt either of us. What we're planning is gonna crush him. It's not that I don't want to be with you, I want it more than I've ever wanted anything…I just don't know how we can do it."

Tom took me in his arms and gently lifted my head from his shoulder. Smoothing back my hair he looked me in the eyes. "Jik, we have a plan. You know this is the time. We have to do it soon—we need everything to have shaken out before another fuckin' campaign. We want people to think of us as a long-time couple when I start to run again. We owe at least that much to Rich."

"I know… but telling him that Pam is finally leaving will be hard enough, and he's been expecting that for years. Telling him about us is gonna kill him. How can we do it?"

"Fuck it, Jik, how can we not? Now's the time—we've talked about it…you know I'm right. I don't want to go on livin' this way, and you've told me that you don't either. We need to start buildin' a life together—a family, we're not gettin' any younger. I think we should tell him before I leave for D.C."

I inadvertently sighed. "It's just that I guess I'm scared. It's going to change everything. A long time ago you told me that Rich wanted to be my Svengali. Do you remember? It was on Thanksgiving, when we lived in the duplex. I didn't know what you meant—it was back when Rich wanted me to hide everything I didn't know by keeping my mouth shut." I gave a small sad huff, "God, I'm surprised I talked at all … Anyway, I've learned a lot over the years about the Svengali story—Tom, you're even more of Rich's creation than I am. If he gives up on you, he could take you down, just like Svengali took down Trilby, the woman he'd made into a star. Will you still want me if you lose your career? I'm invisible, but you're not. It could get so ugly—will you be able to forgive me if it does?"

"Jickster, give me more credit than that—I love you. And, it's not like I don't have connections. I've already had offers that pay a hell of a lot more than bein' a Senator. But, if you wanna be poor I can always teach—we'll start a family and build a life outside of politics. Rich'll be okay—he's got a reputation for bein' one of the best political operatives in D.C. He'll just create another politician."

"Don't say that Tom, you know that you're more than that to Rich. I didn't mean a politician when I said he was your Svengali—well, maybe I did—but there's so much more between you guys … God, how am I going to do this when I don't even know how to talk about it … Rich has been my only family for so long. He's not much of a husband, but he's been like my big brother for a huge chunk of my life."

"Maybe that's enough for him. Maybe after Pam leaves we can work somethin' out so that nothin' much has to change with the three of us. We all love one another, right. It could work—right—com'on, Jickster, tell me I'm right … "

As Tom's words trailed off, I shook my head and quietly mumbled, "Maybe … I doubt it … but maybe. Just promise me that we'll tell him together."

"Jik, I can't make that promise. If it works out that the time seems right during this trip, I'm gonna tell him this weekend. There is absolutely no point in puttin' off the inevitable. I've already told Pam about us—she knows everything. Rich has gotta know soon. I'd just as soon have him know before I go back to Washington so that you can come join me now that Pam's talkin' about movin' to a place of her own. It shocked the hell outta me that she's willin' to give up the townhouse."

* * *

I WALKED THROUGH the kitchen door, dropped my canvas bag of papers and hung my coat on the first peg of the coat rack. The answering machine light was blinking. The red glowing numbers said that I had missed three calls, but I had only one message. I pushed play.

In a ragged voice, I nearly didn't recognize, Rich said, "T-T-Tom t-told me. So you want h-him n-n-now—just know h-he'll f-f-fuck almost anybody." After a sob and an interminable pause he continued, "You l-live with T-T-… it, I c-c-can't anymore." Then he hung up.

I walked to the living room, turned around and walked back to the kitchen not knowing why I'd walked to the living room. I tried calling Tom at the hotel where they'd stayed for the last two nights. He didn't answer. I checked with the front desk and was told that the Congressman and my husband had checked out earlier. Originally I'd been expecting them back later that night, or more likely in the early hours of the morning, but I didn't know what to think now. Rich had sounded so upset in his message that I'd a hard time imagining that he and Tom could share an eight hour car ride. Was Rich even coming home? Would it be Tom bursting through the door at one-in-the-morning to sweep me off my feet?

I was concerned, yet relieved. The worst was over—I hadn't wanted Tom to tell Rich without me being around, but he had. I'd try to forget Rich's cryptic words and focus on the positive.

AT ELEVEN-THIRTY I was startled from bed by someone pounding at the front door. It was too early for Rich and Tom to be back, and, anyway, neither of them would have knocked. It was my boss from the paper, George Jenkins. His first words were, "What have you heard?"

"Heard?—What's going on?" I said while rubbing my face, trying to come round enough to carry on a conversation.

"Is Rich home, Jicky?"

"No, he's with Tom Streator—they're on their way here. They've been off on a victory lap…for Tom's win…"

"Jik, I think you better sit down."

"What?…com'on, George, what is it?"

George handed me the curled paper he'd been clutching. It was a UPI printout, and it didn't take me long to understand why George Jenkins was in my living room.

UPI—Ravenna, Nebraska, USA—It has just been reported that the newly elected Junior Senator from Nebraska, U. S. Representative Thomas L. Streator, and one other person, as yet unidentified, died from injuries sustained in an automobile accident that occurred just outside the town of Ravenna, Nebraska, 35 miles northwest of Grand Island at approximately 9:30 p.m. on Saturday, November 21.

Highway Patrol Captain Paul Olson said it appeared that the driver of the vehicle fell asleep before driving into a concrete bridge abutment on Nebraska State Highway 2. There were no tire marks indicating any attempt had been made to slow Rep. Streator's late model sedan. No other vehicles were reported to have been involved in the collision.

Both men were thrown from the vehicle and believed to have died upon impact. It has not been determined which of the men was driving at the time of the accident. Neither man was wearing a seatbelt. Alcohol does not appear to have been a factor.

Rep. Streator (Dem.), age 37, has represented Nebraska's first Congressional district since 1989, and this November won a seat in the the U. S. Senate. He was married to Pamala A. Streator, a policy development specialist with

the American Medical Association in Bethesda,
Maryland. Rep. Streator had no children.

GEORGE SAT ON the couch with me while I told him that I
was sure it was Rich in the car with Tom. He said that he was
sorry to be the bearer of such sad news, but he'd been hoping
he'd been wrong in his assumption that the other person had
been my husband.

I asked George if he would like coffee, stood quickly, and
walked to the kitchen before he could answer. Dazed, I
touched the answering machine, turned and walked back to
the living room, picked up the Thermofaxed UPI article from
the coffee table and stared at it without comprehension or
tears. George asked if he should stay with me, but seemed
relieved when I told him to go home.

I know that I should have called Rich's parents that night,
or I should have called Pam to confirm what I'd read, but it
was so late that I did neither. As soon as George left, I walked
to the answering machine and replayed Rich's message. Before
anyone else could ever hear his words I deleted them.

I had no doubt who had been driving Tom's car. Rich's
broken voice replayed the answer over and over inside my
head: *"You live with it. I can't anymore."*

CHAPTER EIGHTEEN

WHEN RICH AND TOM died, I lost everything. I lost my family and my lover. I lost my past and my future. I lost my two best friends.

I sat on the Weckwerth's couch in an unresponsive stupor. I was grief stricken, but I was also horrified, and so angry with Rich and with myself that I thought it would be a blessing if I were to die, too. Rich's answering machine message kept playing in my brain. My husband, who had never been intentionally cruel to anyone, had decided that the last act of his life should be a murder-suicide dedicated to me. He wanted me to know and to always remember that I'd done this to us.

Rich's parents, though devastated, had taken over immediately and made all of the final arrangements. They'd had a traditional Methodist funeral for their only child at the church where he'd been baptized and where we'd attended services every Sunday since moving back to Chadron. When the former governor of Nebraska, Bob Kerrey, requested to speak at the service, Gloria had turned him down. Bob respectfully attended the service anyway. He and Rich had been close for years—starting when Rich had become active in party politics shortly after his return to the State.

The church was packed. Many of the town folks came to pay respect to Rich's parents, but they also came because Rich was Rich. Though he was just "one other" to the national news outlets, to Chadron he was "one of their own." He was a successful attorney and the respected leader of the Democratic party in the State. While many of the townspeople didn't agree with his politics, they admired his abilities and his undeniable intelligence. But most of all, in his small hometown, he, like his father, was known as a good man.

I would keep it that way. No one would ever know what he had done. Or was it, what *we* had done…

WHEN I'D HEARD about the plans that Pam had made for Tom's services, I'd sat in bewildered awe. How she'd put the ceremonies together so thoroughly in just a few days was unfathomable to me. She held memorials in Lincoln and, later, in Washington, D.C. Bob Kerrey gave the eulogy in Lincoln, and the newly elected President of the United States, Bill Clinton, spoke at Tom's D.C. service. Tom was buried on the ranch in Colorado where Streators had been buried for the last hundred years. There, along with his parents, Pam had planned a small family service.

I should have, at the very least, attended Tom's service in Lincoln, but Rich's funeral had been held the day before and I was afraid—afraid that my emotions would betray me, or my sanity might completely escape me. Rich's parents made the long drive to Tom's Nebraska memorial; I spent the day curled in my bed holding Tom's picture.

Weeks passed while I did nothing but sit on the Weckwerth's couch. It was hard for me to be around Rich's parents, but it was harder to be alone in Rich's and my house with reminders of Rich and Tom all around me.

Gloria wrote beautiful acknowledgement notes to the people who had sent cards and flowers. When appropriate, she would set them in front of me to sign. She put food and drinks on the coffee table and urged me to eat. She said Rich wouldn't have wanted to see me this way. I didn't tell her that she was wrong, that this was precisely what her son had wanted for me. What I didn't deserve from Gloria was her kindness.

* * *

I HEARD ON the TV news that Pam Streator had been tapped to be Tom's replacement in the Senate until a special election could be held. The people of Nebraska had been impressed by the young widow. Political columnists had written glowing accounts of her behavior. Things like, "Not since Jackie Kennedy have we witnessed such grace and dignity." It seemed offering Pam Tom's seat was, to quote the *Omaha World-Herald*, "the right and proper thing to do." The announcement made me want to scream from my rooftop—*NO, SHE WAS LEAVING HIM!!! WHAT DO YOU MEAN RIGHT—THIS ISN'T RIGHT! IT'S ALL A SHOW!*—She hadn't loved him for years, and from what Tom had told me, she hadn't even liked him. I thought *she doesn't deserve the honor.* But, of course, I said nothing. I just cried into my pillow.

By the time Pam called me in late November, I'd started to change my mind about her. We had never been close friends, and, though I'd always assumed she'd made fun of me behind my back, in public she'd always been unfalteringly pleasant. I'd also come to realize that she was carrying a burden and a secret, too—and hers had to play out in a much more public fashion than mine. She was forced by political circumstances to act the grieving widow. It couldn't have been easy, and I envied her ability to perform the role so well. I had no reason to be jealous, or even care, if she took Tom's Senate seat.

* * *

"JICKY, YOU HAD to've known that Tom and I were having problems. I know Rich knew. I'd wanted out for awhile, but he and Tom kept saying no—they both insisted we stay together until Tom was established in Washington. The thing is, Jik, Tom had changed in his last term in the House. He'd wanted out, too. I'm pretty sure he had a lover. He'd always had his flings—he'd started cheating on me back at the U—but this time it must have been serious. I think he really wanted to be with her. I hope she's not crazy like some of the others and planning on giving me problems—nah, she's probably just some *pathetic little whore* stuck in a lie and crying her eyes out."

I didn't know what to say. Tom had told me that he'd told Pam about us. If she meant what she'd just said, Tom had lied to me. I thought it more likely she knew that I'd been Tom's lover and was sending me some sort of vicious message. Either way it played with my head.

"Jik, are you still there?" Pam didn't wait for a response. "I didn't mean to lay this on you, but I don't have anyone else to talk to. You know what he was like—Rich must have told you about all Tom's flings. I mean, no one knew our husbands and our lives like you do. I'm so mad at Tom for dying and I'm so sorry for you that he took Rich with him." She paused; I thought I heard ice cubes clink. "I'm just glad Tom didn't kill you, too … I'd thought you were going to be with them taking pictures."

Finally, I spoke. "I decided not to go—sort of at the last minute … And, Pam, I don't blame Tom for the accident … we don't even know if he was driving. It could have been Rich. You know we all drove on those long trips."

"Oh, obviously you haven't heard the latest findings. The cruise control was set to eighty-five. Rich never drove much over the speed limit, did he? I remember how Tom laughed and laughed when you guys bought the Firebird—he said Rich would never drive *her* the way *she* deserved. That fast, it had to be Tom behind the wheel."

I thought, *Yes, and Rich always wore his seatbelt, but he didn't that night when he set the cruise control and aimed for that f-ing bridge abutment.* I just said, "It's okay Pam, I'm not blaming anyone." I don't know how I'd managed to choke out those false words.

"Jicky, there are a few other things that I wanted to talk to you about. You might have guessed already, there's someone else in my life. I'd wanted a divorce so that we could marry. Obviously, we can't now—Tom's death screwed that up. So, I'm going to take the Senate seat for the next two years and live this lie for a little while longer. What I've been wondering is, would you like to come to D.C.? You know most of Tom's staff nearly as well as I do—certainly, the Nebraska staff. You could be my liaison—I'm sure they all like you more than me —you could smooth my way."

I tried to break in to say "no," but Pam just kept talking.

"I know it's a lot to think about, but I thought maybe you'd like a fresh start away from Chadron. Besides, I need someone who knows the whole story—somebody I can trust." I heard Pam take a drink. She cleared her throat and said, "I promise; *I'll take care of you.*"

"…Um, Pam, I don't know. Can I call you in a few days?"

I said goodbye and cried for hours. Why had Pam unloaded on me, and what in the hell did it all mean? I couldn't figure out if she was feeling guilty and needed someone to talk to like she'd said, or if she was trying to trap me in a corner and play with me like a cat toying with wounded sparrow. The innuendo was obvious, but there was also something in her inflection that had chilled me. And, the crap about Tom having lovers—it couldn't have been true—I would have known. After all these years, I still didn't understand how Pam's mind worked.

One thing I did know, politics was a thing of my past. There was no way on earth I would be moving to Washington, D.C., and maybe that had been Pam's plan all along. One bizarre phone call and poof!—she'd never have to think about Jicky Weckwerth ever again.

CHAPTER NINETEEN

BY EARLY DECEMBER, when the sympathy cards in the mailbox were being replaced by Christmas greetings, I'd finally moved off the Weckwerth's couch. I was living in my old place and had started back at the *Register*. George was happy to have me back, not only for my photos, but also because with me around he didn't have to answer the phone. For a man interested in what was happening in the world, he was not the least bit inquisitive when the phone rang.

At home, I'd completed my move to the guest room. I'd been sleeping in that room for years, but I'd always kept my things in the master bedroom so that Rich's parents thought we shared a room—it had been important to Rich that Gloria and Wes not know we slept apart. After my things were out of both, I closed the doors to Rich's bedroom and office. That part of my life was over.

Ironically, in the past, the only times I'd sleep with Rich were when Tom was using the guest room. When I'd first started using the spare room as my own, I'd dutifully washed the sheets before Tom arrived, but in the last few years it hadn't seemed important. Tom said he loved sleeping in a bed that smelled of *Jicky*. Whether he'd meant the perfume or me, I'd never been sure. He'd gifted me with a bottle of the expensive perfume when he'd moved to D.C. (just after we'd made love for the first time). I had never smelled the scent that

I'd been named for and, at first whiff, hadn't been sure that I liked it. But, Tom did, so I wore it for him.

It got so that I wouldn't change the sheets for days after Tom had left. If he *liked* the way I smelled, I *craved* the way he smelled—smoke, soap, and English Leather. I missed his scent nearly as much as his tobacco and Gentleman Jack tinged kisses. I wanted to smell him, to taste him, to make love to him. Despite what Pam had told me, I ached for Tom and missed him more than I grieved for Rich. That ache was a condition I couldn't share and a shame that I couldn't escape.

* * *

"OH, THANK YOU, Dad, but I can't take the money—I don't know why, but it just doesn't feel right, and besides, I don't need it. Rich took good care of my business—I've got money coming in from my photos and I've got my job at the paper until I figure out if I'm going to stay in Chadron."

"But, Jicky, this money is for you. That's why I bought the policy—to secure your future and, well, Gloria and I were hopin' to secure the futures of our *grandkids* if anything should happen to Rich … "

"I'm so sorry about that—I know you and Mother would have been really good grandparents."

"Hon, it's okay. We all know it's not your fault babies didn't happen for you two."

I didn't know how to respond to his comment. Thankfully, Wes kept talking.

"What do you say I put the money away for you? You don't ever have to take it if you don't need it, but if sumthin' happens you'll know you've got the cash to handle it. How's that sound?"

"Sure, Dad, I don't think anything's gonna to happen to change my mind, but you can just stash it for now."

"Oh, I almost forgot to tell you, you might be gettin' a call from an insurance investigator. Just standard stuff, but they're tryin' to figure out who was drivin' the car. There're two different insurance companies involved, so they'll be fightin' it out tooth and nail."

"Oh? I thought it'd been determined that Tom was driving? That's what Pam told me when she called."

"Don't know where she got that idea. As far as I know the driver hasn't been named. Maybe Pam just assumed it was Tom 'cause it looked like they were goin' pretty fast. Rich always said Tom had a lead foot."

"Do you think if they find something strange the insurance company's gonna want the money back?"

"Nah—what could they find? The only way they could claim it was a bad payment is if the investigators could prove that the boys were involved in a felony. If drivin' fast and feelin' woren out is gonna be classified as a felony, this country's full of felons."

"Umm, well, just stash the money somewhere, okay…and, thank you… thank you for everything… I'm so sorr—," my words were cut short by a sob.

"Jicky-girl, we all are. We all are," Wes said as he hugged me.

I'd just told Westerly Weckwerth to bank a hundred-thousand dollars. It may have been stupidity on my part, but it felt like blood money to me, or at least, money that I didn't deserve. And, I was worried. Maybe fast driving couldn't be considered a felony, but I thought a murder-suicide would be. Whatever happened, I had no intention of ever spending any of the settlement money on myself.

* * *

IT HAD BEEN weeks since Pam had called making me feel like I should run away, and the sad Thanksgiving dinner that

I'd shared with the Weckwerths on the day following the call had only increased my desire to escape. I'd decided to go see Pops, Joel, and Gary for Christmas, and to Gloria and Wes's credit, they encouraged me to go, saying a visit with my family might do me good. I hadn't celebrated Christmas with my real family since my brothers and I were kids. Rich and I had flown to Waterbury in 1988 when Gary graduated high school (just before he went into the Marines), but that was already four years ago. Gary was back in Connecticut now, living with Pops and planning on starting at the local college. I was so proud of him; he had done an excellent job of raising himself.

Joel had married a while back, but, from what I'd heard from Pops, he still lived in the area. I'd never spoken with his wife. Pops said she was a "nice gal." He liked her. I was hoping marriage would be good for Joel. He'd never really pulled his life together and seemed to have bounced from one thing to another after high school. Maybe having a wife would finally give him some stability. No part of growing up had given him much grounding. Our mom was pretty messed up most of his really early years and had left us when he was only seven—then I left, or rather they left me, when he was twelve. The stint with Louisa hadn't lasted long, and after that... well... I suppose Pops had done the best he could.

I LET GEORGE Jenkins know I was leaving the paper for good. If he was upset by my sudden change in plans, he didn't show it. He just started looking for a new receptionist right away. With the advent of better point-and-shoot cameras, my position as photographer was not what it had once been. George had always been proud to have a famous photographer on his staff, but he'd found a couple of hobbyists happy to take my place whenever I'd taken time off to work on Tom's campaigns. He was probably relieved when I told him that I was moving on—at least he wouldn't have to juggle my erratic schedule any longer.

When I told Rich's parents that I wasn't sure when I would return, Wes offered to keep an eye on my house. I think he liked the idea of having another hideout in the winter where he could enjoy reading his Larry McMurtry novels and drinking the kinds of beverages that didn't meet with Gloria's approval. And, I think Wes felt Rich's presence in our old place, in the same way that Gloria had told me she sensed Rich when she sat upstairs in his childhood bedroom. While I didn't feel Rich's or Tom's presence anywhere in Chadron, I couldn't escape their ghosts. So much guilt, grief, loneliness, and confusion—I didn't know what to do about my feelings. Leaving seemed like the worst and only answer.

DECEMBER
1992

CHAPTER TWENTY

I'D PURCHASED A ticket to Waterbury, Connecticut, planning to visit my father and brothers whom I felt I barely knew any longer. Joel would be turning twenty-seven on January eighteenth and Gary was twenty-three. Truth be told, I didn't know how old my Pops was. He'd always seemed old to me, but he would've only been in his fifties, because, as I remembered the story, he'd left college when Mom had gotten pregnant with me. I'd never thought much about it when I was a kid, but I've wondered as an adult if our lives would have been different had our father completed his education and had a degree to fall back on instead of always bouncing from one manual-labor job to the next? Pops was so darn smart, and yet, when I answer my own question, I doubt things would have changed much. Pops would've still been Pops—the irresponsible, unreliable, inebriated, lovable father he'd always been. And, I'm afraid without major intervention, our Mom would've been just as depressed and absent.

I FLEW TO New Haven—it was the first time I'd ever flown by myself. Gary had borrowed a car from a friend to pick me up. He met me at my arrival gate and we walked arm-in-arm through the festive airport to the baggage claim. So close to Christmas, the airport sparkled with decorations and activity.

Perhaps it was because Gary was steering me through the hubbub, making it so I didn't have to think for myself, that I suddenly felt the way I had in the weeks just after Tom and Rich had died. It was a feeling that would come over me in Chadron when I'd see strangers driving their cars or pushing carts in the grocery store. I couldn't understand how people could smile and go on as though life were normal. Why weren't they as stricken, as chest-empty numb, as me? Didn't they know that the world had ended? I closed my eyes briefly, then looked up at my brother. The world hadn't ended for him, and in my rational mind I knew it hadn't ended for me either. I realized that I would feel this hollow pain for a while, maybe the rest of my days, but the world was still spinning—life was going on, and I had to, too.

I'd been surprised when I'd first seen Gary. He looked good, but so much older than he'd looked when Rich and I had seen him at his graduation. He'd filled out since high school. His hair was still sandy-red, and freckles still littered his high cheek bones, but now the head that hosted those features was on a neck with the circumference of a sequoia. When I mentioned my surprise at his new look, he'd responded with a grin, and in a low-pitched resonant voice said, "The U. S. Marine Corps will do that to a kid."

My kid, I thought; my, now, grown up brother.

GARY UNLOCKED THE passenger door, then walked around back and tossed my suitcase in the trunk of the newish Camry. As he folded his six-foot-four frame into the driver's seat, I told him to thank his friend for the use of the car—it was nice getting this time to talk, and I was happy not having to take a bus, my luggage in tow. I'd thought about renting a car when I first talked with Gary about coming to visit, but he'd recommended I wait. He hadn't said why.

I watched the lights of the city go by and held the side of the seat as Gary took the winding approach to the interstate. It wasn't that he was a bad driver—he was just a fast driver and the heavy traffic and wide interstates unnerved me. I'd seen heavy traffic on my trips to D.C. with Rich, but I was sure that I would never get accustomed to it. I wondered why I hadn't thought about that when I'd envisioned a life with Tom in Washington. There was so much that I hadn't thought through. I was still lost in thoughts of the past when Gary spoke up.

"Jicky, I'm so sorry about Rich and his friend. I shoulda come to the funeral, but, well, you know … "

"Yeah, it's okay," I said shaking my head from side to side, "I wasn't in very good shape then. It wouldn't have been much of a visit for you."

"No, but you know what I mean—somebody from the family should've been there. From what you told us over the years and what I saw of Rich when you guys came to visit—well, he seemed like a good guy. We're really sorry."

"Thanks, Gary, he was a good guy and so was Tom. I can't believe they're both gone—or maybe it's like I can't believe they're never coming back. I don't wanna believe it. I want to think when I head home to Nebraska they'll be there waiting for me. Like this has been a big nightmare."

We were quiet, both caught-up in our own thoughts, until I broke the silence.

"How'r Pops and Joey doing?" I'd spoken with our father recently, but I hadn't talked to Joel since last December.

"Joey's okay, you know Joey, he's kind'a like Pops when it comes to workin'—sorta off and on— except he's a kitchen hopper. He's a damn good chef, but his temper always seems to get the best of him. His big news is that Sherry's pregnant. Joel's gonna be a dad."

"Wow, that's great … maybe … or just a little scary … and, it makes me feel O-L-D. My little brothers aren't supposed to be parents before me."

"It'll prob'ly be okay—Joel turned out to be a pretty decent big brother, and Sherry, she really seems to have her head on straight."

"So, how's Pops?—What's he think about becoming a grandpa?"

"Oh, he's happy about it, though he's getting forgetful, so if you ask him, he might not know what you're talking about."

"Gee, Gary, forgetful? Isn't he a little young for that? Pops has always been so sharp."

"Yeah, well…Pops isn't doing so hot. I didn't want to tell you until you got here, but he's pretty sick. I've been wanting him to see a doctor, but he doesn't wanna go—says it's too expensive, but I think that's just an excuse—the man's never paid off a medical bill in his life. I think he's afraid of what the doctors are going to tell him."

"What? What do you think's wrong?"

"Truth, Jicky?—Truth is, I think Pops has AIDS."

"Pops? How?"

"God, Jik—it's more like *how not*. You know if there's something sketchy out there to try, Pops is gonna try it. He sorta held things together when I was at home—bein' a good example or somethin', but he really went off the deep end when I went away to bootcamp. That's when the drugs really took over from what Joel's told me. Heroin mainly."

"Really? Heroin?"

"Yeah, that's what Joey said."

WE PULLED UP to a three-story wood-frame building that a century ago would have been a fine house in a fine neighborhood. Neither of those things held true in 1992. The painted façade of the building was peeling and the side walls were sprayed with graffiti. The front porch sagged and one of the first floor windows was covered with a large sheet of flaking particleboard. Wires, held aloft by nail-encrusted wooden power poles, criss-crossed the air over our heads. So many of them! It seemed that every wire and cable installed since Edison had invented electricity still littered the sky over that part of Waterbury. The burned out shell of what had once been an apartment building neighbored Pops's building. Its front wall was missing, and the visible rooms, some still furnished, made the structure look like a derelict doll house. A tattered curtain fluttered through a shattered window, and a broken toilet hung from the edge of a second floor bathroom. I asked if it had burned recently. Gary said it hadn't; as far as he knew it had been that way when Pops and Joel had moved into the apartment shortly after he'd left for bootcamp.

"I promised my friend I wouldn't park outside of our place any longer than I'd have to to get your stuff unloaded. I think he's being overly cautious, but I'm gonna respect his wishes— I might need his car again." As soon as he'd helped me to the apartment landing, Gary took off to return the Camry, but not before he'd admitted that the neighborhood was the reason he hadn't wanted me to rent a car. He thought that a nice car sitting on the street night after night might have tempted fate, or, at the very least, somebody with a crowbar.

IT WAS GOOD that Gary had warned me about Pops, but I was still not prepared to see the person our father had become. Never a heavy man, he was now skeletal. His pale Irish complexion, normally so much like Gary's, had gone from rosy to grayish, and he had a festering sore on his forehead.

We didn't kiss when greeting one another at the back door, and he hugged me only gingerly. I don't know if his hesitancy was from concern for my health or if he didn't want me to feel how much of him had wasted away over the past four years. His voice, however, was still strong and he seemed overjoyed to see me and genuinely sad when he told me he was sorry that I'd lost my husband at such a young age.

"At least I was an old man when I found out your mom'd died."

"What Pops?… Mom's dead?… When?" I asked.

"Sorry Jicky, I thought you knew." All of a sudden Pops seemed confused.

"I knew she'd left us, but I sorta hoped she was still out there somewhere. I alway thought I might see her again."

"No—no, she died a while ago. Are you sure your brothers never told you?"

"Yeah, Pops, I'm sure. That's something I'd remember."

He rubbed his jaw as his eyes teared, "Guess you'd better talk to Gary about it…. Would you mind if I laid down, sweetie. I'm beat after all the excitement of waitin' for you to get here."

Pops walked from the kitchen to the living room couch and pulled a worn blanket over the lower half of his tracksuit clad body. A beat-up kitchen chair sat beside the couch covered with crumpled tissues, old newspapers, and a stained coffee mug. From the looks of it, the couch was where my father spent most of his days. As soon as Pops appeared to be sleeping I walked back to the kitchen, washed my hands, and got myself a glass of water. I wasn't sure where to take my suitcase, so I sat at the kitchen table and stared out the window watching trash and dust-like snow blow down the alley behind the apartment.

GARY WAS BACK within the hour carrying a bag of groceries. He stocked the ancient fridge with eggs and wieners, and one of the metal upper cupboards with store-brand Wheaties, mac-and-cheese, and cans of tomato soup. He then filled two cracked plastic ice trays with water and set them in the freezer before joining me at the table with a can of warm Coke. We talked over Pops's condition while I gathered the nerve to ask Gary about Mom.

"I didn't realize you didn't know, Jicky—Pops found out while I was away. I think she died from a heart attack—she was back in South Dakota living someplace on the Pine Ridge Reservation. Somebody named Marlys called Pops with the news—evidently our mom still had her address among her things—she's the person the morgue notified."

"Yeah, Aunt Marlys was who I lived with when you guys moved east—she's Mom's sister. I wonder if she knew where Mom was?"

"I don't think so, Jicky. From what Pops said about it at the time, it sounded like it was a surprise for Marlys, too."

"I wish I'd known Mom was on Pine Ridge. You wouldn't know this, but that reservation is just north of Chadron. Mom was so close, but I never knew…I could've seen her if I'd known."

"I'm sorry for you, Jik; I really am. But, honestly, her death didn't mean much to me, and I didn't see any point in talking about it—none of us did: I didn't remember her, Joel said he didn't like her, and thinking about her made Pops sad. But that's still no excuse—one of us should've told you. I'm sorry we didn't."

GARY SHOWED ME through the apartment which was surprisingly large. We walked from the kitchen, situated at the back of the house, past the bathroom and into the living room where our father was still sound asleep. Gary carried my suitcase down a long hall passing several doors. At the end of the hall he opened a door to a room with windows that faced the street at the front of the building. It was a bright, clean bedroom—obviously, Gary's. On the wall, above the twin bed, he'd taped the "R-eagle" poster that I'd sent to him while he was in high school; at least I assumed it was the same one. Judging from the layers of tape and missing corners it looked as though it had been taped on many walls over the years. The poster read *"FREEDOM"* in large script letters that appeared to wave across the blue sky above Mt. Rushmore.

"Did I ever tell you what the poster company wanted to write on the picture?" Gary shook his head. "The morons wanted to write *Let Freedom Wing*. Rich told them that if they insisted, they weren't going to get the licensing rights to my photo. He told me that he thought their design team must have been a bunch of *'wascally wabbit'* idiots. He wasn't going to let my photo be turned into a joke."

"Rich was a smart guy."

"Yeah, he was … " a ragged breath escaped my lungs. "Well, anyway, I'm really pleased that you still have the poster."

"Of course I do, along with my T-shirt." Gary pointed to a very worn souvenir T-shirt from the Badlands of South Dakota with a scene of rugged peaks framed by a rainbow. The shirt was on a wire hanger, hooked over the closet door knob.

"Don't tell me that hangs there all the time."

"Aw, you got me—I just put it there in your honor, but I think it should stay."

"No, no that's okay … I'm happy to see that you cared enough to keep it, but you can prob'ly put it back where it came from. So, this is your room—where do you plan on sleeping?"

"I'm moving down to Pops's room."

"Really? You sure sharing a bedroom's a good idea?"

"Yeah, he's pretty much on the couch all the time now. It's closer to the bathroom and the TV. I've cleaned his room top to bottom—it'll be fine. The other thing I like about this new arrangement is that I'll be closer to Pops if he needs me at night. Right now—from this room—it's hard to hear him when he gets up."

I told Gary he made a good case for giving me his room, but I still felt like a crappy big sister kicking him out of his bed. Gary hugged me and said that he'd never thought of me as anything near *crappy*, and admitted he wanted to make me comfortable enough so that I'd consider hanging around for a while.

* * *

I LAY IN GARY'S bed that night listening to the sounds of engines revving and tires squealing, broken only occasionally by the sharp wailing of police sirens. I thought about all I had learned in the past few hours: Pops was sick, very sick, and Mom was dead. Already a widow, it looked like I was going to be an orphan in my early thirties as well.

But, of all the emotions I felt that first long night in Connecticut, my physical longing for Tom was what consumed me. As I kicked at the blankets and twisted my pillow, it was the pain of knowing that the future Tom had planned for us would never be. I couldn't go back to the sameness of the life I'd left behind in Nebraska, yet, without Tom, the only future I could envision was pointless wherever I went. Empty. For the first time in my life I felt completely empty.

* * *

I DIDN'T SEE Joel or meet Sherry until Monday, the down day for the restaurant where they both worked. Joel, like both Gary and Pops, had changed over the past four years. His face had thinned and he now sported a neck tattoo which, along with an ever-present scowl, made him look a bit dangerous. Joel was about my height and probably not much heavier than me, but wiry. And, while Gary took after Pops's clan, Joel and I shared features from both our parents. It wasn't hard to believe we were siblings—had we been the same sex (and had Joey smiled a little more) people probably would have thought us twins. Named Jicky and Joel, I suppose some people assumed we were.

Sherry was petite and just starting to show. She seemed nice and greeted me with a hug. Joel's eyes had beamed with pride when he'd introduced us—it was like they were saying, *look who I married—I'm not a loser after all.* Sherry said that they had met at a restaurant where they'd both been working—not the one where they worked now. "Joel is such an amazing chef. He's going to make us lunch—we brought all the stuff." They had come through the kitchen door laden with bags full of food and pans.

Joel interjected, "Yeah, I borrowed a few things from the restaurant." He pulled two small pork loins wrapped in plastic and a few fancy onions from a bag at his feet and plopped them on the counter. I figured he'd used the wrong word, "borrowed" usually meant that one intended to return the items—I didn't say anything, knowing I'd be a hypocrite. I felt I'd long ago given up my right to a perch on moral high ground. Besides, he really didn't need a preachy big sister anymore.

We all went into the living room to see Pops. It had evidently been awhile since Joel had visited. He looked surprised by our father's condition. If Sherry was put off by it, she didn't let it show; she walked to the couch, hugged Pops and told him all about her last prenatal check-up.

When Joel, Gary, and I went back to the kitchen to get chairs to take to the living room, Joel hissed at Gary, "Bro, why didn't you tell me Pops was in such bad shape. I'm not sure I wouda brought Sherry down to this shit hole."

"Damn it Joel, I told you—you just weren't listening. I asked you to come by weeks ago and have a talk with him—and, what do you mean, shit hole. You're the one who rented this place and moved Pops here. Don't get all prissy on me about it."

"Sorry, I just didn't...I didn't think Pops would've gotten so bad so fast."

That's when I broke in, "Don't argue guys...it's gonna be okay." To Joel I said, "Gary and I have talked Pops into seeing a doctor. He's got an appointment on Wednesday. We'll get it sorted out. There's gotta be something they can do to make him feel better."

"Oh, yeah, Jik — and who's gonna pay for that." Joel asked, more of a statement than a question.

"I will if I have to—I've got insurance money from the accident, but Gary's gonna look into getting some assistance from the state or the hospital, too. Maybe Pops'll qualify for somethin' ... I'm going back to the living room. You guys can stay here and argue if you want—nothin' ever changes between you two, does it?"

I grabbed one of the kitchen chairs and headed back to Pops and Sherry. Gary came into the room a short time later with a kitchen chair of his own. As he sat down beside me, he whispered, "You should've never let Joel know you've got money," then he turned to Sherry and Pops and said, "Joey's starting lunch—sure looks like it's gonna be terrific!"

CHAPTER TWENTY-ONE

POPS HAD BEEN quiet through the tests and examinations which we'd already deemed irrelevant after we'd been greeted by a receptionist and immediately shown to a private waiting room so that Pops wouldn't be seen by other clinic patients. Pops, always a gregarious Irishman, shut down immediately. To him, the receptionist with her brusk greeting and hurried isolation had made clear the results of his AIDS test even before it had been administered.

In actuality, it took a few days until we had Pops's official diagnosis. He had HIV/AIDS and a related cancer called Kaposi sarcoma that was causing the purplish sores on his face. The clinic doctor said, because the cancer had been left untreated for so long it was most likely attacking Pops's internal organs, too, although he couldn't know for sure without further tests.

"What do you see as the next step?" I asked Gary once he'd hung up the kitchen wall phone and told me the doctor's assessment of Pops's condition. Pops, not party to our conversation, rested as comfortably as he could on the living room couch.

"I guess I, or rather we, take care of him. I can stay and do the day-to-day stuff, and you can help with the money part of things, if you're still willing."

"Of course I'm still willing, but here's the thing…what are you gonna do once you start at UConn? Second semester must start…when? In a month? I've never gone to college, but I've worked at one—it's not like your schedule is gonna be your own—classes are held when classes are held. Pops is gonna have appointments, and I hate to say this, but what if he gets worse before he gets better? He's gonna need someone around here full time."

"Oh, yeah," Gary frowned, "like we could get a nurse to come to this part of town even if we could afford it. You don't have that kind of money do you? Doesn't matter—no one would come."

"Don't be like that, Gary. I wasn't thinking about hiring anybody; I'm thinking about staying, if you and Pops will let me. There's no one but my in-laws back in Nebraska, and they're doin' okay. I've got a car, if I can figure out how to get it here, and other than that, I pretty much brought all my stuff with me—at least the stuff I thought I might need. So, what d'ya say, little brother, you want your big sis back?"

"God Jicky, are you sure? It could get really ugly. What am I saying—it's already gotta seem really ugly. But, if you're willing to re-up, well, that's what I was hoping for."

"It's settled then, let's tell Pops."

WHEN I'D CALLED Rich's parents in Nebraska, I told them only that my father had cancer and that I'd decided to move to Connecticut to care for him so that my younger brother could go to college full-time. They were sorry for us, but supportive. Wes sounded almost pleased when I asked him to put five-thousand of the insurance money into my checking account: "Well Jicky-girl, looks like you get to spend it to help your family. That's how it should be!" I could almost hear a big affirmative nod as he finished the sentence.

"Yeah, I guess… What do you think I should do about my car? I'm thinking now like I shoulda driven it back here, but I wasn't sure when I came east that I'd be staying for long and it would've been such a long trip by myself. The big, multi-lane roads out here scare me, but I'll likely get used to them. Most of my trips will probably be drivin' my Pops to see doctors or goin' to the grocery store. I can prob'ly avoid the interstates."

"Don't worry Jik, you're a good driver, but I get ya not wantin' to drive across half the country. It's a long haul on your own, 'specially in the winter, but I got an idea. It's just an idea, mind you, but the Maddox kid flew back from Yale for Christmas—maybe if we pay him a little bit he'd be willin' to deliver Rich's Firebird to you. Young guy like him might enjoy the drive. It sure as shootin' wouldn't scare him."

"You think, Wes? Do you s'pose he'd mind bringing the Chevy instead of the new car?"

"I don't think it'd make much difference. I can take care of everything on this end. If it doesn't work with the Maddox kid, maybe I can pay someone else, or I could just sell both cars and you could buy a new one out there. The old banana boat is way past her prime anyway."

"Don't worry 'bout her age, Dad. You and Rich kept that old Chevy like new. The banana boat's the car I'm used to driving, and it'll be a lot easier for Pops to climb in-and-out of a sedan than the Firebird. Besides bein' a little older model's prob'ly a good thing around here." I didn't elaborate. "You absolutely sure you're okay with lettin' the Chevy go?"

"She's your car now, Jicky—I've got the memories—I'll just hold on to those."

"Here's an idea for you, Dad. Why don't you pay off the Firebird from the insurance settlement account and keep it for your fun car. I think Rich'd like the idea of you toolin' around Chadron in his sports car. I know the thought makes me happy, and it'd be one less payment for me to make on something that I don't really need anymore."

"Are you sure? That's a big gift you're offerin' up, Jicky-girl."

"It's a small gift compared to all you and Gloria have done for me over the past years."

"Well, if you're sure—I accept! I'll be the snazziest old fart in Chadron in those wheels."

"Yeah, you will be." After a pause I asked, "Did you ever hear anything more from the insurance company on their investigation? Anything come in the mail for me?"

"Oh, sorry Jicky, I forgot to tell you. I think they're done with us, but as far as I can tell they're still fightin' over who's gotta foot the bill. The experts seem to think that Rich was drivin' the car, but that there was some sorta issue with the Caddy's seatbelts. It looks like both company's are graspin' at straws. Or goin' after General Motors; it's more like they're graspin' at big bucks. To them it's all about who's got the deepest pockets—for me, if they're right, it helps explain why Rich wasn't wearin' his seatbelt. I still wish I knew why he was goin' so fast. It just doesn't seem like him."

"Dad, I'm so sorry." I couldn't say *I wish we had some answers*, because in my mind I already had them.

GARY AND I met Stan Maddox at the bus station in Waterbury in early January. He'd been happy to drive the Chevy from Chadron—"It gave me a good excuse to leave a few days early. It's not like I don't like my family and their friends, but it just gets kinda old bein' asked the same questions over and over. You'd think that nobody from that town ever went away to college." I didn't tell him what he already knew—not many kids from Chadron went away to

Yale. It had been a big deal when he'd been accepted, and a year-and-a-half later it still was.

Along with the car, Stan had brought the rest of my photography equipment and clothing that Gloria had carefully packed in boxes gleaned from the grocery store. I was starting my life over—this time in a New England slum. I was happy that we'd chosen to meet Stan at the bus station, knowing that I didn't want reports of my new neighborhood making their way back to Wes and Gloria. Rich had worked hard teaching me how to hide my family's poverty and my own lack of education. After so many years it was a hard habit to break.

CHAPTER TWENTY-TWO

POPS HAD TAKEN his diagnosis surprisingly well. I'm sure he'd already known that he had AIDS—maybe the diagnosis was actually a relief. He seemed apologetic, but happy, that I would be staying on in Waterbury, but he was adamant that we not move from the apartment. He gave me his reasons, and some of them made sense: he liked his downstairs neighbors; it was close to the UConn campus, so Gary could walk to his classes; it would be difficult to find an apartment that he could afford with so much space in a nicer area of the city; but his biggest reason, and one that I didn't understand, was that he said he was comfortable. He said, even though he didn't go out anymore, he could picture the neighborhood and felt like he was still a part of it. He could lie on the couch and think about going down the stairs, out the front door, and walking to the bar on the corner. He said, in his mind, he'd sit with his old pals and talk sports or complain about local politicians. In his brain he was still part of this neighborhood. "I've given up so much, Jicky, don't make me give up my home, too."

So we stayed. I tried to talk Gary into taking his old bedroom back, but he wouldn't hear of it. He said since I was going to be with Pops all day, he'd take the night shift. Gary found an old desk for his bedroom and we scored a large worktable for mine at a used furniture store in the neighborhood. It was so big, Gary and I ended up carrying it home down the cracked sidewalks because we couldn't fit it in the Chevy. We took turns walking backward.

* * *

WE HADN'T SEEN anything of Joey or Sherry since Pops's diagnosis. I think it made Pops sad, but he didn't complain. I'd hoped when arriving in Connecticut that we might all spend Christmas Day together as a family—it had been so many years since I had been with my family for Christmas, but it wasn't to be. Sherry had asked us to come visit them on the Monday following the holiday, but Pops was reacting to one of his new meds and didn't feel like going out in the cold, even though we wouldn't have had to use public transportation because Gary's friend had loaned us his Camry for the day. I'd ended up staying with Pops that Monday while Gary drove out to see Joel and Sherry and deliver my Christmas gifts.

* * *

GARY AND I drove to the hospital on April eighth to meet our new niece, whom Sherry and Joel had appropriately named April. She was a beautiful baby with a head full of dark wispy hair, and without a speck of new-baby *Winston Churchill* in her serene face. With Sherry's permission, I took scads of pictures—some of April with Sherry and some of April with her Uncle Gary. Joel was back at work. Having taken time off for April's birth, he couldn't afford to stick around the hospital on the days to follow. I promised Sherry that I would visit them at their home soon and get some shots of the whole family while April was still new and dewy. It was wonderful to have a baby in the family.

* * *

WES LOOKED AFTER Rich's and my house during my first year in Waterbury, but called me in February of 1994, after he'd been approached by a realtor with an offer. He said that he and Gloria would love for me to move back to Chadron, but they wanted to know if it was "ever going to be in the cards." I told Wes no. I was sure after a year away that I wouldn't be moving back. We agreed, selling Rich's and my house was the logical next step.

I hung up the phone and thought back to the day we'd closed on the house, when Rich had insisted on carrying me over the threshold. I had hoped we would start having a real relationship, blaming his reluctance to have sex with me on us living with his parents. If Rich had loved me in the way I'd wanted to be loved, would we still be in our house in Chadron? Who knows? We might have outgrown it—we might have had children. Or, would I have messed everything up by falling in love with Tom, anyway? Was it inevitable? As guilty as it still made me feel, I hoped so. I loved Tom. He'd made me come alive and renewed my excitement about the future, and, as much as I loved Rich, I knew now that he never could have made me feel that way. That knowledge somehow made giving up the house easier.

When Wes called me a few days later to tell me that there was a buyer for the house, I asked if he would be willing to clear it out for me. The biggest job would be boxing up the kitchen items and the papers and books from Rich's office. Wes told me that the realtor had said that the prospective buyers were interested in some of the furniture. I told him he could negotiate the deal using any of the furniture except the drafting table Gloria had given to me—that I wanted to keep. I promised to sort through all the papers and small stuff when I came back for a visit. I didn't say, *after my father dies*, but Wes

and I both knew that's what I'd meant. He said he and Gloria
would be happy to help me in any way they could.

CHAPTER TWENTY-THREE

ASK ARTISTS THE worst part of mounting an exhibit and I bet the majority of us would say it's writing the *Artist's Statement*. It's a cruel thing to ask of an artist—many of us became visual artists because written words, sometimes even spoken words, don't come easily to us.

I'd been asked to write a statement once before. It was for an exhibit at the art center in Chadron, which consisted of an old gas station on the north/south drag through town, open only on weekends and manned by volunteers. That show had been of photos I'd shot in Nebraska, some along the Platte River (including many shots of the sandhill cranes that flock to the area near Kearney every March) and some from places not far from Chadron: Fort Robinson State Park and Toadstool Geologic Park, one of my favorite haunts. I didn't have much to say about my shots, so Rich had helped me come up with something poetic that made me sound artistic. This time I had to write a statement on my own. At least the gallery owner had promised to proof it for me—I probably couldn't help but sound like a hick, but I hoped his editing meant that I wouldn't have my bad spelling and wonky grammar on display in New York City.

I'd started the statement by writing: "In November of 1992 my husband, Richard Weckwerth, and his best friend, newly elected U.S. Senator Thomas Streator, died in a car accident on a barren Nebraska highway. That night my future changed."

I crossed out those first two sentences and started over:

Jicky O'Connor Weckwerth
Beginnings and Endings: Life with the O'Connors
April 20 thru August 20, 1996
Schuester Gallery, NY, NY

Artist's Statement:

In December of 1992, after a life altering event, I went to live with my father and brothers in Waterbury, Connecticut. We had not lived together as a family since the three of them had moved east in 1977. In the fifteen years that followed I'd only traveled twice to see my family. Due to our usual circumstances (lack of money and time) they had never come back west to see me.

Fifteen years apart makes for many changes. We were all adults now—were (or had been) living on our own. But, because of our father's (Pops's) illness, and the fact that my brother, Gary, and I had no other family commitments, we chose to live with him for his final years. Our Pops had advanced HIV/AIDS and his death within a few years seemed a certainty.

Our brother, Joel, lived just outside of Waterbury with his wife Sherry. When I first met Sherry, she was five months pregnant and glowing. Having just gotten to Waterbury a few days earlier, and being greeted by my Pops's condition, the contrast between these two members of my family, the oldest member and the newest member, was remarkable. (see image #1—Pops on couch with pregnant Sherry beside him on old kitchen chair)

With my father's permission, I started taking photos of the journey through his maze of clinic and hospital visits, and his everyday life battling the disease that was slowly taking him away from us.

Starting on April 8, 1993, the day after my niece, April, was born, her parents gave me permission to document her first years of life with my camera. Because I did not live with April, Sherry and I set aside one day a week for visits, but she called me whenever something momentous happened in April's life—like the day she began to walk on her own. (see image #17)

When I started these two photographic journeys, this exhibit was not something I had in mind. My desire was to interact with my family in the way that I knew best, as a photographer. However, as I started to process the film and look at the shots, often taken on the same roll of film, I couldn't help but notice that I was capturing movement—ebbs and flows in life. As Pops shrunk, April grew; Pops moved from the couch to a hospital bed, April from a bassinet to a crib; Pops got a wheelchair, April took her first steps.

I realized, as an artist, I had something to say—a story to tell.

Patrick O'Connor, my Pops, died April 6, 1995, just a day shy of my niece's second birthday. As a family we had April's birthday party following Pops's funeral. The O'Connors would go on. (see image #30—April wearing pointed birthday hat, standing on chair with her fingers splayed on Pops's closed casket)

* * *

I RAN TO the kitchen to quiet the ringing phone. "Hello, Jicky Weckwerth speaking."

"So, how much is left?" To Joel's credit he'd waited over a year from Pop's funeral to ask me. He knew, as did Gary, that I'd used the life insurance money from Rich's death to pay our father's bills. Whether Joel knew that I'd been helping Gary with school expenses, I didn't know, but it seemed unlikely. Gary had told me that when it came to money, around Joel, I should hold my credit cards pretty close to my vest.

"Jik, I've got a line on a little restaurant. It'd be a chance for Sherry and me to finally have a place of our own and do things right. I just need someone to bank me for a while. Wha'da ya say?"

"Wow, Joey—don't you think you could have at least said *hello?*"

"Yeah, okay—Hello, sis, how you doin'?—Happy now. But, did ya hear what I just told ya? We got a shot at a place of our own, Sherry and me."

"Sounds good Joey, but I don't have anything to give you right now."

"Shit, Jik, that's a lie—Pops didn't use up all that settlement money—no, way. You've got cash—I know ya do."

"Joel, maybe I should'a told you earlier, but I put the money left after Pops passed into trusts for you, Gary, and April. Gary's and April's are to be used for their educations, but school's the only thing that they can access them for. If anything remains in their trusts after they've finished school, it'll be invested until they're thirty-five and they can claim it then. You'll get your whole amount when you turn thirty-five."

"What the fuck, Jik? Thirty-five? You may as well've said dead. Shit. Thirty-five."

"I'm thirty-five—it'll go faster than you think."

"Why the hell didn't you just give me the money. You're lettin' Gary have his."

"No, I'm not—UConn's getting his. I didn't set up the trusts, I had my father-in-law do it. He's the one who picked thirty-five, but I agreed with him. If you want to argue with somebody about it, I'll give you the name of the bank controlling the trust, but I don't think you'll get very far with them."

"How much, Jik? How much am I getting?"

"By 2001, hard to say, but the trusts started at twenty-four thousand each, so with interest, maybe around thirty?"

"Fuckin' A. April's, too?"

"April's should be quite a bit more, since she prob'ly won't use any of it until she's eighteen unless you decide to send her to private schools."

"You have no right to control my life like this, sis—it's my money and she's my kid."

"I'm really sorry you feel that way, Joey. I've never given you money because I wanted to control you, or even because I wanted your thanks—'though, it might've been nice to hear it once in awhile … I gave it to you because I felt bad that we weren't together. I gave it to you because I knew what it was like to grow up poor and not have what other kids had. I wanted to help—that's still all I wanna do."

Joel responded by slamming down the receiver.

* * *

"GARY, JOEY'S GONNA start bugging you about money. He wants to buy a restaurant—I'm not sure it's a bad idea, I just don't know if he and Sherry are ready. But, anyway, he knows about the trusts now, so he's prob'ly gonna be asking you about them. Feel free to give him the phone number of the trust department—they've gotta be used to talking to guys like Joey. I was going to give it to him myself, but he hung up on me."

"He did what?"

"Yeah, he hung up the phone … like I did him dirt by putting money into trusts for him and April."

"That's Joey for you. I love him, Jik, but sometimes I hate him, too."

"Hate's kinda strong … but I know whatcha mean. I keep wondering if it goes back to our childhoods. When I was little, Mom was still okay. She was fun, we did stuff together. I never doubted that she loved me, but by the time Joey came along, she was changing. I don't know if her baby blues started then, or maybe being responsible for two kids was just too much."

"Yeah, and three kids pushed her right over the edge—or at least out the door. You know, I don't remember her at all. As far as I was concerned, you were my mom."

"I always loved you like my own, but maybe that's part of the problem. I had Mom, you had me, but Joey … he had nobody."

"Yeah, but was it circumstance, or was he born a prick? I guess what we're tryin' to figure out is if it's *nature or nurture* —I think it was prob'ly both. But, no matter, Jik, you shouldn't ever feel guilty about Joel. You didn't let him down as a kid, and you aren't letting him down now—and, just in case I haven't said it recently, thank you. I don't think people come much better than my big sister," Gary said as he gave me a hug.

CHAPTER TWENTY-FOUR

AT THE END of August 1996, I left Waterbury. My show at the gallery in New York had closed after a very successful four-month run. I was in negotiations to have the photos of Pops and April made into a book with a publisher in Manhattan, but there was no reason I couldn't continue that process by phone and mail, in the same way that Rich and I had always conducted my licensing business.

I knew I would miss my family, especially my new family. Sherry and I had become close over the two years that I'd photographed April. And, April! I loved my niece more than I could have imagined. I would miss her, but I knew that she was growing up with loving parents (even though her father hadn't shown me much love since our run in over the trust accounts). As for my other brother, Gary and I had been sharing the old apartment in Waterbury off-and-on since he'd started commuting to the UC Storrs campus, but he was ready to move away permanently. He'd finished his Gen Ed classes and needed more time on campus. Or, as he'd put it, "I can't be babysittin' you anymore, sis. Get smart and move outta the 'hood."

Originally, I'd figured that I'd move to a better place immediately after Pops died, but after two years in the apartment, it felt like home, as did the rest of the neighborhood. I still didn't go out much at night, or put myself in stupid situations, but during the day I enjoyed prowling the streets for photos. There was a lot of ugly in our Waterbury neighborhood, but there was beauty, too. I liked capturing both. The other reason I stayed was Pops's downstairs neighbors. The folks below us were a charming couple in their fifties who ran a homeless shelter just down the block across from Pops's favorite bar. Ramon had been a pastor in a mainstream church before developing a drug habit, Stella Ann was an artist. They'd met in rehab. They were loved in the neighborhood, and with good reason; they were the embodiment of caring, and, having both been addicts, they understood at least part of what many of the people coming to the shelter needed. Living above them felt safe, even when the sounds from the street should have made me duck and cover. They had become my good friends—Ramon had even officiated at Pops's small memorial service, and they had both joined the family for April's birthday party afterward.

But now, a year after Pops's death, I knew it was time to move on. I'd once thought I'd move closer to the Atlantic shore—I loved photographing the ocean and the ever changing sky above it. I'd also considered moving to NYC for a while, but after the gallery show and more than a few trips into the City, I'd decided that I needed a break from crowds. I'd contacted my Aunt Marlys in Gareth to see if I could visit. I didn't like the idea of being near Jim again, but I wasn't a teenager anymore and I figured I could put up with him for a few days. I know some famous author once wrote *you can never go home*, or something like that, and I wasn't sure that I wanted to live in Gareth again, but it was definitely rural and could give me a starting point while I searched for my new place in the world.

On my way west I planned on visiting Gloria and Wes in Chadron. It was time to clean out their garage. It would be a big job, but one so much easier than cleaning out the the guilt and pain still rattling inside me from Tom and Rich's deaths. I'd been away from Nebraska for over three-and-a-half years, but when I drove into Chadron, Rich's message from the answering machine played in my head as though I'd heard it only hours earlier: *"You live with it, I can't anymore."*

I had robbed my in-laws—I had stolen their only child, their beloved son. I was a poor replacement, but I was all I could offer. They, of course, didn't blame me, however had they known of my affair with Tom, they might have blamed us both. As far as I was aware, no one knew that Tom and I had been lovers—except, possibly, Pam, and I figured she would never let me know for sure.

Pam and I hadn't spoken since I'd left Nebraska. She, or more likely someone from her office, had asked Rich's parents for my new address when she'd run for Tom's Senate seat in the special election. I'd asked Wes and Gloria to not give it to her—I didn't give them an explanation. When she got married (the December after winning the Senate race), she'd sent an invitation to my old house in Nebraska. Gloria forwarded it to me with a few other pieces of mail—I didn't reply. Perhaps I was being childish, but I'd realized that without our connections to Rich and Tom, U. S. Senator Pamela Streator-Lee and I would have never been friends. After knowing one another for over ten years (basically living under the same roof for nearly a year), we were, at most, functioning acquaintances. I would always be the waitress who filled her coffee cup at a diner she was loath to enter. Yes, she had offered me a job right after she was given Tom's Senate seat, but I'd never been sure of her intent. I figured she was either feeling guilty, thinking that Tom had caused the accident, or, more likely, she was toying with me, knowing that Tom and I had been lovers.

None of it mattered anymore. She was now the official Junior Senator for the State of Nebraska, and she had a new husband. Her life had gone on without Tom and Rich. Like most of the world, she had forgotten them. I knew that I wasn't alone in my grief—the Weckworths and the Streators would forever miss their sons—but I figured I was alone in my guilt.

* * *

WES GREETED ME with a bear hug as soon as I stepped from the SUV. "Nice wheels—glad to see you didn't try to drive the old yellow Chevy all the way back here."

"Hi Dad…no, I traded it for the Tahoe just before I left. It's roomy, but it sure doesn't ride like the banana boat. She was a good car."

"That she was."

I'd started toward the hatchback to get my suitcase, when Wes said, "Just leave your things—Gloria's inside waitin' for a hug."

Gloria stayed seated when we entered the living room, which I found unusual.

"Come over here Jicky, it's been far too long." She reached out for a hug and I bent down and held her. She was thinner than I remembered, but her hug was strong and heartfelt. "I don't know if Westerly told you, but I'm not getting around very well anymore. The doctors around here don't know what's ailing me, and I just seem to be getting worse. Suppose it's just old age, but your father-in-law's older than I am and he's as healthy as a twenty-year-old. Aren't you, Westerly."

"Oh, prob'ly, and stronger than most, considerin' the young bucks seem to spend their days pushin' buttons on video games—my thumbs prob'ly aren't as strong as theirs, but I betcha I could beat most any of 'em arm wrestlin'."

WES SHOWED ME to Rich's old bedroom—my old bedroom, too—having been where Rich and I'd slept that first year after moving back to Chadron. The room was unchanged. Red, white, and blue ribcord bedspreads still covered the beds, and Rich's collection of Cornhuskers pennants still decorated the walls. Wes bragged about putting fresh sheets on my bed as he placed my suitcase on the matching twin and said that he was learning to do all sorts of household chores to help Gloria. "Not that I do them nearly as well as she did," he said, then smiled slightly. "But, ya-know, it keeps me busy now that I've retired." His smile was belied by the furrows on his forehead. I knew what it was like to watch a loved one wither away—I couldn't imagine what it was like to watch your life's partner weakening, not even knowing the cause.

"Jicky-girl, we want you to stay around as long as you like." Wes said those words with a smile too, but I could see the pleading in his eyes.

I LAID IN BED that night and thought of the past. I could imagine Rich's face, but it was like recounting the features of my favorite teacher, Miss Harris—I could remember, but details were fading.

Conversely, nothing about Tom had left my memory—not his smell, not his taste, not his voice, and, especially, not his face: Tom's wide-set eyes didn't sparkle, as much as they sparked. They had a shimmering glint when he smiled that disarmed everyone. His irises were dark, so brown that they looked like deep wells. I could sink into his eyes and lose myself. His nose, like his ears, showed the signs of his years of wrestling—it had been broken at least once and he wore the resulting bump like a badge of honor. His voice, always low, had, from smoking and years of campaigning, achieved the consistency of an unpaved road. Tom murmured when we made love, and it was the only time he called me Jicky; other times I was Jickster, or Jickums, or anything else that popped into his inventive head. I didn't mind. His re-naming game wasn't something he did with other people. It was public, but it was between us—for me it had provided us a unique bond even before we'd become lovers.

Years had gone by and I still missed Tom's kisses. I missed their force and hunger. I missed the way they made me feel desired and engulfed. It didn't happen often, but on some nights, like that first one in Rich's old twin bed, Tom's loss overwhelmed me. I'd curled into a ball and cried until I choked on my tears. The only thing that quieted me was the fear that Wes and Gloria could hear. I knew I would be staying in Chadron, and I didn't want them to feel any worse than they already did.

* * *

I PULLED ANOTHER bankers' box from the high storage shelves that Wes had fastened to the garage wall to hold Rich's papers. I'd developed a technique by the second day. It went something like, pull box from shelf, drop box to left shoulder, balance box while walking to drafting table, slide box into place, remove dusty cardboard lid, ATTACK!

Wes and I had set up my old drafting table as a work space in the corner of the garage to make my search and destroy mission as painless as possible, but I hadn't expected the pain caused by the edges of the heavy corrugated bankers' boxes digging into the flesh where my neck met my shoulder. I was developing a pretty nasty bruise. I should have thought about how heavy the boxes and books would've been for my in-laws before I'd asked them to carry Rich's and my things to their garage when they'd readied our house for sale. I wondered if Gloria had already been having trouble standing. Another something to feel guilty about.

The late summer Nebraska heat and the buzz of houseflies gathering in the garage windows added to the unpleasantness of my task, but I owed it to the Weckwerths to finally finish up what they had so generously started. I knew that most everything I would find could be thrown, but I wanted to make sure that I'd saved all the papers from when Rich had organized my licensing venture. I think, too, that I had wanted to take this time to say my final goodbyes to Rich—and to Tom, who was the main subject of so many of Rich's home-office political files.

Several days into the project, I'd unearthed three boxes from Rich's college days, both undergrad and law school. I looked at the papers and tests topped with *As* and praise-filled notes from professors. I pulled some of the most interesting to take into the house for Gloria, knowing that she'd most likely never seen them. Rich had never talked much about his grades; he was smart, but it was nice seeing that his professors had thought him brilliant. It had always bothered me that his stutter had made some people assume he was mentally slow. Perhaps that was why he'd been so sensitive about me sounding uneducated—it was an unwarranted perception that he had dealt with his whole life. As I hauled the rest of the boxes to join the others already in the Tahoe, I thought about the drive I'd be making to the landfill in a few days to dump what remained of my husband's life. It was a horrible thought; I paused while I wiped the tears and sweat from my stinging eyes.

The next box off the shelf was filled with high school memorabilia and copies of acceptance letters from colleges and universities. They were all from Nebraska schools, and from the exaggerated size of one folder it looked like Rich should have headed to the University of Nebraska in Lincoln upon graduation, not the University of Wyoming. That was something I'd never understood. Rich loved his state, he loved Nebraska football—he was a "Go Big Red!" Husker down to his little toes. Why didn't he go to school in Lincoln? I'd never asked him, but I promised myself that I was going to ask Wes. Of course, had Rich attended UN, we would have never met, so I would have never met Tom—I didn't want to think about that, although in the end, perhaps it would have been better for all of us.

* * *

A DAY LATER while I was sorting the boxes with Rich's political files, Wes walked into the garage just as I was setting a red Pendaflex folder back on the drafting table. The shell-shocked look on my face prompted Wes's first words after, "Hiya!"—

"So, you've seen it—I knew Tom was a player, Rich'd told me a few things—but there were so many women. How thin can you spread the butter and have it still taste like butter? Huh, Jik, tell me that?"

"I don't know … I didn't know … Rich told you? He never told me anything about Tom's affairs. After the accident, Pam told me, but I didn't believe her. I thought she was just trying to justify leaving him. You knew that, right? She was about to leave Tom—I feel like an idiot."

"Why, Jik? it's not your fault—none of it is. When you're kept in the dark, you shouldn't feel bad about not seein' things. So, Tom fooled around, and Rich covered it up. He sure wasn't the first politician to do it, and I'm darn sure he won't be the last. Some mighty fine ones have had a thing for the ladies. I don't know how much of that foolishness you read, but it was all in the past. From what I could tell, Tom'd really cleaned up his act his last few years in office. Maybe all Rich's preachin' finally got to him."

When I didn't say anything, Wes started talking again.

"At least you didn't have to worry 'bout that stuff with Rich, not like he was gonna go chasin' around. You were the only gal for him—his first, you know. His mother use'ta worry 'bout him. He never dated in high school. Gloria was so happy when Tom and Pam got married—I think she was hopin' Tom'd show Rich the way."

I didn't know what to say at that point. Once again I was left wondering what Wes was telling me. The September sun angled through the open door making the double garage stall feel like a preheating oven. The low sunbeam settled on the folder making it glow. Leave it to Rich to make Tom's folder of indiscretions red—Tom's scarlet letter. Were the last few years not mentioned in Rich's file because they were my scarlet letter, too? Was I not included because Rich didn't know about Tom and me, or did he not write about us because he didn't want to incriminate his wife in print? Or, maybe he knew about us and was just happy to have Tom's infidelity in-house where he could monitor it, thinking it would blow over like all of Tom's other affairs? Whatever had been Rich's reason, Tom and I had ruined his political dreams by wanting more.

CHAPTER TWENTY-FIVE

I'D BEEN WITH the Weckwerths for nearly two years. During that time Gloria had been diagnosed with VP—Vascular Parkinsonism, sometimes called Arteriosclerotic Parkinsonism, the result of small strokes leading to Parkinson's-like symptoms. Gloria's problems with walking hadn't gotten any better, nor were they any worse. Wes and I had recently found a home health care nurse to help with Gloria's day-to-day care —he and Gloria had insisted that with in-home help they could manage on their own. Wes had said it was time I started exploring my options; both Weckwerths felt as though they had disrupted my life for too long.

They needn't have worried. I was still at loose ends, and helping my in-laws felt like easy penance. I owed them the devotion of an only child. I spent my mornings helping Gloria ready herself for the day, but after that, I had most days to myself. I would take my cameras and hit the road just like I had years earlier when freed from the newspaper office, or on long weekends when Rich was away with Tom.

When I'd lived in Connecticut I'd started wondering about my mom's life after she'd left Pops and us kids. Hearing that she was on the Pine Ridge Reservation when she died, it occurred to me that she might've had some relatives still living in that area, meaning that *I might have relatives living in that area*. I started making day trips north, and, when I found out through my amateur sleuthing that my mom had actually lived in Oglala, my trips got a little longer.

I found no relatives, but I found people who had known Joeleen O'Connor, and when I introduced myself as her daughter they invariably said I had her eyes. People had liked Joeleen in Oglala; she'd sussed out a living and led a quiet life. No one knew that she had left three children in her wake, but most seemed to know that she'd battled depression when she was younger, because, as I discovered, she'd continued to succumb to it off-and-on until she'd died.

Once, when I'd asked Pops during our last year together why he hadn't looked for Mom, he'd said that early in their marriage she'd told him that someday she would probably leave him, and, if she did, he was to carry on as though she were dead. He'd said, "Jiks, you were old enough—you remember how bad she'd gotten. I couldn't do squat for her—she had to take care of herself. That's how she wanted it." So that's what he'd done—mourned her as though she were dead and hoped she was in a better place. He said that he'd briefly tried to find her after moving to Connecticut when his "lady friend" had wanted to "make things legal." He'd figured he'd need Joeleen's signature on divorce documents, but once Louisa had given him and the boys the boot, he'd given up the search for Mom.

I OFTEN SPENT time in the Badlands of South Dakota. Occasionally I'd stop at the Visitors' Center at the park and sign posters and puzzles featuring my licensed photos. The strange formations of the Badlands and the wooded draws around Valentine and Chadron were some of my favorite subjects. Those landforms, and the magnificent flocks of sandhill cranes that took over the Platte River in early spring, became like obsessions for me during my years with Wes and Gloria. I put thousands of miles on the Tahoe. While moving to Nebraska had been Rich's idea, I'd fallen in love with my adopted state's rugged landscape and migrating birds.

Sandhill cranes are not beautiful birds. On the ground they remind me of wattle-less wild turkeys inbred with giraffes—their mottled light-tan feathers match the ugly stubble in the late-winter fields, and their long legs and necks make them ungainly on the ground. They interact with comical hops and bobs. The bobs always making me think of those little glass drinking birds (minus their top hats). Oh, but when they fly, when thousands of them, tens of thousands, swirl in the sky as they descend onto the flat islands of the Platte River, it's a sight to rival anything in nature.

That's where I'd been that mid-March night, photographing cranes as they'd landed on the khaki-toned, weed-choked islands of the Platte. The hum of the road had seemed quiet after the noise of the large birds landing en masse. I was saying goodbye to the cranes. I knew that I'd be leaving Nebraska soon. I still did not know what I'd do to fill my days, but I was ready to try life on my own again.

* * *

THE AMBULANCE PULLED away from the driveway, sirens screaming. I looked around the living room at the chaos left by the EMTs. Tubes, plastic clamps, wrappers, and blue disposable gloves littered the coffee table and floor. Furniture had been shoved to the walls to make a path for the rolling gurneys. I picked up a crocheted afghan, carefully folded it, and returned it to the couch. I should have immediately followed the ambulance to the hospital, but I'd wanted to regain some semblance of calm—something I'd lost when I'd walked through the door and found Wes on the floor, Gloria splayed out beside him after she'd fallen trying to reach his side.

CHAPTER TWENTY-SIX

WESTERLY WECKWERTH'S funeral filled First Methodist Church to the back row of pews. He hadn't owned the insurance agency for several years, but the care he had given his customers, most of the adults in Chadron, had not been forgotten. The pastor spoke of Wes's love for people and their love for him in return. It was obvious.

I sat beside Gloria, she in her wheelchair parked in the aisle close to the casket, me in the corner of the first pew. It was only days after she'd fallen beside Wes, and the purple bruises on her thinning skin made me realize how vulnerable she'd become. She had thought she would die before Wes; Wes had thought she would die before Wes. But that's not what happened, so we were left to reimagine the plan. Money would not be a concern—Wes had always made sure of that. The home health care nurse would still be coming daily, but I knew, even though it had never been stated by anyone, I was no longer free to leave. I would stay in Chadron as long as Gloria needed me.

As the pastor gave the eulogy my mind drifted to thoughts of my father-in-law. It had only been in the past week when I'd finally remembered to ask him why Rich hadn't attended the University of Nebraska. He'd said, "Don't know, surprised me too, but he changed his mind that summer after he'd graduated—just insisted he had to go to Wyoming."

"But he was always such a big Nebraska fan. Those were the only teams he ever cared about. Besides, he loved this state. It's just always puzzled me that he went away for college."

"Yeah, well, I wondered too, but then I started thinkin' maybe he'd just taken up likin' the Huskers to be like his old man—just like I always thought he listened to those boring opera broadcasts on the radio to have somethin' to talk with his mother about."

"I hate to disagree with you, Dad, but I think he truly liked both Nebraska sports and opera. He listened to both of them when you guys weren't around. When we first met he'd fill me in on how his beloved Huskers were doing, and he had more opera cassettes than any other kind of music—he even carried them in his car—those aren't signs of a fair-weather fan."

Wes shook his head. "Don't know what to tell you, Jicky-girl. I loved my son, but I have alotta unanswered questions 'bout him. I do know he was a good man, though. Always thought that—always will."

I sat with a wet Kleenex balled up in my hand and knew that no one who knew Westerly Weckwerth had any unanswered questions about him. He was as open and straightforward as Nebraska's high plains. He loved his family, he loved his friends, and, as the pastor had said, they loved him in return. He'd lived the way he had wanted and died quickly, without pain. We should all be so lucky.

GLORIA DID NOT have that kind of luck. She had the *blessing* (her word not mine) of a long goodbye. She didn't give up on life after her Westerly died, but she did start sliding downhill again. Sometimes the desire to live has a lot to do with who's standing by your side.

I helped Gloria hire full-time nursing care as her strength waned. Once she was bedridden it was impossible for me to take care of her by myself, even with a day nurse most of the week. By autumn I'd started spending full days at the house editing photos or painting watercolors while she rested. When she was awake, we would sit in the living room listening to opera albums or talking. Gloria told me about her childhood on a small ranch outside of Chadron and the struggles she and Wes had experienced when he'd first started the insurance business. Of course, we talked about Rich, who she still always referred to as Richard. About a year after Wes had died, as we flipped through one of the many family albums, we came to a photo of Rich and his dad dressed all in red, heading off to a Huskers game. The picture prompted me to ask Gloria the same question I'd asked Wes shortly before he'd died.

"Why didn't Rich go to school in Lincoln? I found his acceptance letter when I was going through the papers in the garage. It seems like it would've been a good fit."

"Jicky, I have always disliked it when people ask me that question." After a long pause she said quietly, as though to herself, "It happened a lot that first summer after he'd made the decision to leave the state. We'd made such a big fuss about his going to Lincoln at his graduation party." Gloria's head shook almost imperceptibly from side to side.

"You don't have to tell me if you don't want to—it doesn't really matter anymore. I was just curious."

"No, Jicky—I think I should tell you. Tell you, and thank you."

"Thank me? I don't understand…how could I have anything to do with it. We didn't meet until years later."

"I'm the one who told Richard that he couldn't attend UNL, or if he chose to, he was not welcome to come home again. He picked Wyoming because he could drive there, and they were still accepting freshman students that summer for the fall semester."

"Okay, Mother, now I'm more confused.

GLORIA TOLD ME a story over the next half hour that explained so much. She said that the summer after Rich graduated he'd become friends with Kevin Saxton, the son of the new Music Director at the church. Kevin had just finished his sophomore year at UNL, and Rich was over the moon at the prospect of joining him there in the fall. The two young men were inseparable throughout June, and Gloria was pleased for him. Rich'd had few friends growing up—it was refreshing to see him so happy, and she thought it a blessing that he'd have someone she approved of (a fellow Methodist!) to show him the ropes at the university.

Gloria continued: It was mid-morning, the third of July, she'd been in the back yard working in the vegetable garden. When she went to the garage to retrieve a hoe, she'd walked in on Richard and Kevin. They were in the backseat of the Chevy. Gloria said that she didn't see what they were doing, but from their state of undress, it was not hard to imagine. She said a noise escaped from deep within her, perhaps a scream, she couldn't remember. She turned and fled for the house. Rich came through the kitchen door several minutes later. They said nothing to one another before Rich ran upstairs to his bedroom.

Gloria told me that she'd collected her thoughts while she prepared the family's lunch and decided what would be best for all involved regarding the situation she had just witnessed. After lunch, with Westerly back at the insurance office, she told Richard what was expected of him if he chose to remain a part of his family and community: He would stop seeing Kevin, and since Kevin was attending UNL, Richard could not. She thought it best if he left Nebraska. If Richard did those things, Gloria said she would not shame him in front of his father. If he refused her conditions, she expected him to leave the house and never return.

"You see Jicky, that was why I was so nervous the first time Richard brought Thomas home. I was worried for him, and I questioned their friendship. I felt much better when Tom started dating Pam, and I was thrilled when they married. It was reassuring to know that Tom wasn't a, well … one of those. When Richard came home his second year of law school and told us that he was dating you, well, you can imagine, I was delighted! I was so happy that he'd gotten all that nonsense out of his system. I've often shuddered thinking about what might have happened to Richard with that nasty AIDS business. You saved him, Jicky. We both did."

* * *

But Ruth said, "Entreat me not to leave you or to return from following you; for where you go I will go and where you lodge I will lodge; your people shall be my people and your God my God."
Ruth 1:16, RSV

WHEN PASTOR RICHARDSON praised me during his eulogy for being like Ruth, the devoted widow who stayed by her mother-in-law's side, it made me cry harder. I stayed—who else was going to? *I am not a saint! Far from it.*

I thought I owed my devotion to Wes and Gloria—a life for a life. In a perfect world, in a world where things went as they should, Rich would've been the one helping his parents in their old age—not me. Not me. Never me.

But there were other things, too, keeping my thoughts far from the pastor's long eulogy. My mind was still swimming with questions for Gloria: Why did you send your son away and then force him, and by extension, me, into a life that we didn't want to live? I don't know that Rich would have been happier living on his own, or with a man, but he might be alive today if you hadn't made him feel like a pariah. Maybe you thought you were saving Wes from some sort of shame—that Rich being gay was something that he didn't know about. Gloria, Wes knew—he never told me in so many words, but he had let me know his suspicions. It didn't matter to Wes; he loved his son, just like he'd loved everyone—unconditionally. Why couldn't you? I loved you, Gloria, but at times it was not easy. You could be so unbending, so hard. You died thinking that you and I had saved your Richard. No, Gloria, we didn't—we killed your son. By wanting what we wanted for ourselves, the two of us killed Rich. And Tom.

CHAPTER TWENTY-SEVEN

Jicky O'Connor Weckwerth
Urban/Rural a Study in Contrasts
April 3 thru June 5, 2000
The University of Nebraska, Lincoln

Artist's Statement:

I am an an adult orphan. Both my parents have died within the last five years, but they both left me long before they left this earth.

We had been a family of five, living in one of the most scenic spots in America, Gareth, a small town along the Chief Joseph Byway (Highway 296) in Wyoming. The road winds through the Absaroka Mountains, and while the town is just a main street and a few houses stuck to a hillside, the mountains are magnificent. But the truth is, I never thought much about the mountains or their beauty until I left them behind two years after my last parent had left me behind in that little town.

To me, Gareth and the mountains were just there. They were the only home I'd known and I took them for granted.

Eventually, when I saw the places that my parents had moved, I thought they must have felt the same way—they had taken our home, at least the beautiful part of it, for granted. My mother left us to move to the Pine Ridge Indian Reservation in South Dakota, one of the poorest areas of the nation. My father left to move to Waterbury, Connecticut—sometimes cited as one of the worst cities in America. My parents never lived in the mountains again.

I visited my father in Waterbury in 1992, and stayed in the city until 1996, the year after he died. My first impressions of Waterbury, at that time the largest city I'd ever lived, were not favorable. My father lived in what was considered a rough part of town—the sort of place people didn't want to park their cars, or once parked, didn't want to step out of them. But, as I spent time in the city, especially our neighborhood, I began to see the beauty of the people and even of the streets. Dad traveled to Waterbury to find love, and while it hadn't ended the way he had hoped, he'd found a place where he felt at home.

The story of finding my mother's home after she left our family is sadder for me. Mom left us when I was twelve—she moved from Gareth and none of us ever saw her again. She died in 1992, and that was when the rest of the family learned that she had spent most of her last twenty years on the Pine Ridge Reservation in South Dakota. When my mother left Gareth in 1972, she was in a deep depression that had lasted for years. I think she had gone to the reservation in search of family and explanations. Twenty years later I did the same. My mother's family was not to be found, by her or me, but I learned from her friends, she, like my father, had found community and contentment in this place often dismissed by the world.

When I'd first envisioned this photographic journey, I thought I would create an exhibit contrasting what we as a nation think of as Urban and Rural. I thought too, that I might end up showing some of the differences between Eastern Life and Western Life. Unlike some of the people I met in Connecticut, I knew that the West was not a TV western. I didn't expect to see tepees when entering the reservation or buffalo stampeding on the horizon. I was surprised, however, by the similarities in urban and rural poverty. I had expected them to look completely different; other than the sizes of the buildings and the ways the streets are paved, they don't.

So, instead, I started looking at these two locations as contrasts in what is perceived as ugly and what is viewed as beautiful. In two places, both thought of as beyond repair by many, I photographed what was there. Yes, some of it is ugly, but it is also full of life, and love, and beauty, perhaps proving we are all the same if you look closely enough.

* * *

I SETTLED GLORIA'S estate that spring after the sandhill cranes had headed north. My show closed in June, so I made the long drive across the state to reclaim my unsold pieces before pointing the Tahoe west to begin my solitary drive back to Wyoming. It wasn't the trip I had planned on making three years earlier. Since that time, *Uncle* Jim had died (good riddance) and my Aunt Marlys had moved to a care center in Sheridan. I'd looked into visiting Marlys, but was told that it was very unlikely she would know who I was—dementia, early-onset Alzheimer's, or the byproduct of a life of disappointments and hard living had taken her memory. It may have been a chicken-shit move on my part, but I decided I wouldn't go see her. I didn't go to Gareth, either. Instead I stayed on I-80, passing through Cheyenne and Rawlins, before turning onto US-191 at Rock Springs and heading north. I'd decided to give the Jackson Hole area a whirl. Jackson was a good town for artists and a beautiful location. I could find the beauty in most any place, but I'd decided I wanted to live in a place where I didn't have to look too hard.

I'd felt guilty for so many years—every morning when I'd opened my my eyes, every time I'd looked in a mirror. The weight of the guilt sometimes made it hard to breathe, especially around Rich's parents. My sorrow had lessened, but for years my guilt kept pulling me under like a riptide of remorse. I'd once thought it would be impossible to escape that feeling. I'd ached for the buoyancy of a clear conscience, for the ability to arch my back, inhale deeply, and float.

But now, looking back over the past seven years, I realize just how much I've grown. Much of what I'd learned was tragic and some of what I'd learned made me angry (at least for awhile), but by finally knowing the truth—about my in-laws, my father, my mother, Rich, and even Tom, I've come to grips with my life. I still foolishly wish things could have been different. I wish that I could have been different. I still hurt. A person can't experience so much loss and not hurt, but my guilt is finally starting to ebb. I've made mistakes, but I've done all I can to atone.

Beggars may never ride, but maybe I'm starting to learn to float.

BOOK
TWO

CHAPTER ONE

DAN OGDEN CLEARED his throat then blew his nose. He had just hung up after speaking with his daughter on her twenty-first birthday, and she had ended their conversation by telling him, "I'll see you if hell ever freezes over." Dan had expected the sentiment, but it had hurt nonetheless. He hadn't seen Becky—she now wanted to be called Becca—for seventeen years, not since he'd gone to prison after killing her mother and brother. *When put like that*, he thought, *the fact that she was willing to talk to me at all is pretty amazing.*

When his tears came in earnest, he grabbed his fly rod and headed out the door. If the stream didn't cheer him, at least he could keep crying without being noticed.

* * *

DAN HAD MOVED to Jackson seven years earlier, shortly after getting out of the State Penitentiary in Rawlins, Wyoming. He was hoping he might rebuild his art career, but knew that it would take awhile. Jackson Hole seemed like a good area—it was a tourist destination most of the year. If his paintings didn't sell to the rich visitors, he could find work washing their dishes or changing their dirty sheets. He was pretty sure that his MFA in studio art wouldn't mean much to his most probable employers in Jackson. He hoped like hell that they'd ignore his time in the pen just as readily.

It had been rough at first, even though he knew he'd had things better than many ex-cons; he still had a brother willing to help him. Greg had driven down from Gillette with their dad's old truck, which he would leave with Danny. Beneath a blue tarp he had packed everything that he and his wife, Jody, thought his younger brother might need to start life anew. It was the stuff from their childhood home, their parents having died while Dan was in Rawlins. Greg, knowing that Danny had nothing, had stored items Dan might find useful. Jody'd sorted through the kitchen utensils, dishes, and pans—Greg made sure that Danny got their dad's hand tools and fishing equipment. Greg had also invested Danny's half of the small inheritance left to them by their parents. It would be enough, along with the little he had earned in prison, to give Dan a fresh start.

After two days in an old tourist-cabin hotel, with the help of a guy they'd met at an AA meeting, they found Dan's first home in Jackson, a small apartment over a couple of shops on the main drag. He could park his truck in the alley that ran behind Broadway and get to the second floor from an indoor stairwell only a few steps from the parking spot. It was a nicer place than he had expected. Greg insisted that Dan get a phone so that he could call his AA sponsor if he felt things crumbling. Greg also promised to call Dan once a week to guarantee him a friendly voice.

For nearly a year, calls from Greg in Gillette and wrong numbers were about the only reasons the phone ever rang. But life had gradually changed: Dan made a few friends, worked manual labor jobs (each one a little better than the last), sold some paintings, and purchased a small cabin twenty minutes north of town. By 1998, he had managed to land a job at the National Museum of Wildlife Art. Dan, having started as a volunteer in the museum's downtown location, had been a huge help when the museum moved into its fancy new quarters across from the Elk Refuge on his side of Jackson.

CHAPTER TWO

"DANNY! HEY, OGDEN, is that you?" Jicky yelled across the rock floor, the sound reverberating through the light-filled reception area of the museum. She'd only seen him from the side, but his walk was unmistakable even after the intervening years. Dan turned.

"Do you remember me? It's been forever!" Jicky called when she saw his face.

"Yes—yeah, I do. The U—you're Jicky—wait a second … Jicky Connor, right?"

"Almost. You knew me as Jicky O'Connor, but it's really Jicky Weckwerth."

"You got married? I suppose—you were just a kid when we met. I'm surprised you recognized me."

They had started walking toward one another and she wanted to tell him that she could never forget him—he had changed her life—but it seemed like too much to shout across a public foyer. When they were finally close enough to touch, Jicky reached out to shake Dan's hand and said, "It was a long time ago, but you look the same."

Dan ran his free hand over his shaggy graying hair. "If you say so, Jicky. — I'd really like to talk, but I'm late for a meeting. Are you in the area for awhile? Can I call you?"

"Yeah, I just moved here. I'd love to talk sometime."

"Great! Just leave your number at the desk—sorry, gotta go." With a quick hand gesture toward the reception area, Dan headed toward the door.

Jicky approached the front desk. "Hi, maybe you heard. That man just asked me to leave my number here for him. I'm a little confused, does he work here?"

"Dan Ogden?" the young receptionist said as she lifted her eyebrows. "Yeah, he's kinda' a big-wig." She pushed a notepad toward Jicky.

Jicky wrote her name followed by her new cell phone number. When she returned the pad and pen to the desk, the receptionist gave her a business card and said, "I don't know why Mr. Ogden didn't just give you one himself."

The beautifully printed business card read: *National Museum of Wildlife Art, Daniel Ogden, MFA, Curator of Collections.*

* * *

DAN CALLED JICKY that evening, and two days later they met for dinner at the Salt Valley Grill. Dan had invited Jicky to bring her husband, giving her the opportunity to mention that she was alone. When Jicky asked about Danny's wife, he had said the same. If either of them was relieved, they had tried not to let the other know, but they were both relieved, and they both knew it.

Dan, never a man of many words about himself, asked most of the questions that first dinner, thereby allowing Jicky, who hadn't had many new people to speak to in the past few years, to fill the evening with her story—at least the chapters of it that she was willing to share.

She finally explained to Danny that when they had first met, she was already married. "I don't know why I gave you my maiden name. I remember that I didn't correct myself at the time because I was too embarrassed. What sort of idiot doesn't know her own name?"

Jicky asked Dan if he remembered giving her his old camera.

"Sorta, though I don't know if I'd have given it to you had I known you were married—I wouldn't have wanted to cause any trouble. I just thought you were a talented kid too poor to go to college."

"Well, I kinda' was that, but I was also married… anyway my husband didn't mind the gift and that camera changed my life. I still have it. It still works."

"Now you've got me real curious, Jicky. How in the world did my old Pentax change your life?"

"Your *old Pentax*, and that photography class you encouraged me to take, helped me get started shooting. I'm a professional photographer—it's how I've made a living."

The server placed their salads on the wooden table and their conversation changed to the size of the silverware, which, following the trend, was the size of mining tools. Jicky laughed. "I've always hated little salad forks so I'm okay with this change," she said, while holding a long-handled salad fork aloft. "As for the size of the rest of the silverware, I'm not so sure—I've been told I have a big mouth, but this is ridiculous."

"Well, the steak knives will come in handy if that grizzly suddenly comes to life," Dan responded, gesturing toward the mounted bear in the corner.

OVER DINNER, JICKY told Dan about moving to Nebraska when Rich started working at the law office. She told him about Tom's meteoric rise in the Democratic Party and then about the accident that had left both Rich and Tom dead. Dan said that he had read about it when it had happened—the death of a U. S. Senator was big news. He said he was sorry for her loss and understood her pain—he'd lost his wife and son in the same way, to a car crash. He didn't mention that he'd been the driver. They'd both passed over the details of their culpability, Dan thinking, *I'll tell her someday*, and Jicky safe in the knowledge that she would never let anyone know her part in Rich and Tom's deaths.

Jicky told Dan about moving to Connecticut to help take care of her father. She explained how she and her bother Gary, separated for so many years, had come together to help her father through his battle with AIDS. She told him about Joel's daughter's birth and how she had enjoyed being around April for her first few years of life. When Dan asked about life on the East Coast, Jicky said it had its goods and bads—she hated the traffic, but had learned to love the ocean.

"Is the ocean the reason you stayed?" Dan asked as their after-dinner coffees were set on the table.

"No, I didn't stay. Well, I stayed for a year to wrap up some business, but then I started back west. I'd planned on settling in Wyoming, maybe not Jackson, but somewhere near the mountains, but when I stopped in Chadron to see Rich's parents, my mother-in-law wasn't doing well, and then my father-in-law died. I stayed on to help Rich's mom, Gloria; by that time we knew she had a type of Parkinson's. So, anyway, long story short, it ended up taking me four years to get back to Wyoming."

DAN AND JICKY carried their cooling coffees to the restaurant's balcony that overlooked the town square. Danny lit a Marlboro and held the pack out to Jicky. She thought about refusing, then reached for a cigarette. Jicky hadn't smoked in years, but her mind had flitted back to the night she and Danny had smoked together outside the Art Building at UW—suddenly smoking felt like the right thing to do.

"So you've given up drinking, but still smoke?" she said after Dan lit her cigarette.

Dan inhaled. "It's more like I still smoke because I had to give up drinkin'. What would life be without a few bad habits?"

"I s'pose not much fun," Jicky said, with a smile, as she reached out to touch one of the smoke rings that Dan had just exhaled.

They stood smoking in amiable silence for a few minutes, watching people mill about in the square below. Dan exhaled and said, "We got interrupted just when you started talkin' 'bout your career as a photographer—what did you end up doing? It's not always an easy way to make a living."

"Well, I worked for the *Chadron Record* off and on. But, you're right, I couldn't have made a living with just that. Let's just say I got some lucky shots along the way. They helped pay my bills."

Danny blew another large smoke ring into the night air. "How's that? Did you shoot anything I'd recognize?"

"Think so … I shot the 'R-eagle.'"

"The what?"

"That's what I've always called the Rushmore eagle photo —the *Freedom* poster? You sell it in the museum's gift shop."

"No, shit? So you're J. F. Weckwerth," Dan said as he ground his cigarette into the restaurant's scarred balcony floor.

"No, shit," replied Jicky.

CHAPTER THREE

DAN CALLED JICKY the next day to tell her that he'd had a nice time at dinner. She noticed that he hadn't called their evening meal a *date*. She wasn't sure how she felt about that— she'd been thinking that it was the first date that she'd been on in years, but maybe not, maybe it was just two old friends getting together for a meal. When Dan, in his official capacity as a curator of collections, had asked if she would be willing to show him her portfolio, Jicky thought maybe the dinner had been a business meeting and that she had even misjudged the part about them being friends. She told Dan that she'd pull some things together to show him, but that she didn't make a habit of photographing wildlife—the bald eagle in the Rushmore photo was just a happy coincidence. She didn't try to explain that she'd considered it a sign from the universe when she'd shot it—she figured that would be a little too *woo-woo* for Dan Ogden. He was a pretty conservative guy, despite being an artist who still wore his hair long.

They made an appointment for Wednesday morning and Jicky attempted to put together a presentation to wow Danny, even though professionally there was little reason. There were museums and galleries where her work fit and a lot more where it didn't. Trying to figure out how her photos could work in the impressive National Museum of Wildlife Art, was like the proverbial "fitting a square peg in a round hole." But it felt good to be working—doing more than just calling her professional contacts with her new address and phone number. She knew it was time to start building her business again. Of course, in a sense she had been working—she'd been hiking and shooting photos of the area since arriving. She had probably already taken too many pictures of the antler arches in Jackson's downtown square. She'd had little interest in photographing the famous arches from a distance (like a tourist), but she'd taken multiple closeups—photos that turned the twisting antlers and their shadows into abstract shapes, the sort of shots her old boss at the *Chadron Record* would have called "arty crap." She was also planning on taking some landscape photos, having just signed up for a guided multi-day backpacking trip through the Tetons later in the summer. Day hikes were one thing, but she didn't feel ready to take on an overnighter in the Grand Teton National Park without expert help. She was hoping she wouldn't slow the group with her camera—or her cough—she seemed to be allergic to something in the Wyoming air. Maybe after the guided trip she could venture back on her own and take all the camera time she needed. And, as an added bonus, maybe by then whatever it was that was making her hack would have finished blooming.

JICKY SAT IN Dan's spacious office with portfolios, folders, and a book of her photos balanced on her lap ready to dole out in the order she thought appropriate.

Dan pushed a pair of oval wireframes to the bridge of his nose. "Seems my eyes need a little extra help these days. Thankfully, I can still paint without glasses, though if my arms don't start growing I may not even be able to do that much longer."

"Ahh, you're lucky, they make you look distinguished," said Jicky. "Although I know what you mean—I've always been happy that I've got good eyesight. It makes working with cameras so much easier. I s'pose my luck isn't going to last; I'm pushing forty."

Dan glanced up and smiled. "Could'a fooled me. You still look like a kid."

While Dan looked through her photos, Jicky looked beyond him and out the window on the far side of his massive desk. The room and the view were splendid—the only office that Jicky had ever seen that topped Dan's was the director's office at Mount Rushmore. It looked out toward the carved granite faces from a window flanked on the left by a Sioux Indian ceremonial headdress. The warbonnet sat atop a bookcase, its magnificent feathers hanging down six feet to touch the floor.

Once Dan had perused the numerous photos that made up Jicky's licensed collection, along with a list of items that bore images of her work (mugs, plates, tinware, album covers, book jackets, T-shirts, posters, etc.), she handed Dan the coffee-table-book featuring the photos of her father and niece. It was titled *Beginnings and Endings*, the same as the New York exhibit where the pictures had been first shown. Tears wet Dan's lashes as he turned the pages. He paused, removed his glasses and wiped his eyes.

"I've seen this, but hadn't put two-and-two together—it's always moved me, but never made me cry 'til now. It's just so hard knowing you and thinking about what you and your family must have gone through. I'm sorry for your loss, but I'm so glad that you documented it. These photos do everything that photos of people should do. ... your work is remarkable."

Jicky basked in Dan's praise of her book. While she'd received accolades from art critics and had the royalties to prove that the book had sold well on both coasts, Dan was the first person she knew from her *real life* who had told her that the book was good. Its publication was not something she had ever talked about in Chadron because of its subject matter. As far as she knew, Rich's parents had never discovered that Pops had died from AIDS. She'd told them that she was staying in Waterbury because he had cancer—they'd assumed cancer was the disease that had taken his life. It would have been embarrassing for her in-laws had they known the truth, and she undoubtedly would have been shunned by some of their friends once she'd moved back to Nebraska. Fear of the unknown can be cruel.

She thanked Dan and then handed him the catalog from her show at the University of Nebraska, *Urban/Rural: A Study in Contrasts*, and a portfolio containing larger copies of the photos featured in the exhibit. Dan flipped back and forth through the portfolio, eventually telling Jicky that while it was a good exhibit, he was most enamored with her close-ups. That knowledge made her smile. She handed him her large portfolio which she introduced as her more recent works, primarily shots taken in Nebraska and the Badlands of South Dakota, but, also, including some of her favorite photos from her recent trip west and her latest Jackson Hole explorations. Those photos included her best close-ups of the antler arch. *Bingo!*

DAN LOOKED AT Jicky's body of work and tried to remember the girl from his drawing class nearly twenty years earlier. She had been so talented, but so raw. He could still remember how her eyes lit up when she grasped the notion of negative space. Well, from the look of her photos, she had become a masterful technician of that concept.

Her photos of people, especially those of her family (the pictures that had brought him to tears) were exceptional. He thought of Dorothea Lange's "Migrant Mother," and knew that Jicky O'Connor, no, Jicky Weckwerth, had the same skill and eye as the famous Dust Bowl photographer. But, if he were to be critical, an important part of his job, he would contend that her scenery pictures were good, but commercial. Not to knock commercial. From what he had seen of her licensing venture it appeared those landscape shots were likely paying her monthly bills. It didn't matter that she wasn't destined to become the next Ansel Adams—as she had already pointed out, Dan's museum was interested in wildlife, not pretty, or even dramatic, scenery pictures.

Dan turned the pages of Jicky's large portfolio and looked up every now and then to see Jicky staring out the office window behind him. In her Nebraska pictures he'd seen two photos that piqued his interest, but she had been so engrossed in something over his shoulder that he decided to wait to talk to her after he'd flipped through the last few pages of the oversized portfolio.

On the last page he saw them—Jicky's closeups of elk antlers taken at the arch in the town square. They were stunning. Maybe he had been wrong about her not being like Ansel Adams. It wasn't as though he hadn't seen closeups of antlers before, even closeups taken at the arch, but Jicky had captured something that he had never seen. The way she played with light, shadow, and texture intrigued him. He closed the portfolio, startling Jicky and bringing her attention back into the room. With his hand resting on the black leather of the zippered case he said, "I want to work with you. From what I've just seen, I think you have the beginnings of two exhibits that will be perfect for the museum."

"Two? Really? I thought, maybe, one. Two, huh? Two would be great."

"So, before I give you my thoughts, I want to know which of the photos you thought had potential. What do you want to expand on?"

Excited, and almost forgetting to breathe, Jicky responded in a flood of words: "Well, I hadn't given it much thought until you mentioned that you liked my closeups. That's when I realized that my closeups of antlers might be considered wildlife. You may have noticed that you startled me when you closed the portfolio, that's 'cause I was composing a shot list in my head. You've undoubtedly figured out that I like to do shows with contrasting images. What if I do that with antlers? The exhibit could feature both my closeups and some longer shots taken of the elk herds during different stages of antler growth. Maybe shots of antlers lying on the ground where they fall, and pictures of the piles after they've been gathered. I don't know—call it *Antlers Near and Far*?"

A sour expression crossed Dan's face, followed by a smile. "Yeah, I'll take a pass on that title, but otherwise I'm impressed. You can pull together quite an exhibit in a few minutes. And, you were right—I was intrigued by your antler photos. I'm just surprised you don't know which of your other pictures interest me."

"Sorry, Dan. I don't know, and I don't think I'm gonna to come up with anything 'cause my brain is full of antlers right now. You'll have to tell me."

"I really liked those two shots of sandhill cranes in Nebraska. Do you have more of those?"

"Oh, I feel like an idiot. Yes, I've got hundreds of photos of cranes. I photographed the migration nearly every year I lived in Nebraska. I guess I didn't think about them because the crane shoots were always something I did for myself. Sorta a hobby. Somehow I forgot that my hobby shots would be classified as wildlife art."

Dan laughed, then said, "So, it looks like we're going to be workin' together *Ms. Weckwerth*. Of course, there'll be a few more people weighing in on the subject and a lot of papers to sign, but that's down the road a bit. Gotta tell you, I'm sure happy now that I didn't take my old camera to the pawn shop in Laramie." He stood and extended his right had across the expanse of his desk.

Shaking Dan's hand, Jicky replied, "You and me both, *Mr. Ogden.* Don't worry about slow decisions or lots of paperwork, I know the drill—this *ain't* exactly my first barrel race."

DAN CALLED JICKY'S cell phone later that day to arrange a meeting in a week, giving her time to sort the Sandhill crane photos and create a written proposal for the elk antler project which Dan had suggested mounting sometime down-the-road, giving Jicky more than a year to photograph the elks' shedding cycle. He told her to expect a few more museum people at that meeting, then said, "Enough of the professional stuff—I just wanted to tell you, again, that I had a great time the other evening, and I've been hopin' that maybe we could have coffee on Saturday morning? Have you been to the new bakery on Broadway? Their rolls are good and their coffee's not overpriced. Could we meet? Say, nine-thirty? Or is that too early?" Dan's voice that had been so confident during the first part of the call, belied an almost teenage disquiet by the end of the conversation.

"Nine-thirty too early?" Jicky chuckled. "Did you just forget that I'm a photographer. I'm normally awake before sunrise. Nine-thirty'd be great. I'll be hungry by then."

They said their goodbyes, and Jicky shoved the phone into the back pocket of her jeans as she thought, *So our dinner was a date... I'm going on a second date with Danny Ogden within a week!* She felt like leaping in the air. She felt young. She felt free. And, then it hit her—Danny had always made her feel that way.

CHAPTER FOUR

"DANNY, I'VE BEEN thinking about learning to fly fish. I've always thought it looked like fun, but I've never known anyone who could teach me. My Pops didn't fish, and when my father-in-law taught me to fish in Nebraska—well not many people fly fish there. Would you consider giving me some lessons, or, maybe, recommend somebody?"

Jicky and Dan had been seeing each other for several weeks by the time Jicky made her request, but it was as though their relationship had stalled. Everything was great on the surface, but it seemed, as much as they both wanted to, they were hesitant to push any deeper. Jicky liked to tell herself that it was because they were keeping things professional. Danny knew that he was just scared by the idea of falling in love.

"Sure, Jik, I'll show you. Only, once you know how, don't always plan on taggin' along with me… shit, that didn't come out right, sorry. It's just that I fish to clear my head—I have to be alone for that."

"No it's okay, I understand. Part of why I'd like to learn is so that I can have that experience. There's somethin' about fly casting that's always looked like active meditation to me."

"Yeah, it is—so's fly tying. If you wanna drive out to my place Wednesday for supper, I can go over the basics with you.

If you want, I can show you how to tie some simple flies—like a hopper. That's what the trout are hittin' on now."

Jicky laughed at the thought of a hopper. It made her think of the Hula Poppers that she, Rich, and Wes would cast when fishing stock dams for large mouth bass. They were massive red and white artificial lures with long rubbery fringe that trailed behind while they hopped noisily across the water. Hula Poppers were the absolute opposite of the delicately tied flies that Danny had shown her, but bass loved them. She quickly developed a theory that maybe fish were like people— some folks would see an entree that was nothing like anything they had ever eaten and jump at the chance to dig in. Others had to have only what other people were eating—foods that were in season, and preferably things with which they were familiar. Some people were bass; others were trout. She figured, she, like most, fell somewhere in-between.

WEDNESDAY EVENING, DAN fixed burgers on the grill with the classic sides of ruffled potato chips and canned pork-n-beans. They ate at the wooden picnic table in his backyard that faced the mountains. He didn't own a table cloth, but he'd picked flowers and arranged them in a rustic pottery pitcher that graced the middle of the weather-roughened table.

"I love it when someone else does the cooking," Jicky said as she reached for another burger.

"How do you stay so thin? I'm not complaining—there's plenty of food—but you eat like a teenage ranch hand."

"It's either my metabolism, or the fact that I don't think about food often…sometimes I forget to eat."

"You forget?"

"Yeah, I forget."

"Sorry I can't offer you anything stronger to drink," Dan said as he handed Jicky another ice tea. "I don't keep it around."

"Well, that's prob'ly smart considering you don't wanna drink."

"Don't want to, and tryin' my hardest to convince myself of it everyday."

"I wish some of the folks in my family would've quit. I've watched booze mess up more than a few lives."

"Yeah, it can do that."

"How long you been on the wagon, Danny? I'm thinking, a long time?"

"Since shortly after my wife and son died—so, eighteen years," Dan said, but didn't elaborate.

TWO HOURS LATER, after introducing the fly rod and reel, fly line and backing, leader and tippet, then showing Jicky how all the parts fit together, Dan taught her the three traditional casting grips. They then moved inside to the corner of the living room that housed his fly tying bench. Dan opened his father's old tackle box and showed Jicky his collection of flies, explaining the various types and when and where they might be used. Dan said that he tied most of his own flies. Jicky thought they were beautiful—airy and so delicate. Thin copper wires were strung through brass beads so tiny that she couldn't fathom how anyone could work with them. She thought, while looking at a fly in Danny's hand, that casting was like throwing exquisite hand-made gifts to trout. Of course, often when one of those gifts was accepted, the fish reciprocated with its life, but that was the price. Seems, whether fish or person, you always had to pay the price.

Dan, with his hands beneath the bench-mounted magnifying glass, wrapped the shank of the hook and carefully trimmed the shaggy hairs and feathers that made up the body of the fly. Jicky watched his hands. She had always been intrigued by Danny's hands. They were average in size and inevitably paint-stained, but they weren't the hands of a studio artist or a museum curator. They were the hands of someone who enjoyed hard work. People could tell that Dan chopped wood and fixed his own truck. Hell, people could tell from his hands that Dan was a man who owned a truck. She wondered, as he wrapped the delicate thread around the hook shank, what it would feel like to have Danny run those hands down her bare legs or over her naked back.

Dan broke the silence saying, "The next step is fun—we're going to be dubbing the noodle."

Jicky stifled a laugh and teased, "You sure we know one another well enough for that?"

Dan, so involved in his work, hadn't picked up on Jicky's innuendo. When it dawned on him what she had said, he laughed. "Wow, I'm slow on the uptake tonight—and you're being a bad student. Pay attention—no self respectin' trout is gonna hit on a sloppy hopper."

Jicky drove home an hour later with the hopper from their fly tying lesson. Dan had gifted it to her after dropping it in an old pill container. She looked over to the passenger seat at the little lure rattling in its amber cage and wondered: *Will Danny ever make a move? Aren't we more than friends?*

* * *

THE NEXT SATURDAY they met at Dan's place and headed to a stream not far from the house.

"If this is gonna work you've gotta follow my lead. Just sort of melt into me."

Jicky leaned her back into Dan's chest while he placed his arm and callused hand atop hers where she gripped the rod. She remembered how it had felt dancing with Tom once she'd learned to follow his lead. She relaxed and let Danny's body talk to hers.

He held the rod tip low and brought it back with a smooth pull until the rod bent, then he stopped the rod abruptly—and paused—before bringing the tip forward. He murmured in her ear, "keep straight, keep straight." They rhythmically repeated the back-forth, back-forth, back-forth motion as the line arced further and further over the water. When they stopped, the fly drifted down stream. Dan buried his face in Jicky's hair and kissed her neck before letting go. He walked away saying that he thought she should try it on her own. He was shaken by what he'd just done; Jicky was shaken too by the way her body had responded. Part of her wanted to run after him, but the other part told her to just let him walk away. For now, she would assume he had his reasons for leaving.

When Dan finally walked back to the stream he was all about teaching Jicky to fish.

They practiced casting until Dan felt Jicky could manage on her own. He talked about taking her to one of his favorite spots nearby, one that wouldn't be too challenging to navigate for a newbie, but he didn't set a date. Dan had mentioned earlier that his job was hectic with reports that he needed to complete before the museum's upcoming board meeting. He wondered, had he told her about being busy to hedge against any sort of future commitment? It was true, he was busy, but it was also a convenient excuse.

As they stowed the gear in the back of Dan's truck, Jicky noticed that Dan seemed to be limping more than usual. She had never asked him about his limp, she wasn't sure if he might consider it rude, but she was curious, and it seemed a safer subject than many under the circumstances.

"Looks like your leg is bothering you today."

"Nah, it's okay. I just stepped wrong the other day and twisted somethin'."

"How'd you hurt it in the first place, if you don't mind me asking? I remember your limp from when we first met, so I know it's been with you a long time."

"Since 'Nam. I got it from a cartridge trap, but I've never complained much, because eventually my life was pretty normal again other than the limp. Lots of guys weren't so lucky."

"I'd forgotten you were in Vietnam."

"Wish I could."

"Do you think Vietnam was the reason you drank? I've heard that a lot of vets drink."

"In all honesty, Jicky, I was a drunk before I went to 'Nam. After coming home I drank more, but I don't think I'm an alcoholic because of Vietnam—I don't blame the war, that's too damn easy. I think I'm an alcoholic because I'm an alcoholic. I just can't drink. Enough said."

"Sorry I'm so nosey. My husband once told me I asked too many questions."

"No, I'm sorry, Jicky. I shouldn't have snapped at you. I don't know why I did." After a pause and a drag on his cigarette, he continued, "I've really enjoyed our mornin' together."

DAN PULLED THE truck into his dusty yard beside Jicky's Tahoe. Other than the dust, which was unavoidable in the summer, Dan kept everything as orderly as a German *hausfrau*. He'd even planted red geraniums, dusty miller, and electric-blue lobelia in pots by the front door. Snow-capped mountain peaks loomed behind the charming little house, dwarfing it further. Jicky thought Dan's house was like one of those little pink bows Sherry had liked to paste on April's bald head when she was a baby—cute, but insignificant in contrast to its surroundings. But, then, most thing were insignificant when compared to the Tetons.

"Thanks for the lesson Danny. It was so much fun once I caught on…it's like when I learned to ride a bike. It's sorta like that magic when your body connects with the movement and they combine—like you're not fighting with it anymore… Sorry, I must sound crazy."

"Nah, not at all—I get it." Danny replied. After a pause that seemed a second too long, he said, "Do you have to leave right away? I've got some leftovers from last night—you must be hungry; I am."

"Thanks, that sounds good…I'm not sure that I've got much of anything in the fridge. I'd prob'ly be eating Cheerios for lunch again, although I'm not sure I've even got milk. You're a hero—you're saving me from dry Cheerios."

They walked to the back of the house and Dan let Jicky in the kitchen door. He told her to make herself at home while he reheated last night's chicken stew. She removed her boots and set them on the mat beside the door, then walked to the bathroom. She took the elastic from her ponytail and washed her hands, smoothing her hair while her palms were still damp. Jicky considered leaving her hair down, but thought it might look like more of an invitation than she was willing to offer. But maybe she was just lying to herself. She'd been feeling the low internal tug of desire since Wednesday when Danny had first touched her hand to show her how to hold a fly rod. She put the hair-elastic on her wrist, then gave a big grin to her reflection in the medicine cabinet mirror and ran her tongue over her teeth. As a final touch, she pinched the apples of her cheeks. It was the best she could do on short notice.

DAN SUGGESTED THAT they dish up from the stove and take their bowls to the picnic table. He'd laid out a bag of hard rolls from the bakery on Broadway. "Jicky, would you mind buttering two of those to accompany the stew."

"Fancy…it's a multi-course meal."

"Smart ass." Dan said as he stepped behind her and wrapped his arms around her waist. Jicky set aside the butter knife, turned and kissed him on the mouth with the intensity of a woman who hadn't kissed a lover in years. Danny reached over and turned off the flame under the stew pot, took Jicky's hand, and led her to his bedroom.

CHAPTER FIVE

HE DISAPPEARED. *He just fucking disappeared.*

After three days of not hearing from Dan, Jicky phoned him. When he didn't answer her calls to his home, she called the museum. Jicky swore she could hear the discomfort in his assistant Tammi's voice when she said that he was "out." Tammi had never just said, "out" before. She was the kind of assistant who would tell Jicky, anyone really, what her boss was doing down to details like, "Oh, Mr. Ogden's in the bathroom—he said he had something spicy for lunch, but he's been gone a long time, so he should be back soon—Do you wanna hold?" When Jicky called the office the next day, Tammi squeaked, "He's on vacation," then hung up.

Jicky supposed Dan could be on vacation, but she had doubts. He hadn't mentioned a vacation when they'd talked about their upcoming schedules. He had even mentioned that he had too much work to get away for anything but half-day fishing trips for the next few months. It was obvious that Dan was avoiding her, and while she knew his reasons weren't the same, it felt like Rich all over again—she had gotten close, so he was pulling away. She remembered the night that she had tried to seduce Rich after getting home from their night out with Tom. It was the night Tom had first asked her if she wanted to "flip for the lead"—the night he'd taught her how to follow his lead. Jicky and Rich had been married less than a year when Rich had rejected her advance, and she'd, in turn, shut down toward him.

Well, she wasn't nineteen anymore and she wasn't going to censor herself again. If there was a reason that Dan didn't want her, he was going to have to tell her. She was not going to let another man she cared about turn her out of his bed unless he could give her a reason. Everything that she had gone through in the last few years had taught her that life was too short to play stupid games. But, while she was hurt and confused by his behavior, she wouldn't stalk Danny. Jackson was a small place, and besides that, they were working together to ready her photo exhibits. Jicky knew that she would see him eventually. She'd get her answers then. *Damn him.*

CHAPTER SIX

IT WAS STUPID talk. She was weepy and babbling like an idiot in front of people she had met just days earlier when they'd all started on the back-trail adventure. Jicky felt as though she'd been drinking, although she never drank when she hiked in high altitudes—she knew better. When supper was served, she'd dished up but couldn't eat. She tried to sip water from her canteen, her head throbbed, and when she left camp with her pack-shovel to relieve herself, she'd barely dug a hole and bared her bottom before she'd exploded.

Back at the camp she'd excused herself and headed for her tent. Jicky had all the classic symptoms of high altitude sickness but had chosen to ignore them for the whole day while the group hiked higher and higher into the Tetons. When Kayla, one of the guides, stopped by Jicky's pup tent to check on her, and Jicky had responded by throwing up all over Kayla's jacket, the experienced guide recognized the seriousness of the situation.

The treatment for high altitude sickness is to get the sufferer to a lower altitude, but it was night, and Jicky could barely stand—it wouldn't be an easy task. Kayla and Nick, the other trail guide, had cell phones, but there was no reception so far into the mountains. Nick planned to retrace the group's trail in the dark until his phone worked, then he would call for aid. It was decided that Kayla would stay with Jicky. Nick figured, after having taken Jicky's pulse, that he'd gotten the better task—hiking at night in bear country was preferable to watching one of your charges die in camp.

Jicky couldn't sleep. She lay motionless, trying not to cough, so that dry-heaves wouldn't rack her body again. Kayla kept watch, but there was little that she could do. Around dawn, Nick trekked into the camp accompanied by the Teton County Rescue & Recovery Team, part of the rural volunteer fire department. One of the EMTs put an I.V. the size of a swizzle stick into Jicky's wrist and held a bag of saline aloft to rehydrate her. It took only minutes before she started feeling human again.

"SO, JICKY—MAY I call you that?" the leader of the R & R squad asked, but didn't wait for a reply. "We have a couple different ideas on how to get you outta here. Here's the deal—when we heard about your condition from Nick, our first plan was to carry you by stretcher to an open area and helicopter you from the park, but now, seein's how well you're reacting to the I.V., we'd like you to consider walking outta here under your own power. What d'ya say?"

"I don't know if I can. It's a long hike if we have to take the same route back," said Jicky.

The R & R leader paused to drink from his canteen. "Well, our thinking is you can test your strength by walking to the only place near here where a helicopter can possibly land—the problem is, nobody really wants to have a chopper land in a wilderness area. I don't know if you've ever seen what a helicopter does to the area around it, but it ain't pretty. The problem with walkin' out from that clearing comes from the fact that to make time, you're gonna have to climb—you'll have to hike or be carried at least seven-hundred feet higher to a flat area above the tree line. That's where the rescuers on ATVs can meet us. They'll take you to an ambulance team, and they'll get you to the hospital in Jackson. So, what d'ya think?"

Jicky stared at the R & R leader as though he were speaking Swahili, "Give me a little more time, and I'll let you know. I'm just not sure I can make it."

"We wouldn't ask you if we didn't think you could do it. We'll carry you if you can't make the climb. It's really not a problem, we do it all the time. What we don't want to do is land a chopper in these mountains—but in the end, it's your call. We'll do what needs to be done." The R & R leader walked away to give Jicky time to decide.

HALF AN HOUR later they started walking. By then Jicky felt fine but weak. Her headache was gone, and, with someone by her side, she could take a few wobbly steps at a time. The only pain she felt was when one of the rescuers would try to assist her by grabbing her wrist where the massive I.V. was still taped, tubes dangling. When the rescue party reached the designated clearing, Jicky understood fully why no one wanted to land a helicopter. It was a spot her group had hiked through the day before—a lush glen with a creek so clear that its waters magnified the colorful stones lining its bed. Jicky had been awed when she'd first seen the area and had slowed the group's progress by taking photos. She knew that she didn't want to be the cause of that Eden's demise and told the leader that she would keep walking. She only promised two steps at a time, but said, "if the rescue team's willing to take it really slow, I think I can climb higher."

Jicky stumbled along looking at her GoreTex hiking boots and moving as directed. There was no longer even a narrow path for the group to follow. The team in front chose the route and the men behind caught Jicky when she stumbled. It was early afternoon by the time they arrived at the ATV site. As she squatted to pee behind an oversized tire on the ugly vehicle, the only privacy in the barren area, the I.V. tubes swept the ground. She'd been pleased that she hadn't required an infusion during the trip up the mountain and was hoping that the medics would remove or, at least, clean the tubes soon. Like every other part of her, they were filthy. With a chagrined smile on her face she thought, *at least unlike my hair they don't smell like vomit.*

The guy driving the ATV was sweet. He grinned goofily ear-to-ear when he met Jicky and didn't even seem to mind her odor as he helped her climb onto the back of the metal monster. After strapping her to his back with what looked like an overgrown seatbelt extender, he shouted over the roar of the motor, "Hold onto my back as tight as you can. I guarantee, even though I'll go slow, you're in for a bumpy ride."

Jicky didn't respond, but wrapped her arms around his body and laid the side of her face on his back. The close human contact was as reassuring as the off-road buffeting was painful—her headache was returning. It took forty minutes to reach the ambulance waiting at a narrow, partially paved road that would snake them down the back of the mountain.

As the driver helped her off the ATV next to the ambulance, Jicky thanked him.

"Nah, that's okay. I'm just really happy to help. Our job is called rescue and recovery—way too often it's only recovery out here. You made my day by bein' alive."

In the ambulance on the long ride back to Jackson she finally got to lay down. After Jicky quit coughing, the team of two nurses removed the dirty I.V. and put in another to start more saline and an antibiotic drip. Jicky muttered a weak thank you to the nurse for wiping the grime and dried vomit from her face. The last things she remembered from the ambulance ride were a nasal cannula being wrapped around her ears and under her nose, and a male voice saying, "I think we're losing her."

* * *

THE REPORTER FROM the Jackson Hole News changed the tape in her small cassette recorder and asked Jicky to continue her story, picking up when the ambulance arrived at the hospital:

"Well, obviously, I didn't die." Jicky said as she took a drink of coffee, "The only thing they lost me to was a long sleep—I passed out. I came to when the ambulance finally stopped at St. John's. In the emergency room, the doctor on call assured me that I was suffering from classic high altitude sickness and would be fine by that evening. The only reason he'd thought to run tests was that this was a first for me—I've lived in mountains off-and-on for much of my life and I've never had problems with altitude.

"So, anyway, my blood tests came back looking fine except for an elevated white count. The doctor said it was prob'ly from a slight cold or virus—he'd heard me coughing, but he really wasn't concerned. Then, about twenty minutes later he came back carrying my chest X-rays, and he had this super serious look on his face. He put my X-ray on a light-box on the wall and told me that there was something very wrong.

"I asked him if it was lung cancer. I don't smoke all that much, but it was the first thing that came into my head." The reporter nodded with the understanding of a sometimes-smoker and motioned for Jicky to continue her story.

"So, anyway, the doctor told me 'no'—my lungs looked fine, but it was all the stuff around my lungs that looked bad. He pointed at my X-rays and explained that normal X-rays aren't cloudy. He said mine looked like my chest was full of cotton candy. He also told me that I had the beginnings of something called a 'water-bottle heart'—I had fluid around my heart, and it was stretching the exterior membrane like a water balloon. It was making my heart hang lower in my chest cavity than it should.

"When I asked the doctor what could cause those symptoms, he said he couldn't tell without more tests and a biopsy, but his guess was some type of sarcoidosis or lymphoma. He said that they wanted to keep me in the hospital overnight, contact an oncologist, and schedule a biopsy for the next day.

"I asked which of the two scary-sounding diseases I should be hoping for. He said my best chances would be with a fast-growing lymphoma, but he thought any problem I had would be treatable. That sounded like good news.

"The last things he said to me were that he hoped I could get some sleep and he was sorry that he'd had to give me such rotten news."

The reporter turned off her recorder and said, "The article about your rescue will probably run in Sunday's edition. Thanks for telling me everything, but the paper won't print anything about your health problems other than the part about you having high altitude issues. The editor really likes to do a story on high altitude sickness at least once a year—I guess he figures it's kinda a public service in this part of the world to remind people how serious it can be."

* * *

JICKY SAT IN the pale-green vinyl recliner staring out the hospital window toward the evergreens but not seeing them. Disparate words the doctor had said clanged in her head, tolling her future: *Rot-ten-Cot-ton-Can-dy, Rot-ten-Cot-ton-Can-dy, Rot-ten-Cot-ton-Can-dy* …

Later, Jicky tried calling her neighbor, Peggy, to arrange for a change of clothing and a ride home upon her release scheduled for the following day, but Peggy wasn't home. The only other person Jicky could think to call was Danny. He was the last person Jicky wanted to call, but she needed help—Dan Ogden was her only other friend in Jackson, never mind that by this point he'd been avoiding her for weeks.

Jicky called from the hospital phone hoping that Dan would pick up. She didn't know if his phone was modern enough to show incoming numbers, but he'd seemed pretty adept at avoiding her calls in the past few weeks when she'd made them from her mobile phone.

"Hello, Ogden here."

Jicky spoke quickly, "Hi, Danny. It's Jicky—before you say anything just know that I wouldn't be bothering you except I don't have anyone else I can call. I'm in St. John's and they've told me that they won't let me leave here without a driver. Can you help me out?"

"Sure—of course. What's wrong? Were you in an accident?"

"No, it's kinda a long story, but to shorten it, let's just say I got high altitude sickness and now the doctors think I might have cancer. My X-rays didn't look good."

"Oh, no. Jicky, I'm so sorry—what room are you in? Are you ready to leave?"

"No, it's okay, you don't have to come yet. I prob'ly won't be released until about noon tomorrow—they want to watch me overnight, and I've got a biopsy scheduled for like six in the morning. Sorry 'bout that, I know it's a work day."

"Nah, don't worry Jicky, I'll come get you. What about tonight, though? Can I come see you now?"

"You don't have to, really…but if you want to, I'm in room 216. Visiting hours are until eight."

"I'll be right over."

"Thanks…it's been a really crappy day. It'll be nice to see a familiar face."

CHAPTER SEVEN

JICKY AND DAN avoided the elephant in the room. Weeks earlier she'd vowed to confront him about his disappearance—at this point it seemed irrelevant. She needed him and he'd come. That was enough for now.

Jicky hadn't broken down since she'd heard the news, but when Danny had walked in and hugged her, she'd started to cry. Dan held her, his arms around the faded pastel hospital gown and robe, until her sobs quieted.

"I'm sorry. I don't know why I did that," Jicky said while stepping back from his embrace.

"Don't be silly, Jicky—anybody in your position would be crying. I mean, it sounds like you got some really shitty news."

"Well, yeah, but the doctor thinks it's treatable…and I feel fine. I just wish I could go home and forget about everything."

"Tomorrow—I'll take you home tomorrow."

"What about the forgetting part? How you gonna help me with that?"

"Don't know," said Dan. "That's something I've never been good at."

DAN STAYED UNTIL the night nurse came to the room with a clean gown and toiletries and told Jicky it was time for a shower. When the nurse discovered that Dan wasn't Jicky's husband, she shooed him from the room and told him to go home. She said by the time she'd have Jicky prepped for the next day's early surgery, visiting hours would be over. Jicky didn't know until morning that Dan had stopped at the nurses' station and received permission to come back at five a.m. so that he could be around when she went into the operating room. Dan didn't know how to make the bad stuff go away, but he could make sure Jicky wouldn't have to face the uncertainty of the biopsy by herself.

Dan knew he'd been a coward, disappearing from Jicky's life the way he had, but after they'd had sex he'd been frightened by the way he'd felt. It wasn't that he didn't want Jicky, but he'd convinced himself that she would never choose him if she knew the truth, and he knew he couldn't live a life with her by his side, and in his bed, without telling her that he'd been responsible for the deaths of his wife and son. He thought, *God, why didn't I tell her? Not telling her's created this whole fucking mess.* If he had only said something before they'd made love, she could have decided if she wanted to get involved with him. One of the primary things that he had learned in AA's Twelve Steps was Step Five—admitting the exact nature of his wrongs. He had told the truth about his accident multiple times in the past decades. *Why can't I now?* he thought. He felt as though once again he'd trapped himself by his own negligence. *She deserves better.* He fiddled with the AA token in his jeans pocket and whispered into the night air, "At least I've stayed sober. At least there's that."

JICKY HAD GIVEN Dan the key to her apartment on East Pearl so that he could get clothes for her to wear home the following day. He'd decided to stop by her place that evening to avoid leaving her side after the biopsy. Dan knew how to get to Jicky's apartment—he'd picked her up a few times when they'd gone out for coffee, however, she'd never invited him in. It surprised him when he flipped on the lights to see just how simply Jicky lived.

The door to the one-bedroom unit opened to a small vinyl-clad entryway with a tiny galley kitchen off to the left and an eating area almost straight in from the door. It was hard to walk into the unit without tripping over one of the two dining chairs. The carpeted living room was not much bigger than a small bedroom; a sliding glass door filled one wall, limiting furniture placement. But that wasn't a problem since Jicky's furniture consisted of an easy chair with a fake-leather footstool, a small TV on a three-drawer metal filing cabinet, and an old drafting table. The bathroom and bedroom doors were to the right of the living room off a short hallway. The only color in the rooms came from dozens of Jicky's watercolor paintings tacked to the sheetrock.

Dan went to the bedroom. A full size mattress atop a boxspring sat centered on the far wall. It was neatly made, but with only a blanket for a bedspread. A large plastic tote full of papers served as the nightstand. On it, Jicky had placed a gooseneck lamp and clock radio, along with a thick library book on physical geology, and a partial glass of water. Dan picked up the glass and touched the rim to his lip. He set it back where he'd found it, then gathered Jicky's clothes from two more plastic totes in the closet. She had asked him to get her toothbrush, but he'd noticed that the night nurse had brought one, so he didn't bother.

Dan found a paper grocery bag for Jicky's clean clothes shoved in the space between a lower kitchen cabinet and the refrigerator. He felt like he was snooping when he walked over to look at the things on her drafting table, but curiosity had won his battle of conscience. She owned a light box for examining photo proofs; beside it sat a stack of glassine sleeves filled with negatives. There was a cracked mug full of pens, pencils, styluses, and X-Acto knives and another filled with paint brushes. Two frames sat between the mugs: a small double frame with school pictures of two boys and a newer frame with a picture of a toddler. Dan assumed the double frame held old photos of her brothers who lived somewhere on the East Coast. He knew from Jicky's published photos that the toddler was her niece, April. The item on the drafting table that most surprised Dan (and made him smile), was another library book. This one was about fly tying, and open to a page printed with step-by-step diagrams showing how to construct a basic hopper. Beside it sat the pill bottle holding the hopper that he'd given her. He thought about the day three-and-a-half weeks ago when he'd started teaching Jicky about fly fishing—the evening he knew he was falling in love with her. Again he thought: *Why have I fucked things up so badly?*

CHAPTER EIGHT

JICKY PUT DOWN her phone. The oncologist, Dr. Kearney, had finally called with a diagnosis—Non-Hodgkins Lymphoma, at Stage III, but only because something called her LDH (lactate dehydrogenase) count, which Jicky alternatively coined "Lymphoma *Dung Heap*," was abnormally high. Her other symptoms considered by themselves had placed her at only Stage II. The first tests performed in Wyoming had been inconclusive. This diagnosis had come from the Mayo Clinic in Minnesota, making the doctor confident it was correct. He'd said the good news was that it was a fast-growing B-cell type that was considered very treatable with chemo. And besides, she was young, only thirty-nine, and healthy ("If we exclude the cancer," he'd added). When Jicky, dreading chemo, asked "can't you just cut it out," Dr. Kearney'd responded, "No, sorry. There's no way to cut out the fluff surrounding your lungs and heart. We're going to have to melt it away with drugs. Ironically the drug protocol we use is called CHOP. We can't do surgery, but we can 'chop' out your cancer." He'd told her, if she was amenable, he wanted to start her treatments the following morning at eight.

Jicky knew she should call Danny with the news, but they had argued a day earlier when she had quit stepping around the ever present elephant and finally asked him about his vanishing act after they'd made love. She wasn't sure that she was ready to talk to him yet when she thought about what they'd said to one another:

"It's probably better if we don't see each other for a while. I think you should just go."

"But, Jicky, you need hel—"Jicky had cut Dan off mid-word.

"No, Danny, I don't. I'll be fine. I feel fine. I don't need anybody right now."

* * *

JICKY PULLED THE Tahoe into the front parking lot of the clinic and eyed an open spot by the door. As she eased into the space she noticed the sign—PARKING FOR CANCER PATIENTS ONLY! She put her SUV in reverse, but stopped. She felt an internal punch in the gut take her breath away—then came the burning in her throat as she fought back tears. A minute passed while she stared at the sign.

She slid the gear selector back to drive, finished parking the Tahoe, got out, and pushed open the heavy door to the clinic.

* * *

DAN SAT IN his office at the museum thinking that Jicky had undoubtedly, by then, heard her diagnosis and treatment plan. He tried to figure out what he should do next. Jicky hadn't physically kicked him out of her apartment, but she'd asked him to leave, which among friends amounted to the same thing.

When she'd asked him why he'd gone underground after they'd had sex, he had said that it was because he didn't want to hurt her. She'd responded that if not hurting her was his intent, he had missed his mark by a mile. Her exact words had been, "Danny, avoiding a woman who has just made love to you is about the cruelest thing a man can do. Don't think I'm going to thank you for it."

Dan then changed tack and said, "well, maybe it was because I don't want to hurt myself."He said that Jicky knew he was an alcoholic, she knew that he had lost his wife and child in an accident. He told her he didn't want to grow to depend on her and chance losing so much again—he thought it might push him over the edge and toward the bottle.

Jicky said that she supposed she ought to be understanding, but she really just thought him a coward. "I lost my husband and someone very special to me the same way you lost your wife and son—I know how it hurts. But do you remember when I asked you if your time in Vietnam had made you an alcoholic?—you said something like 'no, nothing but alcohol makes an alcoholic drink.' I think it's really interesting that the horrors of Vietnam weren't a cause, but that I could be? ... Maybe I should be flattered, but if that's how you really feel, especially now that I'm sick, I think you should just leave."

Her last words, "I'll be fine. I feel fine. I don't need anybody right now," repeated like a recorded loop inside Dan's head.

CHAPTER NINE

CHEMO GAVE JICKY time to think. She'd thought she would spend the inevitable downtime caused by treatment painting or reading, but when the strong drugs kicked in she didn't have the energy or concentration for either. She found that closing her eyes and letting her mind drift was about the only thing she could do when she didn't feel well. The location her mind so often landed when it wasn't floating above the Nebraska bluffs or soaring with a flock of cranes, was her memory of three men, her personal trinity—Rich, Tom, and Danny. She supposed it was a way of reassessing her life—a slow-motion version of having life flash in front of her eyes.

Jicky'd told herself that the cancer wouldn't get her, that it was just a blip in the timeline of her life, but she had also forced Dr. Kearney to give her the statistical odds of surviving stage-three Non-Hodgkin's lymphoma. When he'd said "fifty-fifty," Jicky's smile said, "I'll take those," while her brain whispered *as if I have a choice*. She was positive that she would get through this illness and she didn't allow herself to think otherwise... except on nights her insomnia kicked in or she ached all over. At those times she thought about three men—two from her past and one who might be part of her future (if she were lucky enough to fall into the right fifty percent).

JICKY PLACED HER phone on the kitchen counter and walked to the bathroom to change. Maybe she wasn't as sick as she'd feared, but as she stripped off her jeans she started to shake. It was only the second week of October, but the temperatures were already falling below freezing—she'd forgotten how quickly the seasons changed in the mountains. It had been getting cold at night for over a month now. She hated being chilled, and the fever induced trembling made her head throb even more. She pulled her heavy nightgown over her shoulders. She'd taken Tylenol along with a Zofran before she'd made the call. She decided to curl up with her heating pad and sleep, assuring herself that she would feel better by morning and be ready to face her third round of chemo in a few days.

Laying on her side, Jicky stared at her clock radio. She couldn't get warm, she couldn't sleep, and she was afraid to move. Her shivering had finally ended, but she was terrified by the idea of rolling over and touching any part of the sheet that hadn't already been warmed by her overheated body for fear that the shaking would start anew. Along with that fear, any move she made caused her head to hurt more. *How long can a person lay in one position?* she wondered. In the recesses of her mind she knew that her temperature was getting dangerously high. *Where's my phone?* She couldn't remember, but it didn't matter. The idea of leaving bed to find it was horrifying. If tremors wracked her body until she vomited or got the dry heaves, that would make her headache even worse. *Don't move, don't move, don't move.* The fever made the pictures in her mind's eye cut-crystal sharp. *Everything so bright and so clear. So clear …*

… Rich, you're sitting in your regular spot at the Never Empty—you look like you did when we first met … so young and handsome … *'Jicky, un jour, tu m'épouseras.'*

But, why me, Rich? Was I just some lump of clay you could make over to please your mother? I was a disguise in the shape of a wife, but, I wanted more … I wanted to have a family with you—grandchildren for your parents. I wish you could have loved me the way I wanted to be loved … I wish … I wish … if beggars could ride …

… Tom, I'm in your arms on a dance floor, surrounded by people, yet we're all by ourselves … We're in a hotel room … I'm sinking into your dark eyes … I'm sliding my hands up your bare chest … over your shoulders … God, I loved you Tom … You said you loved me, but did those words mean anything to you? Did you see me as the same naive girl Rich saw? You were so good at saying what I wanted to hear … Did you mean any of it? … The red folder … 'I do what I like, and I like what I do.' You never would have changed … would you … did it matter …

… The click of the answering machine. Rich's voice, 'You live with it, I can't anymore' … live … I can't anymore …

JICKY ROLLED OVER and coughed. She'd heard something—*the alarm? her phone?* She glanced to her side and saw that it was a little after eight p.m. Her nightgown clung to her body and her pillow was soaked with sweat. She needed to change into something dry, but she couldn't face climbing from beneath the blankets. Maybe she could get back to sleep if she thought about something pleasant …

… Back-forth, back-forth, back-forth … Danny, your arms are around me, and the slow rocking motion of casting is like a dance … I feel you nuzzle my neck …

we're in your bed … our arms and legs tangled skin-to-skin … afternoon sun streams through the open window … so good, so right … But wait—Danny, you're not being being truthful, I want the truth … Did you really mean that you didn't want to hurt me or yourself? Did I kick you out of my house for telling the truth? No—disappearing is not right … I'm worth more … I'm—

JICKY AWOKE TO someone pounding on her door. Her sheets were drenched and her thinning hair was pasted to the sides of her face. She was freezing again and didn't want to leave the bed, but she was lucid enough to know that she needed help—her fever was raging. She remembered calling Dan for help before going to bed, but hanging up when an answering machine had clicked on. Danny didn't own an answering machine—she assumed in her haste she'd called the wrong number. She didn't know who could be at her door, but knew she was in no condition to be picky.

Jicky stumbled to the entryway snagging the blanket she was clutching around her quaking body on a kitchen chair. She yanked on the blanket as she reached for the door, turned the knob, and crumpled onto the threshold.

CHAPTER TEN

DAN HAD DECIDED to buy an answering machine a day after Jicky had asked him to leave her apartment. He would give her space, but he would be damned if he would miss her call if she ever reached out for his help again, or still better, called to forgive him. If she reached out, he'd decided that he would tell her the truth. Even if she didn't reach out, he would tell her—he just didn't know the appropriate interval to let lapse. He didn't want to seem pushy, and, besides, her plate was filled with more important concerns than those of a lovesick middle-aged man.

All of September had passed, a beautiful month in Jackson, one that he would have liked to have shared with Jicky, but she hadn't called. He had driven by her apartment building several times during the month. Twice her Tahoe had been sitting outside, so he'd figured she was home. He didn't know much about chemo treatments, but assumed they kicked butt. He hoped she wasn't suffering. He'd gone as far as asking the curator of exhibits at the Wildlife Museum whether she had heard anything from *Ms. Weckwerth* about the planning stages of her upcoming exhibition. It was a long shot, the crane exhibit was still months away, but it was the only thing he could think of. He'd considered calling Jicky from the museum on some *official* pretense, but knew he couldn't pull it off. He'd just come across like the idiot he was.

IN THE MORNING Dan had worked on a small oil painting and then spent the rest of the glorious October day wading in his favorite trout stream. The cold water always made his bad leg ache, but not until he was driving home. Fly casting was so all-encompassing for him that his body became secondary. Nothing hurt when he was fishing. It wasn't until he'd pulled off the waders and climbed into his truck that the throbbing began. He thought about the time before the pain—high school and early college—the days before 'Nam, back when the future seemed like a vast open canvas where he could paint the life he dreamed. *Shit.* He lit a cigarette and rolled down the window. It was dark when he pulled up beside his house. He stubbed out his second cigarette in the truck's nearly-full ashtray and stepped down from the cab, good leg first. He was hungry and wishing that he'd kept one of the browns from today's catch for supper. It was going to be another evening of scrounging in the fridge and cupboard for a meal. Did fried eggs and saltines with peanut butter constitute a meal? They might tonight; tomorrow he would have to face the grocery store and clean his dirty truck. Another exciting Sunday in Jackson.

Dan stashed his gear in the corner of the kitchen and walked through the living room on his way to the bathroom. His new answering machine was blinking, something that he'd seen only once before when Bergstrom, the janitor from work, tried to get ahold of him after a sparrow had flown into the atrium and set off the empty museum's motion detectors. This time there wasn't any message, just a missed call. Dan figured there had to be some way to check on the number, but for now, nature was the one calling and he still needed to wash the fishiness off his hands before he started foraging the kitchen for supper. Studying the answering machine instruction manual would have to wait.

DAN WIPED THE bacon grease and egg white residue from the cast iron frying pan that normally sat on the back-left burner of his gas stove. It had been seasoned metal when he'd inherited it from his parents and was even more so after nearly daily use since his move to Jackson. He washed his dirty supper dishes—a worn spatula, fork, butter knife, and plate—refilled his water glass, and walked in stockinged feet to the living room.

It took Dan about fifteen minutes to figure out the correct combination of numbers and symbols to punch into the little plastic machine to get his call history. He was surprised to see Jicky's number as the last incoming call, and he wondered, *since she made the effort to phone, why didn't she leave a message?* Maybe she didn't like machines. He hated to leave messages— lots of people did; maybe she just wanted to talk and would call back. Dan decided to cool his heels by tying flies while he waited for the phone to ring. If Jicky hadn't called back by eight, he'd call her.

At eight o'clock sharp, Danny called Jicky. When her phone asked him to leave a message, this time it was Dan's turn to hang up. He thought from the little he knew about mobile phones that she would be able to see his number and return the call if she wanted to. But, just in case he didn't hear from her, he'd decided to call once more at eight-thirty. If she didn't answer then, he would bite the bullet and leave a message. Dan wrapped the shaft of a nymph hook and thought about what he might say. Something like: *I saw from my answering machine that you called me earlier—I hope you're feeling okay and just wanted to talk—I really want to talk to you*

Jicky—There's something I need to tell you—Jicky, you've got to get better—I think I love you … God, he was pathetic.

When eight-thirty rolled round and he hadn't heard anything, Dan tried Jicky's number again. Even though he had thought about what he might say, when the messaging system kicked in, he hung up. He went to the kitchen, grabbed his jacket from the hook, and drove into town. He'd see if Jicky's Tahoe was outside her place. If she was home he'd knock on her door. If she didn't want to see him, she could ask him to leave, but at least this way he could see for himself how she was handling the chemo treatments. He could see in person the face he saw every night when he closed his eyes. *I think I love you, Jicky. Shit, I know I love you. Who am I kidding?*

CHAPTER ELEVEN

ALONE IN THE hospital room, Jicky began to cry for only the second time since receiving her diagnosis. The tears were stupid, what the nurse, Linda, had told her was only a possibility, and she had far more important things to deal with in the immediate future. But why hadn't someone told her before now? Was it because the news was so inconsequential to most women her age, or was it because all of her doctors had been men?

Linda had been asking Jicky questions about her medical history that she'd been too sick to answer when Danny had delivered her to the emergency room the previous night. When Linda asked about the dates of her last period, Jicky had told her mid-August, before she'd started chemo. Linda reassured her that it was common to not menstruate during chemo, then asked her how old she was. When Jicky replied that she was almost forty, Linda shook her head and said, "Did anyone tell you that you may have had your last period? Often women getting close to menopause stop having their periods altogether. It's like chemo forces early menopause—you might get some spotting in a few years when you'd normally be going through the change. I mean if you're done having kids, it's great—less hassle and fewer monthly expenses."

Linda finished her questions and checked Jicky's vitals before leaving. That's when her tears had started.

At thirty-nine, almost menopausal? Really? She had always thought of herself as young. She'd thought that her dreams of a family and kids were still possible. In fact, she'd spent most of the long drive from Lincoln to Jackson planning, or at least imagining, futures for herself. Forty was going to be her new twenty—like when she'd left Gareth for Laramie—it was a chance for her life to begin. Not all of the visions of her future had included children. She'd never been desperate to have a baby, but she'd always considered it a pleasant possibility, especially when Tom had wanted children so badly. Now it looked as though it wasn't going to happen, and she cried for what had been taken from her. It was another part of her life that had ended before it began—like her marriage to Tom and a relationship with Danny.

WITH AN ANTIBIOTIC I.V. drip controlling the pneumonia that had caused her fever on Saturday, Jicky slept most of her two days in the hospital. Dr. Kearney had warned her that infections were almost inevitable when undergoing chemo, but she'd been surprised at the severity of this first one—she hadn't expected pneumonia. After all, technically, her Pops had died of pneumonia. At this point, she knew she wouldn't die, she was just thoroughly pissed by the timing of the hospital stay. The pneumonia had changed her chemo schedule; now her third infusion wouldn't be for another week. It looked like her plan to fly to Connecticut at Christmas to see Gary, Joel, Sherry, and April was going to have to wait, but she was hopeful that after her sixth CHOP infusion she'd be done with treatment and feeling good enough to fly east in January to celebrate Joel's birthday.

Joel still wasn't talking to her, but this birthday would be his thirty-fifth—she figured that he would have no reason to be mad at her once he had access to his trust fund. Besides, even if he was still upset, she knew that Sherry and April would be happy to see her, and that Gary would make every effort to get away from med school to visit (no matter the consequences to his GPA). Ever the attentive little brother, when Gary had first heard about the lymphoma he'd wanted to fly to Wyoming to see her. She'd talked him out of it, but he'd compensated by calling weekly for updates and giving his "god-damned learn-ed opinion," which Jicky appreciated.

ON THURSDAY AFTERNOON, when Dr. Kearney was finally willing to let Jicky return home, Dan took the afternoon off to shuttle her back to her place. He'd been visiting her daily, and they had been getting along well, however all his good intentions about coming clean with her about his part in the accident that had ruined his family had been put on the back burner because of Jicky's illness. Dan told himself that he didn't want to add to her problems—well, maybe that was just a load of b.s., but he'd tell her soon, as soon as she could function on her own again, in the event she wouldn't want to see him after hearing the truth.

Dan walked Jicky into her apartment and dropped her bag of things on the table. "Jik, why don't you sit down for a while. I don't mean to be insulting, but you look wiped out—like the ride home was grueling."

"Oh, yeah—well it was. Climbing into your pickup for someone with pneumonia is no easy feat."

"Should I have brought your Tahoe instead?" Dan asked in all earnestness.

"No, silly, I'm just giving you a bad time—I think the Tahoe is just as tall as your truck."

Dan put the cube-shaped faux-leather hassock beneath Jicky's feet and got a blanket from her bed to tuck in around her legs.

"Danny, now that you've got me all comfy, feel free to take off. Since Dr. Kearney thought I was well enough to go home, he must think I'm well enough to be on my own. He knows my situation."

"Hmm..." Dan responded, "I know my situation, too, and I don't have any reason to leave. I took the afternoon off to help you, and if you'll let me, that's what I'd like to do. For instance, do you know what you're going to eat this evening? I don't think anyone is gonna come knocking on your door with a tray of Jello tonight."

"I hope you're right about that—it's not my favorite food."

"Well, what is?" Dan called from the front of the open refrigerator, "It doesn't look like you have anything in the house."

"Yeah, you're prob'ly right. I was gonna go shopping on Sunday."

"I'll make you a deal. You help me put together a shopping list and point out your dirty laundry, and I'll leave you in peace while I go to the grocery store and wash your sheets. It'll give you a little test to see how independent you really are at this stage. But, you gotta promise to keep your phone on you —no more calling and hanging up, or deciding calling is too much work. When punching a few buttons is too much work, that's a pretty good sign that you really need help. Got it?"

"*Jawohl, Herr Ogden*! Loud and clear."

Jicky sat in the chair and made a shopping list while Dan stripped her bed and located her other laundry. Dan knew that Jicky normally did her wash at a laundromat a few blocks from her apartment, and it may have made some sense to do that so that he could've done both loads at once, but Dan didn't want to hang around the laundromat while her clothes washed and he wasn't comfortable leaving Jicky's things unattended. He'd drive out to his place to throw in the white load and get it in the dryer before he went to the store. Even though it was a lot of driving, it was a good plan—that way he could take the sheets back to Jicky when he delivered her groceries. He was willing to make another trip to his place to get the second load from the dryer if Jicky needed anything right away, but if not, he planned on dropping them off on Wednesday before he went to the museum. He hoped it would give him an excuse to check in on her in the morning without seeming too pushy. *Jawohl* indeed!

DAN LET HIMSELF in Jicky's door. She was asleep in the easy chair in the living room, feet on the hassock, exactly as he had left her over three hours earlier. He set her groceries on the kitchen counter and went back to the pickup to get *his* laundry basket full of *her* laundry. He smiled when he looked at her old drafting table. On it lay thousands of dollars worth of photography equipment, but the woman was too cheap, or was it too preoccupied and disinterested, to buy a laundry basket? Everything he learned about Jicky made Dan want to learn more.

Jicky awoke when Dan started putting the groceries away. "Oh, hi Danny…sorry I didn't hear you when you came in. Hey, don't bother with those—I can do it. Besides, I want to see what you bought so that I'll know what I have to eat for coming week."

"Sure, Jik—I just didn't want to wake you. Go ahead, take over. I'll make your bed."

"No, really, Dan, I can do that too."

"I'm not so sure—making up a bed is a lot harder than most people think."

"So, okay, I'll make you a deal," Jicky said, mimicking Dan's word from earlier in the day, "you sit down at the table and we'll talk while I put the food away. If I'm too tired to make the bed after taking care of the groceries, then you can do it."

DAN ENDED UP making Jicky's bed and their supper. He'd never had cancer, but he'd had pneumonia. He knew how anything to do with the lungs could incapacitate a person for weeks. He left at eight, after doing the dishes and making sure Jicky took her evening meds. When he promised to come back in the morning before he went to work, Jicky assured him that it wouldn't be necessary. When Dan explained that stopping before work would be the most convenient time for him to return her laundry, Jicky grudgingly said, "Okay, fine, come then." In truth, she was relieved—she'd been hoping to see him in the morning, but she would have never asked for a visit.

CHAPTER TWELVE

DAN SAT AT his kitchen table untangling strands of Jicky's hair from her fuzzy black socks. He had been doing her laundry for weeks now, and judging from the dryer's lint trap and the bottom of his laundry basket, there was no longer any doubt that Jicky was losing her beautiful long mane. She had mentioned that her hair was starting to thin when he'd visited her in the hospital, but he'd assured her that he'd seen no change. After her third round of chemo, a week and a half ago, there was no denying it; Jicky was going bald, and just in time for winter. *Lousy timing*. He'd have to remember to buy her some nice soft stocking caps next time he was at a store.

Dan pushed Jicky's towels and clothes into the pillowcase that she'd told him to use to transport her wash and took his green plastic laundry basket back to its spot in the spare bedroom. He looked around the room—two easels, one with an oil painting he'd finished months ago, the other with a large canvas that he'd prepped for an acrylic abstract on the day Jicky wouldn't let him stay with her while she'd had a chemo treatment. He had taken the day off to be by her side— when she'd dismissed him, he'd decided to paint. However, he'd been so distracted by worry that applying a couple coats of gesso was all that he had managed. The white canvas sat as a reminder of the rest of that awful day: He'd picked up Jicky at the infusion center mid-afternoon. She'd seemed fine at first, only to be retching into her toilet three hours later as Dan held her sweat dampened hair away from her face. He'd stayed at her apartment for as long as she would allow, but she wouldn't let him stay the night. She said that it was because she didn't have a place for him to sleep.

Dan hoped it was that simple—that the lack of a bed was Jicky's only reason for not wanting him to stay the night. If it was, maybe he had a solution. He walked to the garage and got a tape measure from his father's old tool box.

* * *

"JICKY, I HAVE a proposition for you."

"Come on, Danny, we've been through this before. I know chemo has made me unbelievably sexy, but I'm not going to bed with you."

"Ha, ha—no, I'm serious. Can we talk?"

"Sure, you're no fun, but sure. I'm not going anywhere."

"Well, that's what I want to talk to you about." Dan didn't let Jicky say anything before he blurted out, "Will you move in with me?"

"What?"

"I've been thinking that it makes some sense for you to move to my place before winter really sets in, and—"

Jicky cut him off, "No, you're crazy. No."

"Hear me out, Jik. You're coming up on your next chemo on the tenth, right." Jicky nodded. "Well, the last one, as I'm sure you remember, didn't go so well, and you told me that Kearney told you that you should expect them to keep getting worse—that they're cumulative. So, my idea is—" Dan paused and then spoke quickly, "you come stay with me until you're done with treatments."

"No, Danny."

"Please, hear me out. I don't want you to be alone, but coming to town all the time is adding hours of driving to my day. I'm not complaining, but it'll be safer for you if you don't have to be by yourself, and, well, I want you to know I'm not being completely altruistic—having you at my house would make things easier for me."

"But you don't have an extra bed either, and I won't kick you out of yours—or share with you if that's what you're thinking."

"No, no. I've already taken care of that. I moved my painting stuff out of the extra bedroom into the garage—it's heated and I'd been thinking about making it into my studio for years. I've already bought a new twin bed and bedding for the spare room, and I've measured things a couple times now —there's room for your drafting table, so you can move it with you and work whenever you feel up to it."

Jicky exhaled, "…It sound like you've thought of everything, except who's gonna move that table. It's a beast."

"I will."

"By yourself? I won't be much help."

"Jicky, who moved it into your apartment?"

"Well…I did."

"Yeah, that's what I thought. If you can lift it, I'm pretty sure I can."

"You're a lot older than me."

"*Ha, ha.* I'd tell you to go to hell, if I weren't already trying to talk you into moving in with me." Dan took a deep breath, "But seriously, there is something that I need to tell you before you make your decision—it's something that I should've told you months ago, and it's the reason I bolted after we made love. I'm sorry… I'm sorry for so much… but, I'm especially sorry it's taken me this long."

DAN TOLD JICKY his story—his history with alcohol, his DWIs, his decision to drive after drinking while on a family picnic at the beach. He told her about falling asleep, causing the accident that killed his wife and son, and landed his toddler daughter in a pediatric ICU for months. He explained his conviction for manslaughter and the ten years he'd spent in Rawlins. He told her how his in-laws had raised his daughter, and how, now that she was an adult, she wanted nothing to do with him. He ended by asking Jicky's forgiveness.

She had listened without saying anything, tears pooling in her eyes. "Danny, I'm so sorry you've had to live with such pain for so long. I'm also sorry you felt you couldn't tell me. I don't think you need my forgiveness, except maybe for hiding from me, and that would seem pretty petty of me considering everything that you've done since I got sick."

Now Dan was crying, too. "But I killed them Jicky; I loved them and I killed them."

"But you didn't mean to. The accident wasn't your fault."

"No, you don't understand—it happened because of a decision I made. I did something wrong—whether I meant to or not—I did it. Their deaths are my fault."

"Danny, you're a good person who made a horrible mistake. I'm in no position to be your judge."

"I killed people I love. Who's to say I won't fuck up and do it again?"

Jicky got up from the table and walked around to Dan's side, bent down and put her arms around his shaking shoulders. "You won't. I know you. You won't."

JICKY DROVE OUT to Dan's place on Sunday morning. She hadn't yet agreed to move in, but they'd decided that a good test would be a day together in the house and a night for her in the new bedroom before her chemo treatment on Friday. She'd told Dan that she didn't want her first night in the new bed to be one where she was feeling sick—she didn't think that would be a fair test.

Dan made pancakes, bacon, and eggs for brunch, while Jicky poked around the yard and looked through Dan's new studio in the garage. An oversized empty canvas sat on his largest easel, it looked gessoed and ready to paint. Jicky thought, *like he's got any time to do his art between working at the museum and chasing back and forth to take care of me.* Jicky looked at the paintings Dan had chosen to hang over the paper-bag colored insulation stapled to the two-by-four stud walls. One was of two children—a boy, maybe five or six, and a girl not much past the toddler stage. Their faces were almost in profile, and while it was impossible to tell what they were looking at, both appeared filled with joy. Jicky didn't have to ask Dan to know that these were his children—the son he had lost in the accident and the daughter who'd lived, but was still lost to him. Jicky thought of her own parents. She could have hated them—her mom had abandoned her, and, in his own way, her dad had too. And, while being left to fend for herself had made her sad, and sometimes angry, she'd never quit loving them—they were her parents after all. Jicky wondered, *if Dan's daughter could learn to look at the situation in a different light, could she forgive her father? Dan is such a good man. They are both missing so much from their estrangement …*

Jicky turned. The other two paintings in the studio were studies for landscapes, both detailed views of the Tetons in different seasons. From the dates Dan had included beside his signature, she assumed that they must have been some of his earliest paintings of the area. Jicky figured he'd probably kept them for sentimental reasons. She'd have to ask him.

She closed the door on the garage and walked back to the house, past the old clothesline and the picnic table where they'd eaten the first time she'd come to visit—when Dan had shown her the fundamentals of fly fishing. This summer had been a bust for fishing, but by next summer she'd be ready to catch some trout. If she stayed with Dan maybe he could give her more lessons on fly tying. Between the reading she'd been doing and some serious practice over the winter, by spring she could be an expert at tying flies even if she couldn't cast a line yet. Her mind drifted to standing in the stream with Danny behind her guiding her rod, and then his kiss on her neck, a move which seemed to have shaken both of them. *Had that been a mistake? Had making love that day been a mistake? Would moving in with Danny be a mistake? Why couldn't she just quit asking herself so many damned questions and just do what felt good?* She, again, thought of Tom's mantra—"I like what I do and I do what I like." If only her life could be so easy. She'd realized after Danny's confession that she needed to tell him her truth, too. She now knew that without unburdening herself it would be impossible for her to put the past behind, forgive herself, and move on. *But how? After so many years, how?*

BRUNCH EATEN, DAN and Jicky sat in the living room reading the *Casper Star-Tribune*. Danny got the Jackson paper during the week, but made a habit of picking up the *Star-Tribune* on Sundays. At the museum he kept up with the outside world by reading the *New York Times* and an assortment of other papers. Jicky confessed to Dan that she had been taking a break from news, at least political news, since she'd moved to Jackson. "Truthfully, I quit paying much attention to politics once Rich and Tom died. I'd never been all that interested, but it was so important to those two, and, well,

Tom's wife, too, that I got sucked in—kinda like marrying into a family business."

Dan responded, "Yeah, I can see that. I don't know too many visual artists wrapped up in what's goin' on in Washington. But you worked for the Chadron paper, didn't you? Didn't that keep you up to date on what was happening in the world?"

"Well, yes, but it was a local paper—like the *Daily*—not exactly the *New York Times*. I still pick up the *Jackson Daily* to see what's happening around town. I mean newspapers are important; I'm not a heathen."

"Good, 'cause there are too many out there already—folks who don't care and don't read, and, now, with so many papers going onto the computer, I'm worried my Sundays spent readin' are going to go by the wayside in a few years. I hate to think about a world without real newspapers," said Dan, as he readjusted his reading glasses, and took another gulp of tepid coffee.

"Look on the bright side Danny—you'll have more time for fishing."

Dan smiled. "Guess you're right. You always are."

JICKY POKED AROUND Dan's house that afternoon after he'd been called to the museum to see an artist who'd stopped by unannounced. When he'd asked Jicky if she'd like to come with him, she'd begged off; she was tired and thought she might nap, but she'd also liked the idea of being alone while she looked through the house. Dan had told her to look at everything. He had nothing to hide. Jicky still thought it sounded creepy—going through someone's things while they stood and watched. Somehow, snooping while alone seemed far more natural.

She started with the room that was to be hers. It was a small bedroom, but certainly big enough for her, even if she chose to move her drafting table to the space beneath the windows. The walls were painted off-white and the wood trim around the door and two windows was stained a dark brown. The walls were bare; Dan had explained that he'd left them that way so that she could bring her watercolor paintings to decorate the room. He'd add that she was free to put anything she liked in the rest of the house, too—he wanted her to feel at home if she decided to stay with him. Alongside the twin bed's spindly metal headboard sat a rustic bedside table with a lamp and a clock radio exactly like the one Jicky had at home. *Danny didn't miss a beat.* There was one small closet, completely empty, so no problems with storage. She thought that one of her plastic bins would fit on the floor, and she could put her warm clothing on the shelf above the hanging bar.

The bathroom was her next stop. Situated between the two bedrooms, it was at the end of a short hallway. She'd been in the bathroom in the past, but she'd never opened the linen closet or peeked in the medicine cabinet. In the small closet, next to the extra toilet paper and Kleenex, Dan had placed a stack of light-blue bath towels. They looked new, and Jicky wondered if he'd bought them in anticipation of her moving in. Danny had evidently just scrubbed the metal medicine cabinet. She couldn't remember ever seeing the interior of a bathroom cabinet so clean, and she'd lived for years with Gloria Weckwerth, the queen of good housekeeping. On the bottom shelf of the medicine cabinet, Dan's toothbrush and tube of Crest formed a sparse bouquet in a pottery mug with a broken handle. Dan's Mitchum deodorant, electric razor, comb, and brush sat on the top shelf of the medicine cabinet. He'd left the two middle shelves empty, she assumed, for her things. The last things Jicky noticed were the bars of Zest soap on the edge of the bathtub and sink. *Ahh, Zest and Mitchum must be what make him smell so good.*

Like the bathroom, Jicky had already spent time in the kitchen and living room. The living room had no closets, so really, no secrets. She walked to the kitchen and looked in the cabinets and drawers. She saw nothing that surprised her—everything was clean and well-organized, and Danny owned all that she would need for her basic cooking. In a small coat closet located beside the back door, Jicky found a broom, a vacuum, and a container of rags topped by a stack of mismatched towels—the ones that had probably filled the bathroom linen closet until a few days ago. On the single rod, a charcoal grey wool topcoat hung from a wooden hanger. An old-fashioned bag containing clothespins hung beside it. The rest of Dan's coats and jackets were on hooks beside the kitchen door. His shoes sat on a boot tray beneath them.

The only room left to inspect was Dan's bedroom, but Jicky didn't enter. She remembered it from their afternoon together. That was enough for now—to think about anything more was too confusing, and besides, everyone deserved some privacy.

"HI, HONEY, I'M home!" Dan called out in jest, after walking into the kitchen at four-thirty. When Jicky didn't respond, he passed through the living room and peeked into the room he'd decorated for her. She wasn't there. He'd parked beside her Tahoe, so he knew she couldn't have gone far. Dan slipped his arm back through the sleeve of his jacket, walked to the kitchen door and then to the far side of the house. There he found Jicky, sitting at the picnic table, casually cutting off hanks of her long hair with the paper shears from his studio. The last rays of the setting sun reflected off the scissor blades.

The dead grass close to the table was littered with her dark auburn locks.

"I'm losing it anyway, so I figured the birds could have it for nesting material," Jicky said, smiling sadly as she tossed a handful of hair over her shoulder. "I didn't want it messing up your clean house, especially since I've decided I'd like to live in it for awhile … I saw when I was snooping in the medicine cabinet that you own an electric razor… Would you consider finishing this job for me?"

"Sure, Jicky, if that's what you want—but, can we go in? It's cold and it's gonna be too dark out here for me to …" Dan's voice trailed off. He couldn't get himself to say *shave your head*. He gently brushed strands of hair from Jicky's nylon jacket, put the scissors in his coat pocket, and they walked together, his arm around her shoulders, to the kitchen door.

CHAPTER THIRTEEN

"I AM NOT going to eat anything for days," said Dan as they climbed into his pickup. He and Jicky were leaving his assistant's house after attending a late-afternoon Thanksgiving dinner with a group of the museum's employees, several who had closed the museum at four before joining the party.

"Yeah, it was really good. Tammi did a great job with the turkey," said Jicky, "and, I don't care if you eat or not, as long as you keep cooking for me. Dr. Kearney's really happy about my weight gain this month."

"Jicky, you're the only woman I've ever known happy about gaining weight," Dan said grinning.

"Extenuating circumstances—I need to make my doctor happy. Turns out getting off schedule ended up being a good thing this month, even though it screwed-up my plans for Christmas. Remember? Originally I was scheduled for chemo yesterday—boy, that would have been the pits."

"So, if you stay healthy, does that mean your very last session is a few days before Christmas?"

"Yeah, the twenty-second, knock-on-wood. I hope it'll be my last—Kearney isn't saying for sure, but if it is, I'm hoping to fly to Connecticut in January to see my family. I'd wanted to go for Christmas, but that's out now. I'm not sure I could've done it anyway—whether I would've been strong enough. It was just something nice to daydream about when I didn't have enough energy to do anything else.

"Well, assuming you want me around, and you'll be over being chemo-sick, what would you like to do for *Christmas not in Connecticut?*"

"Ha, that's pretty lame. And, just how old are you? That movie came out in the mid '40s, didn't it?"

"Yeah, but it's on TV every year…I figured you'd have heard of it. But, seriously, what would you like to do for Christmas?"

"Let's just celebrate one holiday at a time, Danny. I don't wanna plan too far ahead these days—I'm tired of trying to replace one dream with another."

* * *

JICKY SET THE heavy Sunday paper, thick with ads for holiday bargains, on the coffee table in front of Dan's couch. "I've been thinking about Christmas. I've decided that I'd like to go to Christmas Eve services at that pretty log chapel just inside the entrance to Grand Teton, or if it's closed for the season, maybe that big old white church at the edge of town."

"I'll look into it. It sort of surprises me though—you've never said much about religion. Do you believe in God?"

Jicky looked up from the "Life" section of the paper. "Do I believe in God??? Not into small talk this morning, are you?"

"I mean, do you ever feel like there must be a God?" Dan asked.

"Oh, yeah, of course, but there are probably just as many times I've wonder, if there really is a God, where the heck he hides, 'cause I've gone through some awful things in my life. I often wished some all-powerful being would've stepped in and taken care of some of the crap—not just left it for me or my family to mop up."

Both Dan and Jicky sat in silence for a moment, before Jicky slowly started to speak again:

"...But, yeah, Danny...when I'd watch a huge sedge of sandhill cranes or see ocean waves crash on shore when I lived back East—or, like, even just driving across the open areas near the Badlands or up that back road toward the Tetons, at those times...yeah...I know God exists. I figure God is that feeling I get. I can't describe it—I sure as heck haven't ever been able to capture it on film—but it's like an internal awe at the beauty of the world. When I feel like that, then I gotta believe in somethin' bigger than us.... Not that nature was designed by God, but that feeling of awe and wonder itself— that feeling. *That feeling* is my way of experiencing God.... Does that make any sense?"

"Yeah, I get it," Dan said, "but if it's nature that makes you feel like that, why Christmas Eve inside a church? —I've never heard you say anything about going to church."

"I haven't since I got here, but when I lived in Chadron I went almost every Sunday. My in-laws were about as Methodist as you can get. I went when I was married, I guess, 'cause it was expected of me, and it sort of became habit. I liked parts of being a church member and could see how it helped some folks. I don't think it ever helped me much—but, my memories of late night Christmas Eve services are wonderful. This is gonna sound stupid, but I always considered walking home after those services the best part of Christmas. We'd leave the church and it seemed like it was always cold and clear. The stars'd shine down on us as we walked back to the house. It was only a block away, but it was like God had spread a blanket of peace over our little chunk of the world. I loved the way it made me feel, and I kinda hoped if we went to Christmas Eve services somewhere pretty, I could step out of the church and get that feeling again. Is that silly?"

"No, not silly—it sounds nice. I'll do some checking around."

"Okay, so, now that I've told you what I'd like, what would you like Danny Ogden? If you could celebrate any way you wanted this Christmas, what would you do?"

"That's easy. I'd want you well enough to enjoy a nice meal with me—maybe a baked ham with all the fixings. And then I'd like us to spend a lazy afternoon together reading the paper."

"Danny, come on, you just described a normal winter Sunday. I want you to give me a biggie—if you could have *anything* this Christmas, what would it be?"

"A biggie, huh … okay … " Dan paused, "I would love to spend Christmas with my daughter." He exhaled a bitter huff, "You want to go to church, and I want hell to freeze over."

"What? Does she know that? Does she know you want to see her?"

"Of course she does, Jicky— I sent her letters and paintings at Christmas the whole time she was growing up, but never once heard anything from her. After she turned eighteen I tried to see her, thinking it was her grandparents stopping her—but she said no. Last time we spoke—the day she turned twenty-one—that's when she made the 'when hell freezes over' comment—I think it pretty much says where I stand with her."

"I'm sorry, Danny. I didn't mean to open old wounds."

"No, I'm sorry to ruin our Sunday—I know you didn't plan to upset me." Dan was quiet for a minute before saying, "I'm going out to the studio for awhile."

DAN FLIPPED THE switches that turned on the overhead light and oil heater as he entered the garage, then walked over and opened the top drawer of his drafting table at the far end of the room. Beneath a stack of extra-large sheets of drawing paper lay a manila folder bulging with papers and photos. Dan grabbed it and started looking through the chronologically ordered contents. The first was a drawing of a teddy bear—a sketch, really. He'd made it as a reminder of what he'd drawn for Becky the first Christmas he'd been in prison. She hadn't yet turned four years old when he'd been sent to Rawlins. He'd had no art supplies, just a pencil and paper to make his little girl a gift, so Dan had painstakingly drawn a portrait of her favorite stuffed animal; the one she'd been given on her first birthday and named "Binky Ba." On the back of the original drawing, which Dan had sent to Becky's grandparents, he'd written a note. He no longer remembered what he had said, but he was sure he must have again asked for their forgiveness.

Dan riffled through the folder looking at the other notes, sketches, and photos. Every year of Becky's childhood, Dan had sent her a work of art at Christmas. During his first few years in prison the pictures were drawings. Eventually, when he'd gotten oil pastels, he'd added color. It wasn't until a kind guard had offered to take Polaroids during his last few years in prison that Dan had more than pencil sketches to remind him of his subject matter, which he'd changed every year.

During Becky's young years it was easy to draw for her, but as she'd gotten older Dan had to do research to figure out what she might like. Starting in November, he'd pay close attention to toy ads in the Sunday newspaper flyers, and every year he'd ask his brother's wife, Jody, for ideas. Greg and Jody didn't have any contact with Becky either, but at least Jody would understand his interest in 'girly toys' and not think him a pervert (his fear, if he'd ever said anything to the other inmates or guards). The year Becky was six, Dan drew a picture of two Cabbage Patch Kids playing on a swing set. A few years later he drew American Girl dolls having a tea party in a garden. By the time Dan was out of prison he figured that Becky would have aged out of liking pictures of toys and baby animals. Had he known what kind of music Becky liked, he could have done portraits of the artists, but there was no way of guessing; musical taste was personal—he didn't want to get it wrong. He'd decided to paint landscapes for her. He still had the studies for his first two efforts hanging on his garage studio walls. In his daydreams, Becky had been so enamored with what she saw in his paintings, she'd wanted to come to Jackson Hole to see the area for herself.

Damn, Dan thought, *I'm such a self-delusional fuck-wit. I thought my teenage daughter would be impressed enough by my scenery paintings to want to reach out to me.* And, even though Dan thought it possible that Becky had never seen the artwork and notes that he'd sent during her childhood, he didn't want to upset her with the knowledge that he had tried to stay in touch, but that her grandparents hadn't allowed it to happen. It didn't seem fair to Becky for him to insinuate that her grandparents were the bad guys. He was the only bad guy in Becky's life—he wouldn't deny it.

Dan looked at the large painting of his children on the studio wall. He'd done it from memory a few years earlier. It was the way they'd looked their last day together— sunburned, tousled, and full of joy. The family had spent the day at Lake Hattie swimming and fishing. Carol had packed a cooler with sandwiches—peanut butter for the kids, and ham and Swiss for the two of them. Dan had thrown in a six-pack of Bud and a couple of loose ones for good measure. *Best be prepared,* he'd thought—Carol drank too, and it was forecast to be a hot day. By six-thirty, when it was time to head home for baths and bed, they all were exhausted. He'd asked Carol if she wanted to drive, but she'd said that she was too tired. So, he had driven—his kids, curled up together on the backseat, and his wife, dozing beside him, in the front … He remembered the tangy smells of sunscreen and sweat and the rhythmic sounds of his family's slumbering breaths …

Dan's mind skipped ahead to the days following the accident, those long weeks after the funerals, while Becky still languished in the pediatric ICU at Ivinson Memorial. That's when he should've gotten his act together—behaved like a father, instead of a drunk. It had taken prison to sober him up, and by then it was too late to convince Carol's parents that he could ever be a father to the only child he had left. He understood. Remembering his behavior, under the same circumstances, would he have made a different decision for an innocent child? His in-laws were good people, and he was thankful that they had stepped up to care for Becky.

He gathered the pictures and photos, put them back in the file jacket, and placed it in the drawer. It was finally getting warm in the garage. Dan shrugged off his coat and hung it on the back of a chair, one he'd borrowed from the kitchen and set in front of the big gesso-prepped canvas secured to his largest easel. He normally stood when he painted but sat when he pondered. Dan took a cigarette from a pack on the windowsill, sat down and lit it. He wasn't smoking in the house anymore, he knew it couldn't be good for Jicky's pneumonia-scarred lungs, but he'd not been able to completely give up what was now nearly a thirty-five-year-old habit. He took a drag and contemplated the canvas. He'd had something in mind when he'd stretched it, but that was so long ago. So much had changed. His mind was as blank as the surface in front of him. He got up and ground out his cigarette in the plaid beanbag ashtray that sat on the sill beside the Marlboros, grabbed his

coat, flipped off the heater and lights, and walked back to the
house.

CHAPTER FOURTEEN

IT WAS AS Dan had feared, the Chapel of the Transfiguration —the little log church at the entrance to Grand Teton Park— was closed all winter. There would be no Christmas Eve service for Jicky to attend, but her other option, the large Lutheran Church, "the big white church on the edge of town," as she had called it, would be having a midnight service. *That should please her,* thought Dan.

He swiveled his chair so that he was looking out toward the elk refuge on the other side of the highway and smiled. It had been a long time since he had felt this content. He'd been pretty pleased with his life when he had landed the curatorship at the art museum, but that was different. Pleased with getting hired and actually starting a new job are two different things. His first two years at the museum had been fulfilling, but stressful. His work life was finally getting easy about the time Jicky called his name from across the museum's atrium and turned his personal life upside down.

Until just recently he'd been an emotional wreck when it came to Jicky. But there had been something about the way his colleagues had treated them like a couple at Thanksgiving, and Jicky's response to it, that had put his mind at ease. So what if they hadn't made love since that summer afternoon. He was certain that they would eventually—when Jicky was ready. In the meantime, they'd been developing a special kind of intimacy. Dan thought about how they had both cried when he took his razor to Jicky's balding head the day she'd moved in and the way they'd laughed until tears flowed watching a video of *Scrooged* while curled up on the couch together after Jicky's fifth chemo treatment at the beginning of the month.

She would beat the cancer. *She had to.*

* * *

JICKY WALKED BACK to the Tahoe. This wasn't supposed to be happening! She'd felt fine when she'd started out from Dan's place in the morning. She needed to get her Christmas shopping done during the week so that the package to Connecticut would have a chance of arriving by the twenty-fourth. At least she'd found gifts for everyone by the time she'd tired so completely that she could barely put one foot in front of the other. Maybe the backgammon set she'd bought for Dan was a mistake, but she had no clue what to get him. She'd thought about a sweater, but had never seen him in one, meaning, she supposed, he didn't wear them. Maybe a game that they could play together was a copout, but she remembered playing board games at the Weckwerth's on Christmas Day and it made a game for two seem like a good idea. Besides, the set was handmade and gorgeous—if Dan didn't like playing the game, at least he'd appreciate the multiple woods and artistry of the intricately inlaid case.

She managed to put the bags of gifts into the back of the Tahoe and climb into the drivers seat before she passed out.

"DAMN IT JICKY, you can't push yourself so hard." Dr. Kearney scolded in his not so gentle bedside manner. He and Jicky had always had a decent rapport, and after she'd confronted him about not warning her that she could be thrown into early menopause by chemo treatments, the doctor had decided to be thoroughly candid with his information to her.

"Dr. Kearney, you have no idea how happy I'll be when my treatments are over and you can't boss me around anymore—I was Christmas shopping, not running a marathon."

"From what I know, a marathon'd be better for you than a crowded store in the winter. Your blood counts are low, both red and white." Kearney glanced at the bag hanging from the pole to the right of Jicky's hospital bed. "This transfusion is going to help with your energy level, but I'd like you to avoid crowds until you have an immune system again."

"Do you think I can still have chemo on the twenty-second?"

"We'll see—you'll have to have a CBC like usual. If your counts are good, and you're otherwise healthy, I'd like to keep you on schedule."

"It'll be my last chemo, right?"

"About that—I'm thinking *no*."

Jicky sighed, "But you said the normal course of treatment with CHOP is six sessions."

"The *normal* treatment is, but it's often followed with radiation. You're doing so well with chemo, I'd like to do seven rounds of CHOP and see if we can get by without making you come in daily for radiation. Those treatments are tedious and could be hard on your lungs—we can always go the radiation route if it turns out that we have to, but I'd just as soon avoid it."

"Okay… what's one more chemo treatment among friends." Jicky said while rolling her eyes. "If you think it's the way to go, I'll believe you. But I want you to know, I'm not particularly happy about it."

Dr. Kearney, attempting to change the subject, asked Jicky about her Christmas plans. When she told him that she and Dan planned on spending a quiet day at home, he'd seemed pleased. When she'd added that they were going to Christmas Eve services at the big Lutheran Church, he was less happy.

"Jicky, I hate to tell people that they can't practice their religion, but you really shouldn't be going to church on Christmas Eve. Those services are packed with people coughing and sneezing all over one another," Kearney faked a shudder, "not to mention all that blasted hand shaking. There's no way I can recommend that you put yourself in that position only two days after chemo."

"Gee, you're no fun at all today, are you?"

"Sorry, just doing my job."

"Yeah. Got that loud and clear. Merry Christmas, Dr. Grinch."

JICKY WAITED UNTIL Dr. Kearney left to call Dan. When she'd come to, after having slumped over the steering wheel, she had driven herself to the hospital emergency room. She didn't think she had pneumonia again, but she'd thought *better safe than sorry*. She'd given the registration nurse Dan's name as her emergency contact, but waited to phone him—there was little point in him driving to town from the museum if she would be released within a few hours. Now that Dr. Kearney had told her that he wanted her to stay the night, Danny needed to know, however, she still didn't think he needed to come into town. "Hey, Danny," Jicky said after having had the prerequisite chat with Tammi, "don't panic, but I'm at St. John's again."

"What happened? Should I come?"

"I got faint while I was shopping. Well, let me rephrase that—I fainted while I was in town. I took myself to the emergency room when I woke up. It's nothing really. I don't appear to have an infection, just a very low red blood cell count. I've had a transfusion and I'm already feeling a lot better. Kearney just wants me to stay overnight to see how my counts are in the morning."

"Jik, I can leave work now and be there in—"

"No, don't you dare—I'm fine. I just wanted you to know that I won't be back tonight. There's nothing you can do for me here. You know how good the nurses are on this floor; all I have to do is push a button and someone comes running. Stay home and take a break from being at my beck and call."

"Like you're so demanding—I fix a little extra food and wash a few more dishes."

"Well, take a break from that then. And, since I won't be around to make you feel guilty, maybe you can go hang out in your studio. It's been forever since you've painted anything, and I think it's because you don't want to leave me alone in the evenings. Here's your chance."

"God, you're frustrating … but since I'm not coming to see you, can you at least tell me what else Kearney told you? Did you ask him if this next chemo will be your last?"

"Yeah, I did, and unfortunately, it won't be. The only good news that came with that disclosure is that if I have seven treatments instead of six it's less likely that I'll have to have radiation treatments. Kearney said he's trying to avoid them, unless it's necessary, which I assume means if the cancer isn't all gone or if it comes back again. I don't want to think about that. I just want all this to be over and done."

"I'll second that. It would be nice if you don't have to do radiation. So, maybe one more treatment's a good trade-off?"

"Yeah, I s'pose. Oh, but I forgot to tell you Kearney's other news—he doesn't want me to go to church on Christmas Eve."

"What? Why on earth should he care?"

"Germs—he says churches are full of them, especially in the winter. Since I'll only be two days out from my chemo treatment he's afraid that my immune system will be wonky. I know he's right, but I'm disappointed. I was really looking forward to the Christmas Eve service."

Dan hung up his office phone and thought about what Jicky had told him—more chemo and no Christmas service. He knew Jicky well enough by now to know how depressed she must be feeling, but he also knew that surprising her at the hospital would not help her mood since she had already made up her mind that he needed an evening alone. He grabbed his coat from the hall tree by his office door and told Tammi that he was leaving early—she should tell anyone who phoned that he would return their calls the next day. Dan nearly flew the fifteen miles home, dashed to his room to change clothes, grabbed a banana off the counter for his dinner, and rushed to the studio. If Jicky couldn't go to church for Christmas Eve, the church would come to her. He finally knew what he was meant to paint on the large canvas that sat gessoed and waiting.

CHAPTER FIFTEEN

DAN DROPPED JICKY at the clinic infusion center for her sixth round of CHOP. She'd given him orders to be back by noon with lunch. When he'd balked at the idea of eating in the infusion center, Jicky explained that people did it all the time. "Most people are feeling fine while they're getting treatments, it's the aftermath that stinks." She added that the first time she'd come for chemo she'd had the same notion that he did— that the room would be full of sad, bald people looking miserable. "Well, yeah, some of them were bald, but they were still snarfing burgers and fries out'a greasy takeout bags, and generally having a pretty decent time. The rule with cancer is, 'eat what you can, when you can'."

Jicky had never let Dan come with her to treatment. She'd always said that there was no need. This time had been different. Physically there was still no need—Jicky had felt fine since the transfusion, but mentally it was getting harder to face the ordeal, which she didn't understand. "I'm almost finished," she told Dan. "I know what to expect, but I don't want to do it—it's like I'm scared for the first time. It's s'posed to be 'forewarned is forearmed,' right?—well it feels like the opposite."

"You've always told me the aftermath of chemo is like having the flu. I think it's understandable that you don't want to willingly do something that's gonna make you feel awful. It makes sense to me. I mean, usually when people choose to do stuff that make them feel bad the next day, like eating and drinking too much, well, at least they're havin' fun doin' whatever it is that's gonna eventually make them sick. I don't imagine having poison pumped into your veins is a barrel of laughs."

"It's not, but it's not that bad either—just a lot of sitting around. I guess what I'm trying to say is 'thank you.' It's the pits this time, and having you as my lunch date is gonna make it easier for me."

Jicky climbed from Dan's truck and walked into the infusion center with her latest library book on physical geography. It was a thick one on the physiography of volcanoes.

DAN DROVE BACK to the town square and parked. He had a few errands to take care of before his Christmas gift to Jicky could be fully realized.

He walked around to the back door of the Salt Valley Grill and let himself into the messy entry off the kitchen. He called out for Larry, the head chef, who was, himself, busy yelling at one of the prep cooks. The restaurant would be slammed by customers over the next few days, every one of them looking for some special way for Larry to impress the people they loved. Dan Ogden was no exception, other than he and Larry were old friends, and he had a very interesting meal in mind. Dan gave Larry the final details and a check to cover all the expenses, including a healthy tip. Dan had worked in the restaurant industry long enough to know that generous tipping was appreciated, even among old friends.

The next stop on Dan's agenda was the KJAX Radio station just outside of town on Highway 22. "Vance the Voice," the nighttime DJ was not around that morning, but he'd left the tape that he'd prepared for Dan with the receptionist. Vance was a friend from the days when both he and Dan had spent hours at AA meetings. Like Dan, Vance had gotten his life in order. KJAX was a new configuration of an old station and Vance was now in on the ground floor of what looked like a very successful venture. Dan was happy for him, and Vance was happy to be doing Dan a favor.

The next few stops on Dan's agenda didn't go quite as smoothly as the first two had, but then, they weren't prearranged like the earlier ones. Dan wanted white or off-white candles. In his mind he had envisioned a forest of glowing tapers and columns; after scrounging around two stores he'd only found seven candles and a pair of inexpensive pressed glass candle holders. They would have to do. He needed to get downtown to buy Jicky's lunch. While she had told him about chemo patients eating burgers and fries, her request had been for soup and a fruit pizza from the bakery on Broadway. Dan picked up their meals and headed back to the clinic, where he found Jicky hooked to an I.V. bag and thoroughly engrossed in her book on volcanos.

"Hi Jik, how's it going?"

"Not bad. This part usually isn't. You already missed the big show."

"Big show?"

"When the infusion nurse comes in wearing welding gloves and carrying the syringe of Adriamycin like it's going to explode any minute. The stuff's the color of cherry KoolAid, but a lot more lethal—I mean, the nurse looks scared just holding it, which isn't super reassuring as she pushes it into my I.V. line."

"So I thought you were getting chemo drugs that spell out CHOP. How does this red Adria-whatever fit in."

"I've no idea. I just know it's nicknamed the Red Devil, and my pee is going to be a strange color for a little while … So, what's in the bag? I'm starving."

"You amaze me—it's hard to believe you're hungry after what you just told me." Dan handed Jicky a paper carton of chicken noodle soup and a plastic spoon.

LUNCH FINISHED, DAN excused himself, telling Jicky that he needed to call his office. At the pay phone in the lobby he called Tammi's cell. He'd have to succumb to pressure and get a mobile phone soon—it seemed they were not proving to be the passing fad that he'd hoped they'd be. He hated the idea of always being tethered to the outside world.

"Hey Tammi, did you and John get the delivery made?"

"Yup, it's all taken care of. We set it right inside the garage door on the tape-line where you'd marked the floor. — Gotta tell you, Mr. O, I saw your new painting! Wowzer, it's awesome! Don't get me wrong, I've always liked your stuff, but this one's great. It made me feel like I was right there even though it's not realistic like your old stuff. I mean, like, I like your old stuff, too, but this is just *sooo* good. Jicky's gonna love it. And, hey, don't worry about gettin' the bench back to us. John and I can stop by sometime after Christmas and get it."

"Sure, Tammi. Thank you, and thank John for me. Merry Christmas."

Tammi held the phone to her chest and yelled to her boyfriend, "Dan Ogden says thanks!" Then, once again speaking into the receiver, she said, "Merry Christmas to you, too, Mr. O. See you on Tuesday."

* * *

"DANNY ARE YOU ever going to tell me what we're doing tonight?" Jicky had awakened from her afternoon nap to find

Dan dressed in dark grey slacks, with a shirt and tie under a navy blue V-neck sweater that she had never seen before.

"No, but don't worry—you'll figure it out as we go along. Now, get dressed in whatever you woulda worn to that church service we don't get to attend," Dan said, with a fashion show like gesture toward his attire. He might have suggested 'warm clothing,' to Jicky if she'd been the kind of woman who wore sandals in the snow, but, this far into their relationship, Dan knew that she was practical to the core. He didn't even recall her wearing sandals in the summer.

Jicky walked into the kitchen just as Dan came in from warming the truck. She was dressed in dark-blue corduroy slacks and a heavy winter-white turtleneck sweater. Her slouch stocking cap matched her sweater and she wore it covering her ears. For a change, Jicky had on makeup, which she'd started using occasionally after losing most of her eyebrows to chemo. She'd filled in her sparse brows and brightened her high cheekbones with blush. Her afternoon nap had been all she'd needed to erase any trace of the ill effects from her treatment two days earlier.

"You look beautiful, Jicky!" said Dan. "Grab your coat, it's time to go."

"Aren't we going to eat first? I'm finally hungry."

"Don't worry, you'll be fed." Dan said, still smiling.

Jicky didn't say it aloud, but thought: *Oh, no, not a restaurant. If I'm not s'pose to go shopping or to church, I can't imagine that Dr. Kearney would approve of me eating out.*

DAN PULLED INTO a spot near a corner of Jackson's festive town square. He helped Jicky step from the truck to avoid a snowbank, and took her arm as they walked past the twinkling antler arches and through a forest of lighted trees to the front door of the Salt Valley Grill. Jicky hadn't been to the restaurant since she and Dan had eaten there on what she now thought of as their first date, and, although it was an excellent restaurant, she wasn't excited about eating in the crowded venue. Jicky was just getting ready to voice her concerns when she realized that the interior lights were off.

"Danny, they're closed."

"Not for us," he said as he knocked three-shorts-and-two-longs on the heavy doors.

"Welcome to the Salt Valley Grill," said the impeccably dressed waiter, Kevin, as he let Jicky and Dan through the restaurant's double doors, which he quickly re-locked. Kevin escorted them to a linen-clad and beautifully set table positioned in front of one of the restaurant's stone fireplaces. The blazing hearth provided light and warmth to the small section of the room that was theirs for the evening. As Jicky looked around the space she noticed theirs was the only table covered with a white cloth; all the other tables in the vast room were dark wood, their tops decorated with small crystal rose bowls holding lit votives. The dancing flames, refracted by the cut glass, looked like earthbound stars in the darkened room. In the middle of Jicky and Dan's table sat a silver and crystal bud vase with a single long stemmed red rose accented by sprigs of pine and holly. *Danny or his elves have thought of everything*, thought Jicky. Kevin helped her out of her parka and pulled a chair out from the table, gesturing for her to sit. He then took Dan's topcoat and left the room.

"Danny this is amazing, thank you. No one has ever done anything like this for me."

"You're welcome Jicky—let's just say you bring out the creativity in this burned-out old codger."

"So tell me, will there be food?—cause, while this is all very lovely, I'm starving."

"Oh yeah, food. I knew I forgot something. Of course—" before Dan could finish his sentence Kevin was back with their salads. That's when Jicky noticed the silverware. The table wasn't set with the restaurant's massive utensils, the ones they'd made fun of during their first date, but with the full complement of traditionally sized knives, forks, and spoons. When she reached for her salad fork, Jicky saw, instead, two full sized forks; she looked over at Dan's silverware—he had a salad fork. It was then that she remembered telling Dan that she didn't like little salad forks. *He remembers everything,* thought Jicky. She lifted her fork into the air as though she were making a toast and smiled at Dan. He lifted his fork in response before they both dove into their salads.

"THAT WAS A beautiful experience and delicious, too," Jicky said as Dan opened the truck door for her and helped her step up and over the snow on the curb. "The lobster pasta and the chocolate mousse were my favorites."

"Yeah, Larry's a great chef—I can't take much credit for the meal, other that telling Larry to do something 'surf and turf.' Lobster linguine and tenderloin steak kabobs were his idea. Oh, and chocolate—I did ask for chocolate."

"Of course you did. So, what's on the agenda now." Jicky paused and shook her head, "Let me start over, that didn't come out right. This was a lovely evening and I'm not expecting more—except that it's fun being out after dark for a change, and after my long nap this afternoon I feel so good."

"How 'bout if I drive around and we look at Christmas lights."

"Sure, that sounds like fun."

Dan fiddled with the radio until he found a station playing Christmas music. The tunes were a far cry from the lovely piano versions that had played in the background at the restaurant, but they filled the silence in the pickup as Jicky and Dan drove around Jackson in search of decorated houses.

It turned out that there weren't many, and the few they saw couldn't compete with the decorated trees and lighted arches in the town square.

Jicky looked over at Dan who was focused on his driving. She wondered what she had ever done to deserve such a gentle, attentive man in her life. She thought of all that Dan had been through and all that he had lost in his life. She wished she could've given him what he most wanted for Christmas—his daughter, Becca—but there were some things that just weren't possible. Giving the love and attention of another person were two of them. "Danny, I think it's time we give up the search and go home. At this point I feel like I'm just making you waste gas."

"I thought there'd be more lights, like when I was a kid. Of course, I didn't live here, so maybe Jackson's never been into Christmas lights. I've never paid much attention before." Dan turned the truck toward the highway.

SNOW SQUEAKED AND crunched under the tires as Dan pulled into his yard and parked next to Jicky's vehicle. He looked over at Jicky who was already opening her door—he thought about telling her to wait, but it seemed a little silly, so he just hurried out of his side of the pickup and got to her before she'd had time to head toward the house. "Jicky, wait up. I'd like you to come with me to the studio if you aren't too tired."

"No, I'm not tired. Sure…"

They walked to the studio following the path Dan had shoveled earlier in the day after the snow had tapered to flurries. Dan opened the door and flipped on the light in the already warm garage. There, at the end of the room, hung the four-by-five foot canvas that Jicky had seen in November when she was first contemplating moving in with Dan. At that time it had been blank. Now it was filled with an image of the wooden chapel at the base of the Tetons, the grandeur of the snowcapped mountains behind it. The piece was painted not in the realistic style Dan normally employed for his landscapes, but in a heavy pallet-knife technique, reminiscent of his abstract works. And, the colors were bright: turquoises, golds, and purples. It was spectacular!

Dan spoke first. "I thought since you couldn't go to church this evening, I'd bring the church to you. Merry Christmas, Jicky."

"Danny this is magnificent! Did you mean it's for me?—no one has ever given me anything so special. I don't know what to say."

"I'm glad you like it. I painted it the night you wouldn't let me come see you in the hospital."

"In one night? You must not have slept."

"I didn't, but it was worth it to see your smile just now." Dan said, grinning. "You're worth it, Jicky."

Jicky shook her head at Dan, and her heavy knit cap slipped down over her eyes. When she started to lift her hand to slide it back to her forehead, Dan gently held her arms to her sides. "This is perfect," he said as he backed her onto the small church pew sitting in front of the closed garage doors. "Mind leaving your hat over your eyes for just a sec?"

"Okay, but don't tell me you have more surprises, 'cause I'm starting to think that my gift for you is pretty inadequate."

"Just one more." Dan said, as he grabbed his lighter from the otherwise empty windowsill and walked around the studio lighting candles. When he finished he walked to the switch by the door, flipped off the overhead fixture, and joined Jicky on the small pew. He reached down and pushed play on the boombox sitting on the floor beside the pew, then reached over and slid Jicky's stocking cap back to her forehead, uncovering her eyes.

Jicky looked around the studio; it was bathed in candlelight and dominated by Dan's painting of the Chapel of Transfiguration. Strains of a choir singing "O Come, O Come Emmanuel" floated up from the tape player at her feet. Jicky looked at Dan, who smiled back at her and said, "I know I'm probably mixing up religions here, but I thought since Muhammad couldn't go to the mountains, I'd bring the—"

Jicky held her finger to her mouth in the universal sign for hush. Dan didn't say anything more. When the music ended, a resonate voice on the tape announced that he would be reading the Christmas story from the Book of Luke: "In those days a decree went out from Caesar Augustus that all the world should be enrolled …" As the last of Vance the Voice's words vanished into the air, a recorded choir filled the room with "Silent Night," ending the abbreviated service in the same way Dan had remembered midnight services concluding at the small church his family had attended when he was a child.

Dan asked Jicky to remain seated while he blew out the candles and turned off the oil furnace. He walked across the darkened studio, took her arm, and they made their way back to the house while gazing at the winter stars filling the velvety indigo of the Wyoming sky. As they stood on the stoop by the kitchen door, Dan was the first to speak. "Is it like the Christmas Eves you remember?"

"It's more … Even the stars seem more wonderful in the mountains."

"Why's that, Jik?—you can't see the mountains at night."

"No, but I can't see the stars during the day either—it doesn't mean they aren't still in the sky shining down on us.

That thought has always made me happy. Just 'cause you can't see something doesn't mean it's not there, Danny."

They kissed beneath the shining arc of the Milky Way, then walked into the house.

CHAPTER SIXTEEN

"DO YOU MAKE New Year's resolutions?" asked Dan as he and Jicky ate breakfast on New Year's Day.

"Not really. When I was in my teens, I'd always resolve to quit smoking, but it never worked. I finally quit when Rich and I moved to Nebraska and were living with his parents—it didn't have anything to do with being a New Year's resolution."

"So what gave you the ability to quit then?"

"Rich's Dad, Wes. I've told you 'bout him—early on he and I were smoking buddies. He finally had to give up cigars, not just because Rich's mom was on his case, but because his doctor got really serious about him quitting—his heart I think. Anyway, we quit together. We'd both tapered way back, so it wasn't too bad when we finally made the break. Funny thing, what we both ended up missing the most was our alone time together in the garage, just talking."

"How'd you deal with it? Missin' talking?"

"We started sneaking away for *non-smoking* breaks. One of us would give the signal like we were gonna go smoke—just like we did when we smoked. Then, we'd go meet up in the garage and talk. I mean, it didn't happen often, maybe once a week or so, but it helped knowing that we could still take those breaks from the world."

"Yeah, it's funny how you need to give yourself permission—sometimes even force yourself— to do the things you need to do for your own sake. I wonder how many smokers could quit if they knew that it's really okay to go take a ten minute break without something burnin' in their hand. No one really gives a shit if you take a mental health break— or at least they shouldn't."

"You know, Dan, you didn't have to stop smoking inside the house—I appreciated it when I was really sick, but I feel bad about it. I mean, it's your house and all. You should be able to smoke in here if you want. I'd never ask you to quit smoking."

"I know that, Jicky, but when I wanted you to move in, I wanted to make it a good environment for you. I figured someone so susceptible to lung problems shouldn't be hangin' 'round my second-hand smoke."

"Yeah, well, I haven't noticed any first-hand or second-hand smoke lately. Where've you been smoking?"

"I haven't been."

"What? You quit and didn't tell me? I don't mean to tell you what to do, but are you sure quitting all together is good for you? I kinda got the idea that smoking helped you not drink."

"At first, maybe—I don't think it's true anymore. Besides, just like your former father-in-law, a doctor told me I should quit."

"No! Don't tell me you're sick, too! What doctor have you been seeing?"

"Yours—Kearney."

"Dr. Kearney told *YOU* to quit smoking? Why?"

"Yeah, he was just tryin' to watch out for you. He saw me smoking outside the clinic last time you had chemo and stopped to talk. He asked me what my intentions were for the future as far as you were concerned."

"What? Like, are you gonna make an honest woman outta me? Really?"

"Well, not exactly, but he knows you've been livin' at my place. I think he just wanted to know if you'd have help in the long run, or, maybe, if you'd be livin' back in town if you've gotta do radiation… Hell, I don't know, Jik. He just asked."

"Then he told you to quit smoking?"

"He said that if we were gonna stay together, I should quit smoking."

"What a busy body. He had no right to tell you that."

"I disagree—he's your doctor and he's just watchin' out for you. I mean, I knew all along my smoking wasn't good for you. Kearney just gave me that extra shove. It's been over a week now since I've had a cigarette. I'm doin' okay."

"I'm happy for you if it's what you want, Dan. Just don't do it for me, okay?" said Jicky, but it wasn't what she was thinking. She was thinking that no one had ever done as much for her in her whole life as Danny Ogden had done in just the past few months.

* * *

DAN DROPPED JICKY off at the clinic on January twelfth for her last chemo treatment. Jicky had thought she'd be overjoyed, celebratory even, but that wasn't the way she felt when she walked out the clinic doors to Dan's pickup four hours later.

"You don't look happy, Jik. Do you still feel okay?"

"It's okay. I don't feel sick yet, but I thought I'd feel great. You know… happy… free…. Instead, I'm just scared. It's like I've been fighting this thing tooth and nail with this whole big medical team behind me and all of a sudden they're saying, 'We don't know if the cancer's gone, but, hey, we're done with you. Go home. We'll see you in month.' It kinda feels like I've been kicked out of the lifeboat to sink or swim."

"Well, if it counts for anything, you've still got me around for as long as you like."

"Thanks, Danny—it counts for a lot, but I still feel kinda . . . " Jicky's voice trailed off as though she'd forgotten how she'd planned to end the sentence.

Dan broke the silence. "Can you still eat? I'll take you to the Bakery for a late lunch."

"You're on." Jicky smiled. "I'll even be thoughtful and order something light colored, so you won't be too disgusted when you get to clean it up later."

"Oh, you are so thoughtful—and so damn gross." Dan said, shaking his head as Jicky laughed.

JICKY AND DAN sat across from each other in the little bakery eating bowls of chicken soup and hunks of fresh French bread with unsalted butter. Dan had wanted to get gooey caramel rolls for dessert, but Jicky had begged off, saying she'd have a bite of his if it still sounded good after the soup; she was thinking more about the passage of time than the food—she never knew when the side effects of treatment would kick in. *But, maybe, hallelujah, it's all over—maybe this was the very last chemo treatment. Maybe, after today, the cancer will be gone ...* She tried to relax and enjoy feeling like those *maybes* were a sure thing.

Dan reached out for Jicky's hand. "So, what now?"

"Well, after you finish that roll, you'd better take me to your place."

"That's what I want to talk about. Now that you're done with treatments, would you consider really moving in with me —making it *our* place?"

Jicky shook her head. "No Dan, it's too soon. I can't make a commitment like that until I know for sure that the cancer's gone. I hope it is, but we won't know for weeks, maybe months. I've thought about giving up my place, but if it turns out I need radiation treatments, well, then I'll want my apartment in town."

"So, you're saying you've thought about moving in with me permanently? I guess I'll take that as a good sign," Dan said, smiling at her from across the table.

Jicky looked at him—she'd seen the look in his eyes before. Danny Ogden loved her. She was sure of it, and it made her scared all over again. Dan wasn't the only person in their relationship who'd concealed a secret, but he'd managed to confess his guilt. She thought, *he thinks he loves me, but he really doesn't know me. How do I tell him the truth about Rich and Tom? What will he feel then?*

CHAPTER SEVENTEEN

JICKY HAD REMEMBERED Joel's thirty-fifth birthday was on Thursday. She'd thought about calling him, but in the end she'd been stubborn and chosen not to, hoping Joel would capitulate and call her once his trust money was released. It wasn't like she didn't keep up with her brother. She'd spoken with Sherry and April just after Christmas when they'd called to thank her for their gifts. Sherry had said that Joel was busy, but she and Jicky both knew that work wasn't what was keeping Joel off the phone. He and Jicky hadn't spoken since Joel had hung up on her before she'd moved back west. Jicky's only consolation was, that according to Sherry, Joel and April seemed to be doing well.

When Jicky's phone rang on Friday afternoon, shortly after she'd returned from her first post-treatment appointment, she was delighted to see that the call was coming from Connecticut. Maybe it was Joel, maybe now that he had the money their cold war could finally end…

DAN CAME HOME to find Jicky curled on the couch looking stricken. It was obvious that she had been crying, but there were no tears in her eyes when he walked toward her.

"Jik, what's wrong?" Dan asked, "Don't tell me the cancer's back."

"No, I'm good. It's too soon to know anyway." She paused and said, "It's my brother—he's dead. Joey's dead… he overdosed—yesterday."

"Oh, Jicky, I'm so sorry."

"It was his birthday. His thirty-fifth." Jicky took a ragged breath, "Gary—Gary called me, he said that Joel was celebrating with friends—his partners from the restaurant. I guess they got some coke that was stronger than he thought. Cut wrong or something—they don't know. He had a massive heart attack—he was dead before the ambulance arrived."

Dan sat down beside Jicky and put his arm around her. At that, she began to cry anew. Neither of them said anything, until Jicky sobbed, "It—it's my fault."

"How can it be your fault, Jicky? Don't tell me it's because you abandoned them when you were kids—you did what you thought was best, and from what you told me, it was about the only thing you could do."

"No, it's the money…I'd set up trust funds for Joel, Gary, and April with the insurance money I got when Rich died. Gary's been using his for school, but Joel's trust was made so that he got control of it when he turned thirty-five. That's what he was celebrating… not his birthday…the money…the damned money. God, Sherry must hate me."

"I'm sure Sherry doesn't blame you, or hate you. How could anyone hate you? From what I know about you, you're practically a saint."

"Don't say that Dan! I am no fucking saint. You don't know me. You don't know what I've done." Jicky pulled away from Dan and walked to her room.

The old Dan Ogden would have let her go. He would have gone to his studio, or grabbed his fishing rod and left the house. But he was changing. Dan knocked lightly on the doorframe as he walked through Jicky's open bedroom door.

He sat down on the edge of her bed, and put his hand on her shoulder. She was facing the wall, the black cotton stocking cap that she wore inside the house had slid off her bald head and onto her pillow. Her teeth were clenched and she was trying not to cry. "Jicky, you can tell me. Whatever it is, you can tell me." Dan said. They stayed in that position, a cocoon of silence, until Jicky started to speak—her words tumbling like rapid-fire.

She told Dan things that she had never admitted to anyone. She explained that she wasn't just responsible for Joel's death, but Rich's and Tom's, too. She told Dan about her affair with Tom—that she had initiated it, and that when Rich found out that she was leaving him for Tom, he'd chosen to commit murder and suicide to stop it from happening— maybe it had been his way of avoiding a public scandal, but he'd let her know it was to punish her. She told Dan about Rich's last message to her, the one she had erased and never reported: *You live with it, I can't anymore.* She explained her feelings about the life insurance money—that Wes had purchased a policy on Rich payable to her, but that she hadn't wanted the money. When Wes wouldn't take it back, she'd had him help her give it away: first by paying for her father's treatments for AIDS and then by putting the remaining amount in trust accounts for her brothers and April. But, now, with Joey's death, she felt like even the money carried a curse. She knew that she was cursed; she deserved it—she'd brought on the deaths of people with her decisions. Maybe she was really meant to die from the cancer so that she would quit killing everyone she loved.

Dan let her talk. He thought she was wrong, but he knew enough about the rage of guilt to let her tell her story without interrupting. When he finally spoke he said, "I know you think you caused all of this to happen, but are you sure that

Rich caused the accident? Couldn't it have been like the authorities said—he just fell asleep."

"Danny, you don't know how much I want to believe that, but it's not true. I heard the phone message, and while I didn't know what he'd meant at first, when I heard about the accident and how it had happened, I knew … Then, when the findings came out, they proved me right. Rich was driving. He wasn't wearing a seatbelt and he'd set the cruise control way over the speed limit. There were no skid marks, he hadn't slowed down at all when coming to the bridge. None of those actions were like Rich—he always wore his seatbelt and barely ever drove over the speed limit. He would've never set the cruise control over the limit. If he'd been acting rationally he wouldn't have done those things. He ran into the bridge abutment on purpose. He killed Tom and himself on purpose, and it was my fault."

"Okay, Jicky, maybe he did it. But it's not your fault, and Joel's death isn't your fault either. They made the decisions that caused their deaths, and in Rich's case, Tom's, too. They were grown men, who made bad decisions. I know a lot about that. You didn't do anything."

Dan held Jicky while she cried.

CHAPTER EIGHTEEN

Jicky O'Connor Weckwerth
Sandhill Cranes of the Platte
March 16 thru August 26, 2001
National Museum of Wildlife Art, Jackson, WY

Artist's Statement:

In the summer of 2000, I moved to Jackson, Wyoming. Before that time I'd lived in several different states, but nowhere longer than I'd lived in Chadron, Nebraska. Nebraska is where I was living when I became a professional photographer, and it was in Nebraska that I first learned about Sandhill Cranes.

Cameras and cranes speak to me in the same way. They both give me a sense of freedom. My cameras let me pursue a profession that allows me to live where I choose and work when I want. Cameras give me professional freedom. Sandhill Cranes, on the other hand, don't seem to have the freedom to fly where they choose, or when they want—they always take the same paths on their migratory trips at roughly the same time of year. But, they can FLY, and, oh what a sense of freedom it is to watch a sedge of cranes, swoop and circle to make a landing on the Platte River in central Nebraska or fly from their nighttime perch at dawn's first light! It is a freedom and wonder of which I never tired.

I was so enamored with the migratory fight of the Sandhill Cranes that I photographed it nearly every single year of the fourteen years I lived in Nebraska, starting in 1982. The photographs in this exhibit were all taken during those years and are tagged with the appropriate dates.

If you are familiar with my work, you know that I am not known for wildlife photography. Sandhill Cranes are one of my few exceptions. I am not a student of birds—having once described Sandhill Cranes as "pale wild turkeys crossed with giraffes." So, while I can talk about landforms and geological structures with ease, my knowledge of ornithology is obviously limited. To supplement the information in this exhibit I worked with the avian biology experts at the University of Nebraska Cedar Point Biological Station. Their knowledge is unlimited. My thanks goes out to them.

Lastly, I'd like to thank Dan Ogden, the Curator of Collections here at the National Museum of Wildlife Art, for taking a chance with this exhibit. Dan and I have a history together in that he was my first post-high-school art instructor. Dan is also the person who gave me my first camera and told me that he thought I would be a good photographer. In 2000, when our paths crossed again, Dan asked to see my portfolio. I hadn't thought that I had anything appropriate to share with the National Museum of Wildlife Art. Dan saw my Sandhill Crane photos and convinced me otherwise.

Thank you, Dan, for always seeing my potential and helping me find pathways to freedom.

* * *

WINTER WAS SLOWLY turning into spring. Saturday night's opening reception had been a huge success with locals, and with the few late-season skiers who had taken time away from the slopes to attend. Nebraska's Sandhill Cranes were a hit!

Jicky, always looking ahead, was making plans to photograph the elk as their new antlers emerged from the pedicles of their skulls. Though her next show was over a year away, she needed to photograph all the stages of the shed for the exhibit to work. Though still weak from chemo, with Dan as her weekend assistant, she had already bagged two good shots—"photos that might make it to the wall" as Jicky liked to say.

* * *

DAN, A PILE of Sunday paper on the floor beside his chair, polished his reading glasses with the bottom edge of his flannel shirt and looked across the living room at Jicky curled in the corner of the couch. She had a calendar and spiral notebook in her lap and held a pen.

"Jicky, you've been at whatever it is you're doin' for a while now. Are you ready to take a break so I can beat you at backgammon?"

"You think, Ogden—when have you ever beaten me?"

"Sunday—two weeks ago—twelve-forty-three p.m., but who's keeping track?"

"Ha, ha… I'll play you, but just give me a couple more minutes with the calendar. I'm trying to schedule shoot days for the antler exhibit. It's tricker than scheduling scenery shots… it's more like when I was shooting pictures of April—I had to catch her at stages, too. But there are some big differences: I knew where April'd be, I didn't have to contend with the weather, and if anything really noteworthy was happening, her mom'd call me. Did you know, elk don't have phones?"

"Wow— elk don't have phones? Sounds like you've really been studying up on this wildlife shit."

Jicky wrinkled her face at Danny and pointed to her notebook then to the kitchen door, signaling Dan to go refill their coffee cups and give her some space.

Minutes later, when Dan handed Jicky a fresh cup of coffee, he glanced at the calendar in her lap. "Has your three month check-up been scheduled? That's the biggie isn't it?"

"Yeah, it's the biggie. I see Kearney on April eleventh, and the big test—it's called a gallium-spec scan—it's the next day. I'm not sure how many days it will take to get the results."

"You mean the day we can make it official."

"Me moving in? Danny, please don't put the horse in front of the cart. We don't know what the tests will say."

"No harm in being positive."

"Maybe, no harm, but a lot of disappointment if you're wrong."

"Shit, Jik, disappointment is always a possibility. I may as well look ahead to the story ending the way we want."

"Besides me being cancer free, what is it *we* want, Danny?"

"Well, I was hoping you wanted us to be together. That's what I want."

"I was just teasing. You know that's what I want, too."

"Since that's the case, I'm gonna go out on a limb here and tell you what I really want."

"To win at backgammon?"

"No—well yes—but, what I really want Jicky, is for you to marry me. Let's make our arrangement permanent."

"Danny, no … Moving in is one thing, marriage is another. I'm not sure I'm cut out for it—I've already screwed up once."

"I thought you weren't going to blame yourself anymore."

"I'm trying not to blame myself for their deaths, but I still blame myself for cheating with Tom. I mean, what kind of wife falls in love with her husband's best friend. I did that Danny. There's no way around it. I'm not a safe bet."

"Jicky, I don't know what went on, and I don't care. This is our chance to be a family. Yours and mine. It's our chance to start again."

"I want you to be right, I really do. I want to start over, but it's still too soon. Please, just let it go for now. Mid-April will be here before we know it—I'll give you my answer then."

CHAPTER NINETEEN

JICKY HAD JUST finished straightening the kitchen after her late breakfast when Danny rushed through the door, newspaper in hand.

"Are you okay, Danny? It's way too early for lunch."

"Yeah, I'm fine. Have you had the TV on?"

"No, you know I never watch TV during the day. What's up? Should I turn it on? Has something happened?"

Danny handed Jicky the morning edition of the New York Times. Emblazoned across the front page the headline read:

Sen. Streator-Lee Arrested

Washington D.C. — April 10, 2001

U.S. Senator Pamala Streator-Lee (D-Neb.) was arrested Monday at her home in the Georgetown district of Washington, D.C., on suspicion of murder in the November 1992 deaths of her husband Congressman Thomas L. Streator (D-Neb.) and his chief of staff, Richard W. Weckwerth, a Chadron, Neb. attorney. The two men were killed in a one-vehicle rollover on a rural highway in Nebraska. At the time, the accident was attributed to the driver, Mr. Weckwerth, having fallen asleep while driving over the speed limit.

The arrest of Sen. Streator-Lee on two charges of aiding and abetting in the commission of a homicide was made after a long investigation aided by the recent confession of an individual hired by Sen. Streator-Lee to tamper with the cruise control of her late husband's 1991 Cadillac Brougham. Along with purposely causing the driver to lose control of the speed of the vehicle, the mechanic stated he was also requested by Sen. Streator-Lee to disable the car's seatbelts and airbags.

Pamala Streator was appointed to the U. S. Senate in January 1993 to hold the seat to which her late husband had been elected the previous November. She served two years before being elected to the office for a four-year term in a 1994 special election. She was re-elected in the November 1998 general election.

In December of 1994 Sen. Streator married Charles Lee and changed her surname to include his. Mr. Lee is a Virginia lawyer and political consultant. Although, also under investigation, Mr. Lee has not as yet been charged with criminal action in the deaths of Congressman Streator and Mr. Weckwerth.

Sen. Streator-Lee has been released from jail after posting a $750,000 bail. A trial date is pending.

* * *

JICKY SET THE paper on the kitchen table, and shook her head at Danny. "It wasn't Rich? Rich didn't kill Tom. Pam?—" Jicky stopped speaking, but her head kept shaking.

"Don't you see what this means, Jicky—besides not causing their deaths, Rich and Tom must have been getting along—at least well enough to get in a car together for the drive home."

Jicky could see Dan's mouth moving, but couldn't hear his words—the words she had just read so much more powerful, tearing apart everything she had believed about Rich and herself for the past ten years. She sat down at the table mumbling, "Pam killed them...Pam killed them..." It was starting to make sense.

"But, Danny, what did Rich's message mean? I was so sure..."

"He was upset, Jik. People say weird things when they're upset. Maybe Tom talked him down. Who knows? What I do know is, you can quit blamin' yourself."

Dan put his arms around Jicky.

"She thought I was going to be in the car, too, Danny. She told me that. Pam wanted to kill all of us." After a pause Jicky continued, "There were so many things I didn't understand... Tom'd told me that Pam would never give up the townhouse in Georgetown, but a week before the accident he'd told me Pam was moving out." Jicky shook her head again, "She never planned on leaving... and the memorial services. She must have been planning those for months... I'm such an idiot."

"Jicky, you are anything but an idiot." Dan held her until she quit shaking her head and rubbing the tears of her long-held sorrow into the shoulder of his dress shirt.

* * *

DAN POURED TWO juice glasses of sparkling cider while Jicky hung her coat by the kitchen door.

"Congratulations! Are you ready to celebrate?" Dan asked as he handed a glass to Jicky.

"More than ready—I've already started. I rolled down the windows and shouted 'Yippie!' all the way home from town. My face is cold and my new hair's all spiky, but it was worth it." Jicky lifted the glass.

"Hey, Jik. Don't drink yet. We have to toast—it's not everyday a person gets a second chance at life."

Jicky paused, her glass in mid-air. "What was I thinking? Of course—you speak Danny, you've obviously been planning something."

Dan lifted his glass, "Here's to new beginnings and grand adventures!" They clicked the heavy rims of the juice glasses together.

As Jicky raised the sparkling cider to her mouth she saw something move at the bottom of the textured glass. "Oops, we might have to start this over. It looks like a bug got into the cabinet."

"Look a little closer."

Jicky, puzzled, held the glass up to the light coming from the kitchen window. "It's a ring."

"I know." Dan took Jicky's free hand and said, "Jicky Frances Weckwerth, will you marry me?"

"Oh, Danny—I want to say yes, but it's way too soon."

"I thought that'd be what you'd say, but it's not too soon Jicky. Tell me one thing that's gonna change if we wait, other than we both get older. If you want to say yes, please, just say yes."

Jicky stood by the table in silence. After minutes had passed with no words, Dan took Jicky's juice glass and slowly poured the cider into the sink. He rinsed the sticky diamond ring and dried it with the kitchen towel.

"You stubborn, stubborn man. Give me until tonight—I'll let you know then. I promise you, I'm not going anywhere, unless you decide you want me to. Now, will you refill my glass so we can finish our toast—I've heard it's bad luck to not drink once you've clinked."

Dan finished his cider while Jicky drank her fresh glass, but, with the ring back in his pocket, he'd lost part of the thrill of the celebration.

* * *

DAN HADN'T MEANT to force the issue of marriage, but weeks prior, when he'd told Greg about his desire to have Jicky move in with him permanently if her post-treatment tests came back negative, Greg had been delighted for him and passed the phone to Jody so that Dan could tell her his good news, too. Four days later Dan had pulled a small package postmarked "Gillette" from his mailbox. His sister-in-law had sent his mother's gold and diamond engagement ring with a note explaining:

"Your mom and dad wanted you to have anything of theirs that they thought you could use. I think it's time you used this. It's not doing anyone any good sitting in my jewelry box, and I haven't been to a wedding in years. I'd love to attend yours!"

Maybe Jody's desire to attend a wedding wasn't a good enough reason to propose marriage, but being married to Jicky was what Dan wanted. When he'd held his mother's ring in his hand it was though she had reached out through all the years of their shared pain to give him the confidence he needed to try again. He understood some of Jicky's reticence, but he refused to accept it as an excuse. Yes, she had guilt issues, but hers were no greater than his, and, unlike his, some of hers had been resolved when Pam was accused of murder.

* * *

IF THE DIAGNOSIS turned out to be as she'd hoped, Jicky had planned to spend part of the day moving her things into Danny's bedroom. This was going to be the night. While they had been kissing and cuddling since Christmas, they'd put off re-consummating their relationship until Jicky had the "all clear" from Dr. Kearney. Now, after refusing his proposal, she didn't know how Danny felt about her. She knew that she was going to say no again this evening—maybe Danny wouldn't want her in his bed. What if he asked her to go back to her apartment? *Danny, why did you have to complicate a day that was going to be so good?* thought Jicky as she straighten her room.

***

JICKY CHEWED HER celebratory steak and thought about how skilled she and Dan had, once again, become at dancing around elephants. After dinner they would revisit Dan's proposal and her response. She thought Dan seemed upbeat, a good sign, unless he'd convinced himself that she had changed her mind. Dan for his part had no idea what Jicky was going to say, but he thought, as he patted the ring in his jeans pocket, that he had prepared good rebuttals to any of her possible objections.

"OKAY, LET'S TRY this again— Jicky, will you marry me?"

"Danny, I love you, but my answer is still no."

"I thought you might say that, but, now, after thinking about it all afternoon, can you tell me why? I won't say I deserve an explanation, but I'd like one."

"I just don't think I'm marriage material. I told you, I cheated on my first husband with his best friend… I'm not a good person."

"That's where you're wrong, Jicky. A bad person wouldn't still be beating herself up over something that happened ten years ago, and I figure, you must have loved Tom Streator a lot to choose him over your husband."

"Yes I did, and, even though I probably shouldn't, I still do. I still love Rich, too—he was a good person—prob'ly a better person than Tom. What does that say about me? Do you really want to marry a woman who's still in love with two other men?"

"You said you love me, too. So, yes, I still want to marry you. I understand loving people who are no longer with us. Remember when you told me that you liked looking at the stars in the mountains and I asked why, since you can't see the mountains at night. You said, 'you can't see the stars in the daytime either, but it's nice to think they're still up there shining down on us even when we can't see them.' Well, I've finally started to think that loving someone who's gone is sorta the same thing. I can't see Carol or the kids, but I know I still love them. That hasn't changed. Loving people, even if they die or leave you, doesn't make love disappear—it's still up there shining down. And, Jicky, just because I love them, doesn't mean I can't love you, and me loving you doesn't mean you can't still love Tom and Rich. I don't think you're the kind of person who's jealous of ghosts—well, I'm not either."

Jicky didn't respond. She bit her lower lip and mulled over what she should say. Dan sat across the table from her, giving her time, as he listened to the ticking of the cheap plastic wall-clock that hung on the soffit above the kitchen sink. Jicky finally spoke.

"There's another issue you should know about, then. Maybe you'll understand my reluctance… back in March—when you first proposed—you said you wanted us to be a family. I didn't say anything then…but… did you mean you want to have children with me?"

"Not necessarily—I hadn't thought about it. You and I can be a family—just the two of us, but don't you want kids?"

"No, that's not it; I think I've always wanted kids. It's just that after chemo, I'm not sure I can get pregnant. At my age, the odds definitely aren't in my favor—I'm getting used to the idea, but since we're talking marriage, it's somethin' else you need to know about me." A single tear ran down Jicky's cheek.

Dan put his arms around her. "Jicky, honey, you're enough for me—you're more than enough, but if you want children, let's try. I'm gonna be one mighty old dad at PTA meetings, but from what I understand, it's not so uncommon anymore."

"But, what do you mean? I don't want to do anything out of the ordinary or expensive—no fertility treatments, if that's what you meant."

"I just meant let's be old fashioned—no extreme measures, but no birth control, either. Just let nature take its course."

"Yeah, but there's something else. You talked about being old—it's a lot bigger issue for me. Pregnancy in women my age, even those who haven't had cancer, well, there can be complications for both mom and baby. Are you ready to deal with that?"

"It's not what I would wish for, but, yeah. You and I have already weathered so much in our lives, I think, together, we can handle anything else that might come our way."

While Jicky wiped her eyes, Danny reached in his pocket for the ring. "Jicky Frances Weckworth, this is my third, well fourth, and final offer— Will you marry me?"

Jicky sniffed, then grinned, "Yes, Daniel, whatever the heck your middle name is, Ogden. I will marry you."

"Edgar—it's Edgar," Dan said as he slipped his mother's engagement ring on Jicky's slim finger.

"It's a perfect fit," she said as she took Danny's hand and led him toward his bedroom.

CHAPTER TWENTY

JICKY RIFLED THROUGH the top drawer of Dan's worktable looking for hot press watercolor paper. She needed the smoother grade paper so that the details of the painting she'd planned for the wedding invitations would reproduce clearly. As she dug though the piles of paper and folders in the drawer, she wondered if she'd remembered correctly—had Danny said to look in the first drawer or the second? She had just lifted several large sheets of drawing paper when she saw the folder. The tab was marked with the words Becky/Christmas. She knew immediately that the folder contained information about the artwork Danny had made for Becca while she was growing up.

Jicky sat down on the paint-smudged kitchen chair that Dan kept in his studio and looked through the loose sketches and Polaroids. Even from fading photos and rough drawings, Jicky could see the love Danny had put into the gifts he had created for his daughter. How could Becca have ignored a father who'd so obviously loved her? When Jicky reached the bottom two sketches, she realized that the landscapes on the walls of the studio were the studies for the last two pieces from the Christmas collection. She had forgotten to ask him about them. Now, she knew.

With the file back in order and once again hidden beneath the drawing paper, Jicky checked the lower drawer. Here were the watercolor papers Dan had promised. Jicky took a stack and headed back to the house. She had intended to start on the illustration for the invitation that afternoon, but she had something much more important to do. Maybe Danny had given up on ever seeing his daughter, but Jicky hadn't. She would find Becca. She would ask her once again to be a part of her father's life.

* * *

June 2, 2001

Dear Becca,

You don't know me, but I would like to know you.

Your father has just asked me to marry him. Please don't make that a reason you quit reading this letter. Your dad did not ask me to write to you, but he has told me that you want nothing to do with him. He's not upset with you about that, he's just very sad and, unfortunately, he feels he deserves your silence. I, on the other hand, do not feel that way, and I would like you to hear me out.

I know your father was driving the car when your mother and brother were killed and you were badly injured. He told me that he had been drinking and fell asleep behind the wheel. He, also, told me that he spent ten years in prison for his transgression (you may want to call it a crime, knowing your father, I cannot). There was no malice in what he did, no intent to harm. Yes, he'd had other DUIs, and, yes, he shouldn't have been driving. But in the end, what caused the accident was him falling asleep while driving his family home from a day at the beach—something he could have done even had he been sober. He made a dreadful mistake and he has been paying for it for twenty years now.

Becca, you should know that your father quit drinking when he went into Rawlins. I'm sure that he hasn't told you, but he has a good job now as the Curator of Collections at the National Museum of Wildlife Art outside of Jackson, Wyoming. He's a successful artist and a respected citizen of Jackson. He's the kind of man any child would be proud to call father—he's a caring and responsible human being, and he has never stopped loving you, or your brother and mother.

Did you get the drawings and paintings he sent to you each Christmas until you were eighteen? I'm asking you, because if you did, you already know that you were never forgotten by him. If you didn't get them, your grandparents kept them from you. I have no intention of insulting your family, but if you didn't ever see the artwork that your father made especially for you, you should. If the pictures weren't destroyed by your grandparents, by looking at the artwork, now, through adult eyes, you'll see how much he cared. You'll see the thought, love, and attention he gave to you in the only way he knew how.

Please, Becca, give your dad another chance. I'm saying this because I know how much it hurts to have a loved one leave your life with issues unresolved. My brother and I had an argument over money that ended our relationship. He died in January and now we will never have a chance to make it right between us. Don't let that happen with your dad. Life is too short to give-up on family.

If you want to ask me any questions, I'll be happy to try to answer them. My phone number and address are on my business card included with this letter.

Sincerely,

Jicky Weckwerth

CHAPTER TWENTY-ONE

JICKY SEALED THE last envelope in the stack and smiled to herself. The invitation had turned out beautifully. Printed on card stock that mimicked cold press watercolor paper, it featured an iridescent rainbow trout lunging at a hopper fly. She and Dan had agreed that it was an odd choice of design for a wedding invitation, but they'd also agreed that, for the two of them, it was perfect. The simple inscription read:

Jicky Frances Weckwerth
&
Daniel Edgar Ogden
Invite you to join them as they join their lives
in marriage
on
the twenty-fifth day of August, Two-thousand-one,
four o'clock in the afternoon
at the
Chapel of the Transfiguration
Moose, Wyoming – Entrance to Grand Teton
Reception, Dinner, and Dance to follow
National Museum of Wildlife Art
2820 Rungius Road
Jackson, Wyoming

* * *

DAN GOT UP early on August twenty-fifth. The small house was full of Jicky's family. Sherry and April were asleep in the spare bedroom, and the recently official, Dr. Gary O'Connor, M. D., slept filling every inch of the sofa. As Dan snuck through the living room in his stockinged feet he glanced at Jicky's prone brother and concluded he had a giant, snoring leprechaun sprawled across his couch. The evening before, Gary had cheerfully asked Dan if he'd like company on this morning's fishing trip—he'd seemed visibly relieved when Dan had replied "no, not necessarily." Dan was going fishing specifically so that Jicky could have some time alone with her family—something that she'd requested. Something that after two days of pre-wedding hubbub, he was more than willing to supply.

THREE HOURS LATER, when Dan walked in the kitchen door, the table was covered with dirty plates and crumpled napkins as if the family had just gotten up and hidden as soon as they'd heard his pickup crunch onto the gravel pad at the side of the house. Dan had the uncanny feeling that he was walking in on a surprise party, but that made no sense—it was his wedding day, not his birthday. He set his rod in the corner beside the coat hooks and called out, "Hey, Jik, I'm home. Whose car's out front? I thought Greg and Jody were still driving the old Blazer. Do we have any other relatives coming?" When he got no response he walked to the living room to find a young woman sitting on the couch with Jicky—both of them smiling.

"Yeah, Danny, we've got a house full of family."

BECCA STOOD AND walked toward her father, her arms outstretched, "Hi, Dad. It seems hell froze over today. I'm sorry it's taken so long—I hope someday you can forgive me."

EPILOGUE

IT HAD TAKEN over a year to build, but Dan had managed to nail down the last piece of interior trim just before the autumn snows swirled in '02.

The new living room is everything Jicky and Dan had envisioned—large, light, and open, with a cathedral ceiling and a huge stone fireplace flanked by vertical windows facing the Tetons. The old living room off the kitchen (which a realtor would now undoubtedly describe as a formal dining room) quickly filled with the couple's enlarged fly tying bench, and Jicky's old drafting table and photography equipment, thereby allowing the spare bedroom to be a bedroom again.

The large painting of the Chapel of Transfiguration that Danny'd created for Jicky four Christmases ago hangs above the fireplace mantle. Even with all the rustic grandeur of the new room, the painting is always the first thing guests notice. But, on this late spring day, casting their eyes lower, visitors might spot a framed wedding picture on the mantle—a group shot of smiling people: Jicky and Danny, in their wedding finery, surrounded by Gary, Sherry, April, Greg, Jody, and Becca. And, looking closer still, those visitors might notice a multi-colored card leaning against the picture's frame. The card is an announcement printed on card-stock matching that of Jicky and Dan's wedding invitations. This time, instead of a trout jumping at a fly, the five-by-seven card features Jicky's watercolor of a red-crowned sandhill crane carrying from its long beak a cherubic baby cradled in a blue blanket. Everything about the announcement radiates joy:

Welcome!

the newest addition to our family

Connor Westerly Ogden

Born April 4, 2003
7 pounds 2 ounces
20-1/2 inches

proud parents

Jicky Weckwerth and Dan Ogden

ACKNOWLEDGEMENTS

Thank you to all who have helped me with this second novel: My very first reader, business consultant, and the love of my life, Mike MacDonald; My second reader, a fabulous writer, and my favorite daughter, Samantha Solberg; The wonderful women of my multi-generational book club who have served as my early readers and cheerleaders throughout the creation of two novels—especially Carolyn Johnson for her early editing and cover modeling and Melissa Nachtigal Godber for her never-ending support and promotion of my work. My final shout-outs go to my brother, Dale Nordlie, for his beautiful cover photos and nature photography and the remarkably gifted, Romy Klessen, for once again working her magic on the computer to make the interior and exterior of *And One Other* look so good. As has often been said, "It takes a village to raise a child." Most authors would say, "It takes a village to publish a book." I'm blessed to live in a literary village inhabited by exceptionally talented friends and family!

www.ingramcontent.com/pod-product-compliance
Lightning Source LLC
Chambersburg PA
CBHW061643190726
48289CB00006B/1718